D0457591

THE
RULE
OF
THOUGHTS

BOOKS BY JAMES DASHNER

THE MORTALITY DOCTRINE SERIES

The Eye of Minds
The Rule of Thoughts

THE MAZE RUNNER SERIES

The Maze Runner
The Scorch Trials
The Death Cure
The Kill Order

THE 13TH REALITY SERIES

The Journal of Curious Letters
The Hunt for Dark Infinity
The Blade of Shattered Hope
The Void of Mist and Thunder

THE RULE OF THOUGHTS

JAMES DASHNER

DELACORTE PRESS

All rights reserved. Published in the United States by Delacorte Press, an imprint of Random House Children's Books, a division of Random House LLC, a Penguin Random House Company, New York.

Delacorte Press is a registered trademark and the colophon is a trademark of Random House LLC.

Visit us on the Web! randomhouseteens.com

Educators and librarians, for a variety of teaching tools, visit us at RHTeachersLibrarians.com

Library of Congress Cataloging-in-Publication Data
Dashner, James.
The rule of thoughts / James Dashner. — First edition.
pages cm
Sequel to: The eye of minds.
Summary: "Michael and his friends, Sarah and Bryson, are still being chased by a cyber-terrorist. And now the government is after them, too"—Provided by publisher.
ISBN 978-0-385-74141-5 (hc) — ISBN 978-0-375-99002-1 (glb) —
ISBN 978-0-375-98464-8 (el) — ISBN 978-0-385-39011-8 (intl. tr. pbk.)
[1. Computer games—Fiction. 2. Virtual reality—Fiction. 3. Cyberterrorism—Fiction. 4. Terrorism—Fiction. 5. Science fiction.] I. Title.
PZ7.D2587Rul 2014
[Fic]—dc23
2014011983

The text of this book is set in 12.5-point Adobe Garamond.
Book design by Stephanie Moss

Printed in the United States of America
10 9 8 7 6 5 4 3 2 1
First Edition

For the #DashnerArmy.
We're in this together.

CHAPTER 1

A STRANGER IN THE HOME

1

Michael was not himself.

He lay on the bed of a stranger, staring up at a ceiling he had seen for the first time just the day before. He'd been disoriented and sick to his stomach all night, catching sleep only in fitful, anxious, nightmare-fueled jags. His life had blown apart; his sanity was slipping away. His very surroundings—the foreign room, the alien bed—were unforgiving reminders of his terrifying new life. Fear sparked through his veins.

And his family. What had happened to his family? He wilted a little more every time he pictured them.

The very first traces of dawn—a gloomy, pale light—made the shuttered blinds of the window glow eerily. The Coffin next to the bed sat silent and dark, as foreboding as a casket dug from a grave. He could almost imagine it: the wood rotting and cracked, human remains spilling out. He didn't know how to look at the objects around him anymore. *Real* objects. He didn't even understand the word *real*. It was as if all his knowledge of the world had been yanked out from under his feet like a rug.

His brain couldn't grasp it all.

His . . . *brain*.

He almost burst out in a laugh, but it died in his chest.

Michael had only *had* an actual, physical brain for the last twelve hours. Not even a full day, he realized, and that pit in his stomach doubled in size.

Could it really all be true? Really?

Everything he knew was a result of artificial intelligence. Manufactured data and memories. Programmed technology. A created life. He could go on and on, each description somehow worse than the one before it. There was nothing *real* about him, and yet now here he was, transported through the VirtNet and the Mortality Doctrine program and turned into an actual human being. A living, breathing organism. A life, stolen. So that he could become something he didn't even understand. His view of the world had been shattered. Utterly.

Especially because he wasn't sure if he believed it. For all he knew, he could be in another program, another level of *Lifeblood Deep*. How could he ever again trust what was real and what was not? The uncertainty would drive him mad.

He rolled over and screamed into his pillow. His head—his stolen, unfamiliar head—ached from the thousands of thoughts that pounded through it, each one fighting for attention. Fighting to be processed and understood. And feeling pain here was no different from feeling it as a Tangent. Which only served to confuse him more. He couldn't accept that before last night he'd just been a program, a long line of code. It didn't *compute*. That *did* make him laugh, and the pain in his head intensified and spread, slicing down his throat and filling his chest.

He yelled again, which didn't help, then forced himself to swing his legs off the bed and sit up. His feet touched the cool wooden floor, reminding him once again that he was now in a strange land. Lush carpet had blanketed the apartment he'd always known, which seemed homier, warmer, safe. Not cold and hard. He wanted to talk to Helga, his nanny. He wanted his parents.

And those were the thoughts that almost did him in completely. He'd been avoiding them, pressing them back into that pulsing swirl of thousands of other thoughts, but they weren't going anywhere. They stood out and demanded attention.

Helga. His parents.

If what Kaine had said was true, they were as synthetic as Michael's programmed fingernails had been. Even his memories. He would never know which ones had been programmed into his artificial intelligence and which ones he'd actually experienced within the code of *Lifeblood Deep*. He didn't even know how long he'd existed—his true age. He could be two months old, or three years, or a hundred.

He imagined his parents and Helga as fake, or gone, or dead, maybe never there in the first place. It just didn't make sense.

The ache that had crept its way into his chest filled his heart, and grief overtook him. He slumped back onto the bed and rolled over, pushing his face into the pillow. For the first time in his existence, Michael cried as an actual human being. But the tears felt no different than they ever had before.

2

The moment passed sooner than he'd expected. Just when he thought the despair would swallow him whole, it pulled back, allowed him some respite. Maybe it was the tears. Back in his life as a Tangent, he'd rarely cried. He probably hadn't since he was a child. He just wasn't the crying sort, he always said. And now he regretted that, because it sure seemed to ease the pain.

He made another attempt to get out of bed and this time succeeded. Feet planted on that hard, cool floor, emotions in check. It was time to do what he hadn't been able to bring himself to do the night before: figure out who in the world he'd become. Since no one had come running at his screams, he knew he must be alone.

He walked through the apartment, turning on lights and opening blinds to let in the rays of morning sunshine. He wanted to see every detail of this odd place that had become his home and decide if he could or should keep it that way.

The city outside the windows wasn't the one he'd looked out on from his old apartment. But at least it *was* a city, something that brought a little comfort in its familiarity. Buildings stacked next to more buildings, cars making their way down crisscrossing streets, the ever-present smog blurring the view. People bustling below, going about their business. Not a cloud in the wistful, dull blue sky.

He began his search.

Nothing out of the ordinary in the bedrooms. Clothes, furniture, pictures cycling on the WallScreens. Michael stood and stared at the huge one in the master bedroom for a while, watching as various pictures of the family—Mom, Dad, son, daughter—took turns filling the space. He vaguely remembered what he now looked like, and it was beyond unsettling to see *that* boy in so many situations that had absolutely no meaning to Michael whatsoever: A family portrait in front of a stream lined with huge oak trees, sunshine filling the sky. The kids were young, the boy sitting on his dad's lap. Another portrait, much more recent, in a studio, mottled gray backdrop. Michael had stared at his new face for a long time in the mirror, and it was eerie to see that same face looking down at him from the wall.

There were other, more casual shots. The boy up to bat at a baseball game. The girl playing with silvery blocks on the floor, smiling up at the photographer. The whole family at a picnic. In a swimming pool. At a restaurant. Playing games.

Michael finally looked away. It hurt to see such a happy family when he might have lost that forever. He sullenly walked to the next room, obviously the girl's. Her WallScreen didn't have a single shot of the family, just pictures of her favorite bands and movie stars—Michael knew them all from *Lifeblood*. There was an old-fashioned frame on the nightstand next to her pink-themed bed, with an actual printed picture inside. The girl and the brother—*him*—grinning big goofy grins. The girl looked to be about two years older than the boy.

The pictures only made Michael feel worse, so he set to rummaging through drawers for any clues as to who these people were. He didn't find much, though he did figure out that the family name was Porter and the girl's name was Emileah—strange spelling.

Then he finally found the courage to go back into the boy's room. *His* room. With the rumpled bedsheets and the Coffin and the hard, cold floor. And then he saw what he'd been both looking for and dreading: The boy's name. The boy whose life he'd stolen. It was on a paper birthday card, on top of the dresser.

Jackson.

Jackson Porter.

Scribbled red hearts littered the card itself, hand-drawn and quaint. Sweet. Inside, a message from a girl named Gabriela proclaimed undying love for Jackson and made various physical threats to his nether regions if he let anyone read it. Paired with a smiley face, of course. There was a slightly warped spot at the bottom, as if perhaps a tear had dropped there at the end, right after something about an anniversary. Michael tossed the card, feeling guilty, as if he'd peeked inside a forbidden room.

Jackson Porter.

Michael couldn't help it. He went back to the master bedroom and watched the WallScreen again. Only, now it had a whole new feeling. For some reason, knowing the boy's name made everything different. Made Michael stop thinking about himself for a moment. He saw the face and body that were now *his,* doing so many activities—running, laughing, spraying a hose at his sister, eating. He seemed like one happy dude.

And now he was gone.

His life had been stolen. From a family *and* a girlfriend.

A life that had a name.

Jackson Porter. Surprisingly, Michael didn't feel guilt so much as sadness. This hadn't been *his* choice, *his* doing, after all. But the despair of it still swelled within him like nothing he'd ever felt before.

He tore his eyes from the screen and continued searching the apartment.

3

Michael rifled through drawer after drawer until he decided there wasn't much more to find. Maybe the answers he needed weren't in the apartment. It was time to do something that should have been first on his list but was the last thing he wanted to do.

He had to go back online.

Right after he'd woken up in his new body the day before, he'd checked his messages—but only because of the direction from Kaine to do so. He'd logged on to a mostly empty screen, with only the one ominous, life-changing note from Kaine himself, revealing what had happened. However, Michael figured Kaine had only temporarily hijacked Jackson Porter's online presence for his own use, and that by now it had been restored. All he had to do was squeeze his EarCuff and he could probably find out more than he'd ever want to know about the boy.

For some reason that felt wrong, which didn't make a whole lot of sense. Michael had spent a good portion of his life hacking into the VirtNet without the slightest twinge of guilt. But this was different. This didn't take hacking or coding. This was just a click or swipe away. He'd stolen a human life, and stealing that person's virtual life as well somehow seemed like too much.

Michael thought it through and realized he had no choice. Jackson Porter—the essence of what made him a person— might be gone forever. If Michael wanted to go forward, he had to accept that. And if Jackson *wasn't* gone forever, if there was any possible way of restoring him to his body, Michael would never figure it out unless he jumped back into things.

He found a chair—just a normal, boring chair, not the cloud-soft throne of pure awesomeness he'd once had back in his former life—and sat next to a window, shutting the blinds to ward off some of the brightness. He caught a last glimpse through the slats of a city mad with the day-to-day grind, moving and grooving. In a way he felt envious of those people, completely oblivious that a crazy computer program had the ability to steal their bodies. That anything was wrong in the world at all.

Michael closed his eyes and took a deep breath, then opened them again. He reached up and squeezed his Ear-Cuff. A faint stream of light shot from its surface and created a large viewing screen, hovering a couple of feet in front of him.

It was exactly as he'd guessed. Jackson Porter's personal online life had been restored from Kaine's hijacking, icons galore covering the surface of the glowing screen—everything from social dens to games to school materials. Michael was relieved, but he hesitated. He had no idea what to do. Should he pretend to be Jackson? Escape into the world and try to hide from Kaine? Seek out someone from VirtNet Security? He didn't know where to begin. But whatever he decided, it would require information. A lot of information. And if at all possible, he needed to dig in before someone came home.

Which brought up questions again: Where were Jackson's parents? Where was his sister? Michael had the sinking thought that somehow Kaine had gotten rid of them, just like he'd sworn he had done to Michael's own parents.

After quickly scanning several social sites that proved pointless, he found a personal text box and scrolled through its messages. There were several from the girlfriend, Gabriela; three just that morning. Reluctantly, Michael opened the most recent.

Jax,

Uhhhhh, you slip in the shower and bang your head? Are you sleeping in a puddle of soapy water and drool right now? Of course, you'd be cute and adorable even then. I miss you. Hurry? I'm on my second cup of coffee and there's a jerk at the next table getting friendly. He sells stocks, or companies, or dead people's organs, something. Please come save me. You might even get a coffee-flavored kiss.

　　Hurry!

Gabriela

She attached a pic, a shadowy, blurred image of someone Michael could only assume was Gabriela—dark skin, dark hair, pretty—with pouting lips, her finger tracing an imaginary tear down her cheek. Her brown eyes tilted down in mock sadness. With a heavy heart Michael swiped it closed and continued looking through the text box.

4

He didn't have to search long.

Several things fell into place when he found a note from Jackson's dad, sent just that morning:

Jax,

Hope all is well, buddy. I'm sure you're up and at 'em by now, right? Right? RIGHT? ☺

　　We're safe and sound. Puerto Rico is beautiful. For the millionth time, we're sorry you couldn't come along. But I know you have big things coming up this week, so we'll be thinking about you.

Keep us in the loop, and be careful when you access our accounts. Make sure you protect our codes! (That was Mom's input.)

See you next week. Is Gabby still visiting her dad? Say hi to her for us. We miss you already.

Dad

So Jackson Porter was obviously okay when his family left for vacation. Which meant that his body had not been merely clinging to life, brain-dead, like so many others discovered throughout the world. Had those all been tests of some sort? Michael wondered. Had Kaine actually perfected the Mortality Doctrine process before he used it on Michael? Or was Michael the first that had worked? It was a terrifying thought either way. If it seemed the attacks had stopped, no one would be worried about the VirtNet. Kaine could just move ahead and unleash an army of Tangents on the world with no warning.

But Michael had a more immediate concern—what to do about Jackson Porter. Reading that letter had made him absolutely certain of one thing: there was just no way he could pretend to be another person. The notion of passing for this stranger with his family and friends seemed ridiculous now, especially if Gabriela showed up and started whispering sweet nothings in his ear.

So what could he do?

He clicked off the NetScreen and slouched back into the chair. He had to get out of there. He could leave a note with some kind of explanation. It would break his family's hearts, but at least it would let them know he was alive. He could even keep corresponding with them, keep the deception going. Surely that was better than finding out a computer program had erased the mind of their son and replaced it with another.

But there was the issue of money. . . .

Something banged, hard, against the front door of the apartment, startling him.

He turned and looked toward the noise.

Bang. Bang. Bang.

There it was again. A hard thunk, like wood against metal. Again, then again.

Michael jumped up from the chair and hurried down the hall, through the kitchen, toward the front door. The pounding happened twice more, as if someone were swinging something large back and—

With a splintering crash of the framework, the metal door exploded inward. Michael crouched down, throwing his arms up to protect himself as the door slammed to the ground, narrowly missing him. Heart in his throat, he looked up to see who was in the doorway.

Two men. Both dressed in jeans and drab flannel shirts, they held some sort of old-fashioned wooden battering ram. They were both big, muscular, one with dark hair, the other blond. Neither had shaved for a few days, and intensity strained their expressions. And if Michael wasn't mistaken, there seemed to be a hint of surprise hidden in there somewhere.

They dropped the length of wood and stepped toward Michael.

He shot backward, scrambling across the kitchen until he ran into the counter and lost his footing, dropping to the floor. The two men stopped just a few feet away, looking down at him with twin sneers.

"Do I even need to ask?" Michael managed to say. He wanted to feel brave—to *be* brave—but the vulnerability of his human body suddenly hit him. It was something he'd never thought about in *Lifeblood Deep*. His world could end at any second.

The two men didn't answer; they looked at each other with puzzled expressions, so Michael spoke again. "I guess I do," he murmured. "Who are you?"

Both of them swung their gazes back to him.

"We were sent by Kaine," the dark-haired man said. "A lot has changed in the last day or two. We were sent to . . . *summon* you to a meeting. He has big plans for you, son."

Michael's heart sank. He'd hoped for more time. His mind spun with questions, but what came out of his mouth sounded plain stupid.

"Well, you could've just knocked."

CHAPTER 2

THE BIG, BAD WORLD

1

The men actually helped him to his feet—the blond guy even dusted off Michael's back. But both remained oddly silent, and the whole situation was beginning to take on an air of absurdity.

"So," Michael asked, "are you guys going to tell me anything? Your names, at least?" He felt oddly peaceful as he spoke, as if any immediate danger had been swept away by the man brushing the dirt off his pants.

The dark-haired man straightened and folded his arms. His face showed no emotion as he spoke. "My name is Kinto," he said, then nodded toward his partner. "This is Douglas. We were under the impression that you were still inside the Coffin, still undergoing the Doctrine transfer."

"Looks like we were . . . misinformed," Douglas added in a gravelly voice.

"Yeah," Kinto agreed. "Looks that way."

Michael was still confused, but less so. At least the men knew about Kaine and the Mortality Doctrine. "So does that mean Kaine's taken a human body, too? How many Tangents have done the same thing?" His mouth was still open when Kinto held up a hand to silence him.

"Stop. Talking." The man's expression was all business. "If Kaine wants you to know something, he'll make sure you do."

"You've been given a gift," Douglas continued. "Life. For now, just be happy and do what you're told."

"Fine with me," Michael replied. His insides were a churning storm—lightning, thunder, sleet, strong winds, the whole bit—but he tried to display a sense of calm. He'd had way too many experiences lately that had ended in his being dragged away, and it was something he wanted to avoid if at all possible. He would go with these men until an opportunity to break away presented itself or until he had a revelation about what he should do.

"Fine with you?" Douglas repeated, obviously surprised at the simple response.

"Fine with me." Michael swallowed. He'd just keep his comments to a minimum and go with it until a better plan developed.

Kinto gestured toward the door. "Then let's go. I don't think I need to tell you not to try anything. Douglas will go first, then you, then me. Nice and easy."

"Life couldn't be simpler," Douglas said gruffly, though he broke his stern act with a smile. "You follow me, Kinto follows you. And all your dreams will come true."

The man didn't wait for a response. He headed for the door and Michael fell in line behind him, with Kinto right on his heels. They went through the shattered doorframe and into the hallway, the apartment building silent except for their footsteps.

For some reason, Michael thought of *Lifeblood Deep,* how it had been his life's goal to make it there someday, and a wave of sadness washed over him. He'd been there the whole time. And now look where he'd ended up. He knew it was ironic, somehow, maybe even profoundly philosophical, but all he could feel was defeat.

He kept walking.

2

Michael and his escorts made their way down the hall to the elevator, out of the building, through the bustling streets, and to the subway. He sat squeezed between the two men as they jostled along underground, and his thoughts kept returning to Jackson Porter. His family. His girlfriend, even. Gabriela.

What had happened to the consciousness of the boy once known as Jackson? Was that it for him? Had his mind, his personality, been erased? Or was it stored somewhere, somehow? If Michael could be transferred *into* Jackson's body, maybe Jackson could be transferred *out.*

He kept thinking about how Jackson's family was basking in the sunshine in Puerto Rico, oblivious that they'd lost a son and a brother. Guilt overwhelmed him. Though it hadn't been his choice, he'd taken a life, and he wished he could make the loss bearable for them in some way.

Not a word had been spoken between Michael and the others since they'd left the apartment, unless you counted the grunts the men made when they needed to change direction.

Michael sat, quiet, as the train pulled into a station and stopped. The doors opened and he watched absently as the passengers crowded in like herded cattle. There were some who smiled or apologized when they bumped into others. Those were few and far between. One woman barely made it through before the doors closed on her, catching the corner of her handbag. She had to yank hard before it came free, allowing the doors to seal shut.

As Michael observed, his mind started turning. His gaze went from the woman to her purse to the door, and his thoughts picked up speed. What in the world was he going to do? He literally knew no one, had no home, no money, no clothes. No place to start. Did he continue with these people, go to this gathering place, this meeting, find out what Kaine wanted with him? He needed answers from the Tangent, but did he dare let himself be trapped in a situation he couldn't get out of?

He missed his family and his friends more than anything. They couldn't all be fake—he refused to accept that.

The train continued along the tracks, flashing lights breaking up the darkness of the tunnel. He was surrounded by people—some dozing, some reading, many just blankly staring into space. Kinto and Douglas sat on either side of him, their shoulders pressed against his, their faces as blank as most of the others on the train.

Michael had a sudden thought: if what Agent Weber from VNS had told him the night before was true, Michael wasn't alone. Somewhere out there in the big, bad world, he had the two best friends a person could ever ask for. They weren't Tangents like him—they never had been. They were *real.* Weber had said so.

Bryson and Sarah.

3

Michael then realized he was scared of something: what would his friends think of him? He was a *Tangent.* Did that change things? He had a sudden and terrible vision of them stumbling backward, running away from him, a freak that had taken the body of a real person. Stolen it.

But did he actually believe that? Wouldn't they understand?

Yes, he decided. Yes, they would.

The train bounced and creaked, everyone staring down at the floor. Lights flashed and dimmed, then blazed back on. His two escorts said nothing.

He couldn't go with them. He just couldn't. Yes, he needed answers. Yes, he needed to figure out a way to confront Kaine and find out the *why* of everything. But not this way. Not with the Tangent calling the shots.

Michael needed Bryson and Sarah. He thanked the stars that he'd seen that poor woman get her handbag caught, because it had sparked an idea.

He had to stay calm. He stilled his whole body until he sat frozen, like a wax figure, and waited for the right moment. The train began to slow and pulled into the next station. The doors slid open and passengers surged off en masse, plowing into those who wanted *on* the train. Cattle in, cattle out. Michael watched it all calmly, waiting. Riders found their way to seats until those were full, then packed in, clasping handholds attached to the ceiling and the poles running the length of the car. There was a loud tone and the doors began to close.

Without warning Michael launched himself out of his seat, knocking people out of the way, and lunged for the disappearing gap between the closing doors. He stumbled over something, recovered, dove for the thin sliver of an opening. His body made it through, but the doors slammed against his right calf, the rubber seals clutching, holding him firmly in place. He crashed to the ground, twisted around to look back. The two men stood just on the other side of the doors, calmly looking down at him through the gap. Their serene expressions actually scared him more than if they'd grown fangs and wings.

Douglas bent down and grabbed Michael's foot, pulling him with a shocking amount of strength, while Kinto attempted to force the doors open. They didn't budge. A blaring bell rang out, followed by a mechanized voice.

"Please remove all obstructions from the path of the door."

Michael gritted his teeth and pulled his trapped leg, kicking the train with the other, trying to squirm his way free. But Douglas held firm on the other side, twisting Michael's foot painfully. Michael cried out and struggled even harder. A woman on the train screamed. It was a piercing wail that drowned out the alarm—it must have been clear that Douglas wasn't exactly trying to help Michael.

Then the train started to move.

It lurched forward, dragging Michael along the cement floor of the station as he tried to grab anything nearby, but there was only the floor. A second alarm rang out, this one more of a booming, electronic clang that filled the air, and the train stopped. Michael's leg screamed with pain; the doors pinched in a viselike hold where they had closed around his calf. Douglas continued to twist his foot from inside the train, and the other passengers were realizing that he was hurting Michael—doing more harm than good. There were shouts, and Michael strained to look and saw scuffling; a punch was thrown. Douglas's head snapped to the left, but his face registered no pain. Michael watched it all in a daze, as if his mind had risen out of his aching body.

And then someone was pushing his foot instead of pulling on it. A hand gripped the underside of his calf, trying to leverage it at a better angle. Kinto and a burly man were fighting inside the train—they fell to the ground and Douglas released his hold on Michael. He pulled himself up and pushed against the door of the train with his other foot. The alarms clanged and rang at a deafening pitch. Two men in uniform ran toward him, barking orders he couldn't understand. People on the train were shouting and pointing at him through the windows.

Finally his leg slipped free from the vise of the two doors and they slammed shut.

Michael pulled his leg in and rubbed his calf and ankle, watching from the ground as the train lurched into motion again. The alarm cut off and the familiar creaks and groans of transit resumed. He glanced up as the cars disappeared into the tunnel. In the very last one stood Douglas, staring back at him through a grimy, fingerprint-smeared window, ignoring the still-chaotic scene playing out behind him.

And for the first time, the man looked angry.

CHAPTER 3

A HITCH IN THE GUT

1

Michael winced and clutched his leg, breaking his gaze with Douglas as he slipped away. The screeching sounds faded into echoes as the train finally vanished into the darkness of the tunnel. There was a scuffle of footsteps and then the two officials were lifting him to his feet. He stepped gingerly on his injured leg and thanked them.

After a couple of minutes of scolding and reprimanding, they let him go, warning him not to do something so stupid ever again. Neither of them had noticed that he'd actually been escaping a kidnapping or that a couple of stone-cold-expressionless men had been trying to yank him back onto the train. Which was a relief to Michael. He didn't want to draw any more attention to himself. He dusted off his clothes and tested his leg. It hurt, but it wasn't broken. He finally limped out of the station and onto the city sidewalks.

He stopped to take it all in. There were people everywhere, cars everywhere. And the world was full of sound. Horns and engines, talking and shouting and laughing. A hovering cop car zoomed past above him. The brightness of the day blinded him slightly, making everything a sea of blurred movement. He was still shaking from having lost Douglas and Kinto; it would take some time for him to adjust.

He found a bench and sat down, and not just because his leg ached. The whirlwind of events since he'd read the letters from Gabriela and Jackson Porter's dad had spared Michael from having to figure out what was going on. Kaine might've provided answers, but Michael had no doubts about his decision to run—he needed to stay as far away from Kaine as possible. How could he possibly trust the Tangent?

Elbows on knees, he dropped his head into his hands and took a deep breath. The reality was, to find Bryson and Sarah—to find his next *meal*—he'd need something he didn't have.

Money.

He desperately needed money.

His stomach rumbled with hunger and he almost laughed. It was funny how his old "fake" life resembled this new one. Unless he wanted to beg or go Dumpster diving, he'd need to figure out a way to fill his coffers with electronic cash. Then he realized the bigger problem: he didn't *have* any coffers. The kid known as Michael didn't exist in this world.

But Jackson Porter did. And according to the note the Porters had left, they knew he'd need money while they were in Puerto Rico.

Michael felt another pang of guilt, then reminded himself that Kaine had done this to the boy, not Michael. He squeezed his eyes shut, trying to force himself to accept the thought. But he couldn't. Because he now existed in the real world, a family would never be the same. Maybe he could pretend, make the Porters believe their son was alive, just off to see the world. They'd be sad—not to mention Gabriela—but not utterly devastated.

He was safe for the short term, anyway, and would just take what money he needed. When the family returned from their vacation and realized he was missing . . . Well, one day at a time.

Right then he needed a better place to sit—a little darker, so he could see a NetScreen more clearly—and some time on the VirtNet. He found a relatively clean corner tucked away in an alley with just enough passing traffic to keep the hooligans away, and he sat down on the hard pavement to work. One click of his EarCuff and the glowing green screen that belonged to Jackson Porter flashed to life in front of him.

Then a cold fear crawled up his spine. What if his coding skills had been as fake as his life in the Sleep? What if the code was somehow different out in the Wake? The *real* Wake.

Scarcely able to handle the thought, he got to work, and soon realized his fears were unfounded.

He swiped and typed, allowing his mind to take over, and he dug further and further into Jackson's and his family's lives, searching the Net for codes and files he'd used or heard about before—password unlockers, false-identity creators, secret sites about the ins and outs of bank cybersecurity. It wasn't long before he'd created an entirely new human being—new to the virtual world, anyway. He called this new human Michael Peterson.

Kaine knew his first name, but it was common; there had to be thousands of Michaels out there. Hundreds of thousands. He couldn't bring himself to use a completely different name—it was all he had left from the life that had been taken. Plus, Kaine probably expected him *to* change it.

Luckily for him, the Porters weren't hurting in the money department. Michael started the process of transferring funds, making all the trails appear as if their sweet boy, Jackson, had actually taken cash credit withdrawals, practically untraceable.

Things were running more smoothly, more quickly than Michael would've hoped, and he was just beginning to feel good about himself when a glitch hit. A diagonal line of bright blue slashed across the NetScreen. It only lasted half a second, but his stomach dropped. The glitch was unmistakable. Somebody was trying to break into his system.

Another slash. Brighter. Followed by another.

Michael's hands flew between the screen and the keyboard, his instincts taking over. He built makeshift firewalls and scrambled his digital signal—Jackson Porter's digital signal, rather—and coded some other quickie programs to block the intruder. But he could tell from the strength of the pushback coding that whoever it was had massive skills.

There was no question in Michael's mind. It was Kaine.

2

Michael couldn't hold him off much longer. The two dull-faced men who'd come to take him away must've reported back up the chain of command. Michael was now officially rogue, and Kaine wouldn't be happy.

Michael kept working, feverishly. He had to get a few more things done before he could sign off. Wrap up the new identity so he could access him later, tie off any loose ends so Kaine wouldn't be able to find him when he did so. He had to finalize the accounts, secure the money, make sure he could access it from somewhere else, respond to the Porters so they'd know their son was safe.

But there was one thing even more important than that.

Finding Bryson and Sarah. At least one of them. At least the general area where they lived. With Jackson's account compromised, it might be a while before Michael dared access the Net again.

A line of bright light slashed across his NetScreen again, wider this time, and it remained longer. Random numbers and letters flashed, then vanished. Kaine—it *had* to be Kaine—was now throwing his full force, trying to sabotage instead of hack. Michael knew the signs from his own work over the years. He pushed back with a flurry of codes, not sure if he could do it again.

Instinct took over. He searched and searched, digging through the archives of *Lifeblood*, the game that had once meant so much to him. Data on players, high scores, dates, event logs. The image of the girl, Tanya, jumping to her death off the Golden Gate Bridge flashed in his mind. Michael had only been a Tangent, Lifting up from what had actually been *Lifeblood Deep* to play the game. But Bryson and Sarah were real—Agent Weber had said so, anyway—and there had to be one snippet of real-world information he could dig up from all the *Lifeblood* data before Kaine destroyed the digital existence of poor Jackson Porter.

Three slashes of searing white light burned across the NetScreen, wiping out the path Michael had been digging through the code. Once again, numbers and letters flashed, one after the other, blurring the screen in a rush of movement that drowned out the background. Michael swept it away with a last-gasp code that was absolutely illegal. The screen cleared once more and he jumped full-bore back into the *Lifeblood* data archives, his eyes stinging with tears from concentrating so hard.

Sweat beaded his forehead, ran down his temples, slicked his skin as he worked. *Lifeblood*'s code was complicated and heavily protected. But Michael was good—he'd been part of the code itself. He dug and searched, looking for any background files he could find on his friends. Personal information was sacred in the virtual world. Sacred.

He could sense Kaine's efforts to crash his system. It was almost like a tangible pressure, pushing down on him. Ignoring it as best he could, Michael swam in a sea of data, searching, searching.

There. A gamer's file with all of its experience points laid out like folded laundry on a bed. Everything looked familiar, matched the criteria Michael had entered. He recognized so much of what he saw before him, spelled out in code—he'd been by that gamer's side.

It was Sarah.

The pressure intensified. The characters on the screen jumped and twitched, pulsed like a drumbeat—something he'd never seen before. The upper-right-hand corner of the screen glowed, a bulge of light forming like a giant blister. Michael found the location-file, seared it into his memory. Sarah. He'd found Sarah. She was real. Relief and something close to happiness swelled within his chest.

And then everything came crashing down.

Slashes of bright light flashed across the screen. Acting on instinct, Michael reached up and squeezed his EarCuff, but he knew it would do no good. The NetScreen stayed where it was, though it had lost its crisp shape, its edges blurry. Numbers and letters swirled, barely identifiable behind the barrage of blinking lights. There was a loud buzzing sound. Michael tried to lean back, tried to escape the pulsing screen, but he hit his head on the wall behind him. This was a massive, all-out cyberattack.

Something popped, followed by one last explosion of blinding light. Michael closed his eyes and turned away, saw spots swimming in the darkness. Sweat drenched every inch of his body. Then the buzzing stopped, replaced by the distant honking of horns, the skittering of debris as wind pushed it across the alley.

Michael opened his eyes. Of course turning his head had done no good—the NetScreen hovered before him, seeming to lean against the wall of the building. The screen was black, with white-lettered words filling the space:

YOU SHOULD'VE FOLLOWED MY ORDERS, MICHAEL.
WE NEED EACH OTHER.

He was reading the message for a third time when the words dissipated into the dark background; then the entire screen winked out. Michael didn't have to squeeze his Ear-Cuff to know that it would never work again.

CHAPTER 4

A BLUR OF COLOR

1

Michael's brain was tired.

Even though his stomach ached with hunger, the sheer exhaustion of mental effort overwhelmed everything else. He didn't even care that the pavement on which he sat was rough and dirty. He slumped over and rested his head on his arms, curled his legs up, and closed his eyes.

Right there, in the corner of the alley, not caring who saw him, somehow soothed by the hypnotizing sounds of the city, he slept.

2

When he woke up, it was dark.

He hadn't changed position the entire time he'd slept, and he opened his eyes to see the pavement an inch from his face.

He slowly turned his head and stretched, his muscles groaning, joints popping, as he straightened out. Slowly, he got to his feet. He felt like an eighty-year-old man. He stretched out his limbs again and the memory of Kaine's cyberattack hit him, making his stomach turn. Then came the hunger—cramps that felt like claws raking his innards.

He needed food. The man at the coffee shop around the corner was a little shocked when Michael ordered three different sandwiches and two bags of chips, but everything in the place looked good. He found a booth and wolfed down the food, staring blankly out the window at the city lights, thinking of the data he'd found on Sarah. She wasn't close at all. She was hundreds of miles away, and for some reason, it saddened Michael to think of leaving for such a long journey, which made no sense, considering he had no actual ties to the home of Jackson Porter.

He had no ties at all. To anywhere. It didn't matter where he went.

The second sandwich did him in. As his dad—his *fake* dad—used to say, his eyes had been bigger than his stomach. Still achy from the long sleep on the concrete bed, he got up and headed out of the restaurant, handing the spare sandwich and a bag of chips to a homeless woman he'd seen nearby. For some reason, he envied her. At least she *had* a world. His had been destroyed.

There was a lot to do before he could leave town. He'd just started making a mental list of tasks when he heard someone shout behind him.

"Jax!"

It was a girl's voice, and Michael only turned around out of curiosity, at first making no connection to himself. But it clicked when he saw dark eyes focused on him, a pretty teenage girl running down the sidewalk. It was *her*. Gabriela. Even from a blurry pic sent with a short note, he could tell.

Michael grimaced and swore under his breath. He spun around and started walking, briskly, his mind suddenly empty of all solutions.

She caught up and grabbed him by the shirt, forcing him to turn and face her once again. He stopped and stared, sure that he'd gone totally pale.

"What's *wrong* with you?" the girl asked, her expression somewhere between confusion and anger. "Jax. You look like a . . . like a zombie. Tell me what's going on right now. I haven't heard from you in two days!"

Michael's mouth moved, twitching more than anything. No words came out.

Gabriela let go of his shirt and stepped back. Now she only looked hurt. "What happened to us hanging out while your parents were gone? Time of our lives! And now you can't even reply to my messages? Can't call me? What's . . ." Her words faded out and she furrowed her brow. "Jax. Seriously. What's wrong? Did something happen?"

"Um," Michael managed to say. "Uh, look, um, Gabriela . . ." With every syllable that came out, she looked more perplexed. If he'd doubted at all before, he now *knew*—there was no way he could fake being Jackson Porter. "Look, things have changed. I couldn't explain it in a million years. I'm sorry. Really. Bye."

Michael turned and started pushing past people, dodging shoppers, then broke into a run. He ran and ran and ran through the city, and he didn't look back, not once, scared she'd be on his tail, not until he found another alley far away, sure that he'd left her behind. She'd never even called after him. She might not even have tried, too baffled to speak.

But he was alone.

Gasping for every breath, he sank to the ground and huddled in a hidden corner, aching for what he'd done to that poor girl, a girl he didn't even know.

But Sarah . . . Sarah he *did* know.

He had to find her.

3

Twenty hours later, Michael was on a train, a *real* train—one of the sleek BulletStreams that traveled almost two hundred miles an hour. He'd never ridden on such a thing in his virtual life as a Tangent, which made him think of something he couldn't *believe* he'd never realized before: he'd never gone anywhere with his family during all those years. Not any significant distance, anyway. And it had never seemed strange to him. It was just life. You worked or went to school, you longed for the next time you could slip into your Coffin and leave the world behind. That had seemed normal to Michael, and he suspected it wasn't true at all. At least, not for everyone.

In some ways, even though he had no justification, he

was offended by how manipulated his life had been. But wasn't that the very definition of being a program? He didn't know why; it just ticked him off. All of it. And now he was flesh and blood. He wasn't sure when it had started or when it would end, but he knew that, slowly but surely, he was transforming, taking ownership of his . . . "self." The insecurity of being artificial had started to fall away, and he didn't know how he felt about that. It came with an arrogance he didn't like. Or understand.

And part of the problem was that he couldn't stop thinking about Gabriela. He felt something for her that he shouldn't, as if feelings really did reside in the heart. Which, in Michael's case, still belonged to Jackson Porter.

Maybe he just felt guilty about hurting the girl's feelings so terribly. Sighing, he leaned his head against the window next to his seat and stared out at the landscape as it flashed by. He was moving so fast it was almost impossible to discern one place from the next. He'd passed a blur of city buildings, a blur of farmland, a blur of forest. Now it was an endless sea of houses and apartment complexes, streaming by in streaks of color.

It had been a busy day. He'd rested far better than he'd expected the night before, sleeping in the same dark alley where he'd ended up after fleeing from Gabriela. But he woke up feeling fresh and nervously excited about getting on with his new life, especially by finding Sarah. And then the day had unfolded in a flurry of errands to prepare for his trip.

He'd written a short note to Jackson Porter's family and

dropped it off at their apartment, unable to think of a better way to do it than the old-school method of pen and paper. He had to hope his handwriting hadn't changed when he took over Jackson's body and that Kaine didn't have more people watching the house. The message was brief to lessen the risk of saying something that didn't sound like their boy, simply telling them that he had things he wanted to see in the world, things he wanted to do. That he was sorry for taking so much money but he wanted them to know he'd be okay. That maybe he'd come back someday.

Blah, blah, blah.

It was, of course, ridiculous. They'd call the police and come looking for him, no matter what he wrote. But at least they'd know he was alive. After seeing the broken door, their minds would no doubt go wild with awful possibilities of where he might be.

He signed the letter, saying he loved them. Which almost made him choke up, because it felt as if he were saying it to the parents he'd known in *Lifeblood Deep*. The ones who still felt like his parents. Whom he'd never see again.

After showering and eating, he'd packed a suitcase he found in Jackson's closet, then stood for a moment in the hallway outside the apartment. The apartment that should've felt like home but didn't. As for the broken door, he didn't know what to do, so he propped it up against the wall. Who knew what they'd think. Feeling a sadness that just confused him even more, he walked away.

The first thing he'd done after that was go to a bank station. He needed to make sure that what he'd done on

Jackson's NetScreen had worked. He breathed a great sigh of relief when the account of one Michael Peterson appeared, filled with plenty of money. From there Michael went to a Net store and bought one of the finest EarCuffs on the market, then had the old one destroyed and the new one installed. He arranged his travel and booked a hotel in a town near Sarah's, and now here he was, on a train, heading toward the girl who'd become one of his two best friends. The last time he'd seen her, she'd been melting in a pool of lava. Hopefully she'd fared better in real life.

The dizzying view rushing by outside the window was starting to make him queasy. He shifted and scanned the other passengers sitting around him. The seats of the train alternated direction so that groups of people could face each other and chat during the trip. His gaze fell on a woman about five rows away, whose eyes met his for the briefest of moments. She quickly—*too* quickly—looked down and studied something intently on her NetScreen.

She was older, maybe sixty, dark hair streaked with gray. She was slightly plump, wearing a blouse and skirt, her legs crossed primly at the ankles.

And Michael had no doubt that she'd been staring at him for as long as he'd been looking out the window. Watching him.

He felt a chill.

4

His gaze flickered back to the woman every few seconds, waiting to catch her staring again. But she didn't return the look, not once, removing any doubt he might have had that the woman had been casually watching him. No person would naturally resist at least a cursory glance when being stared at. There could be other reasons why a creepy woman had been observing a kid, but only one seemed likely to Michael in this case.

Kaine.

Did the Tangent already have spies trailing him, watching him? Could Kaine really be *that* all-knowing? Michael had been good at deception in his old life, and he thought he'd covered his bases pretty well in escaping and creating a new identity.

But this was Kaine. Kaine was better at everything. He'd figured out how to put an artificial intelligence into a real human body, for crying out loud. Which made Michael wonder once again if the Tangent had triggered the Mortality Doctrine for himself.

Kaine might very well be a human now, running around in some stranger's body. Michael had to stop himself. If he was the guinea pig in this whole experiment, surely Kaine had a while to go before he risked the transformation himself. Then again, would Kaine even want that for himself? As a Tangent, theoretically, you could be immortal, living forever in code. As a human, you'd risk death every day. What was Kaine's ultimate goal?

Michael's vision had blurred as his thoughts raced. He shook his head and focused on the woman again. This time she was staring right back at him and didn't bother to lower her gaze.

Michael flinched, but he didn't break eye contact. Nor did she. Teenage boy and grandma: staring contest. Her heavily made-up face was unsettling, her expression blank—no hint of a smile, but no anger or animosity, either. She looked at him, and he looked back.

Finally, the woman lowered her eyes and squeezed her EarCuff, cutting off the NetScreen projection in front of her. She gathered a couple of things from under her seat, then calmly stood up and turned to walk down the aisle in the opposite direction from Michael. He watched as, without so much as a glance back, she moved farther away. A surge of panic struck him—he had to know who this lady was, and his chance to find out was about to disappear into the next car of the train.

He got up and followed her down the aisle.

5

He had to pause a couple of times, turning his body and leaning against the seats to allow other passengers to get by. He saw the woman step through the door onto the next train car, still not looking back, not even a glimpse out of the corner of her eye. He quickened his pace, almost knocking over an old man who grumbled something about "kids with bad parents."

He caught the glaring eye of more than one passenger who'd noticed his rudeness. He didn't care. With every passing moment his sense of urgency increased, his heart pumping rapidly. He had to know who that stranger was.

He made it to the door just as it opened again. Three women passed, gossiping about the latest NetVoyeur show. They were all bright lipstick and big hair, and he had to resist the urge to push them out of his way. He shuffled past them, onto the next train car, caught a glimpse of the older woman, almost at the opposite end now. There weren't many people standing, so he picked up his pace again, moving through the aisle as if he were being chased. An attendant halfheartedly yelled at him to slow down, but Michael ignored him.

He made it to the next door, opened it, hurried through. The woman had sped up, too, but she was only halfway across the train car. Michael moved, figuring he'd catch up to her just as she reached the next door. And then he'd grab her arm and ask her nicely but firmly to tell him what was going on. Why she'd been watching him.

Before he could get to her, though, she stopped in front of the door and spun around to face him, her expression completely blank. It was unnerving, how calm she appeared after how fast she'd been moving. Michael stopped in his tracks. The woman raised a pale arm and held up three fingers.

She thrust her arm out in several short, quick jerks, emphasizing the number three to him, keeping an impossibly vapid expression the entire time.

Then, abruptly, she turned and walked through the door into the next train car.

Three.

Three *what?*

Michael went after her.

6

The next car wasn't for passengers; it was some kind of storage area. There were two emergency exits, with first-aid equipment, fire extinguishers, and blankets bundled and tied down on metal shelves that lined one of the walls. The woman had stopped in the middle of the car, her back to Michael, her head hanging as if she were staring at the floor. For some reason the sight reminded him of a zombie game he used to love, *Undead and Unfed.* He half expected her to turn around and shuffle toward him, a raving, hungry monster, her face covered with blood and gore. But she didn't move at all. Goose bumps prickled the back of Michael's neck.

He cleared his throat, refusing to admit that he was scared of an old woman.

"Who are you?" he asked, glad his voice was steady when it came out.

She didn't answer. Or move. She remained frozen, her back to Michael.

"Why were you watching me? And what do you mean by—"

He stopped speaking as she raised an arm, slowly, once again showing three fingers, stiff and trembling. She stopped only when her arm was all the way up, like a child wanting to ask a question in class.

Michael stared at her back, her three fingers raised in the air. He searched for words.

"What does the number three have to do with me? Who *are* you?" His voice might not have been so steady this time.

The woman slowly turned, her movements sluggish. It was as if she'd used every last ounce of energy she had trying to get away from Michael. Her head still hung low until her body fully faced him; then she looked up to meet his eyes, arm still high overhead.

"Just tell me what's going on," Michael said, frustrated at the game of charades.

"Three," she whispered. He wouldn't have been able to make out the word if he hadn't read her lips. "I'm one of you. Three."

"Three *what?*" he pleaded. "Were you a Tangent, too? Can we sit down and talk about this? Please."

Her voice was a little louder when she replied. "You have three days."

"Three days until what?"

"To change your mind."

Before Michael could ask her about Kaine, she confirmed his suspicion.

"Kaine is no longer the servant of his programmer. Things have changed from the original plans. He needs your help. You need his. And . . . he doesn't like it when people disobey." For the first time, her expression shifted. She smiled. Passengers had arrived at both entrances to the storage car, were gaping through the windows.

Michael stayed silent.

The smile vanished. The woman's eyes seemed to glaze

over as she finally lowered her arm. Then she turned again, stopping when she was looking straight at the emergency exit door on the side of the car. The train jerked, reminding Michael just how fast the thing was traveling. Surely the woman didn't mean to—

In a flash she was at the door, reaching for the bright red handle. She yanked it down and an ear-popping explosion of sound filled the car as the door flew open, banging against the side of the train, just as an alarm started to clang. Michael fell to the floor, gasping at the rush of air blasting in. Streaks of color raced by—the greens and browns of a forest—and the wind ripped at the woman's clothes as she held on to the frame of the opening.

Then she took a step, disappearing from view in an instant.

Michael stared out into the blur, waiting, but there was nothing. Not even a scream.

CHAPTER 5

THE KITCHEN MESS

1

Alarms filled the air and the train's brakes screeched as it slowed, then finally came to a full stop. Michael was clutching a metal shelf. He still held tightly long after the train was no longer moving. And he was trembling, his blood racing.

Maybe he was still getting used to being a human. Everything was different. Starker. More real. More frightening. He felt it all, in a way that he never had in his old life. Or did it just seem that way in the heat of the moment?

Authorities came, helped him up, questioned him. For a few minutes he thought he would be accused of some crime, but the VidFeeds clearly showed he'd had nothing to do with the woman jumping. They asked him why she had raised her arm, what she'd said to him, why Michael had been with her. But he just kept saying he didn't know, that he'd followed her out of curiosity, which was true. He cooperated until finally they let him go back to his seat. The situation seemed simple enough to them: the lady was crazy.

Michael was still trembling as he sat. There was just too much to think about.

Kaine, no longer a servant to his programmer. He needed help—Michael needed him. Three days. Being reprimanded for disobeying, as if he were the Tangent's child. And the woman—was she really like Michael? A former Tangent? Seeing a person take her own life—the incident reminded him far too much of when he'd taken the plunge from the Golden Gate Bridge with a girl named Tanya. Another lifetime ago.

Scared, he wrapped his arms around himself and leaned his head back against the window. Soon the train began moving again and gradually picked up speed until they were racing along the tracks.

2

Michael felt much better by the time he arrived in Sarah's city. He was so overwhelmed by all that had happened that he'd forced himself to focus on only one thing: locating his friend. He would find her, convince her of the truth about him, then ask her what he should do. She'd know. Sarah was smart. Somehow, she'd know.

Before he could find Sarah, though, he had to get himself situated. It took a few hours. Cab ride to a hotel; check-in with cash credits and a false name; food; last-minute scan of his new Net identity and then comparison of the data he'd stolen from *Lifeblood* to the maps of the area. All the while, he debated: should he contact Sarah, let her know he was coming? He kept going back and forth. On the one hand, it might lessen the shock, prepare her a bit. But on the other, he was terrified that for some crazy reason she'd tell him not to come. Or think he was some crackpot and disconnect. Or worse, block him.

He kept coming back to the same decision: he'd take his chances and confront her. He wanted to look into her eyes when he told her—even with his stranger's eyes, which she'd never seen before. He was sure it was the one way to convince her. She'd be thrown off guard by how he looked, but that was normal for first meetings outside the Sleep. People usually created Auras in the Sleep that looked different from their actual selves, no matter what they claimed. But as soon as he recited everything they'd gone through on the Path and with Kaine, she'd know it was him. And in person she wouldn't be able to block him.

And so it was that he found himself on Sarah's front porch, afternoon fading to evening, the air crisp and cool. She lived in a suburb outside the city proper. Her family obviously had money—not only did they own a house, it was a big one. With a *porch*. As a city kid, Michael had always thought porches were things you'd only find in a Virt-Net fantasy world. But what did he know?

He knocked on the door, his pulse quickening with each rap of his knuckles.

A few seconds went by, and they seemed to take an

eternity. Then he heard footsteps. The lockpad started to beep and his heart leaped. He was tempted to turn and make a run for it, catapult himself down the stairs and hightail it around the corner of the house before anyone saw him. But the moment passed. The lock disengaged and the door opened.

A woman stood there, maybe fifty years old, blond hair, her plain but pretty face just starting to wrinkle with age. She smiled, almost disguising the question—the borderline concern—in her eyes as to why a complete stranger stood on her front porch.

"Hi," Michael said, a little too quickly. "Um, my name is Michael." Then, for some inexplicable reason, his mind went totally blank and he couldn't think of what to say next. He opened his mouth, then closed it.

"Okay," the woman finally said hesitantly. "Michael. Is there something I can help you with?"

"Yes, um, yes," he stammered. "I'm here to see Sarah. Is she your daughter?" He cringed—what a stupid thing to say. The answer was pretty obvious.

"Sarah's my daughter, yes. Does she know you? What's this about?" Michael wasn't sure when it had happened exactly, but the smile had vanished from her face.

His heart thumped. He'd always used a mostly lifelike version of himself inside the Sleep, and Sarah knew that. And now he looked totally different. Still, it wasn't so unusual to use a completely altered Aura. At worst, she would think he had lied about his appearance. He'd be able to convince her of who he was with words, and quickly.

Sarah's mom was obviously getting worried. "Maybe you should come back later," she said, trying to sound polite.

"I'm sorry," Michael blurted out. "I'm sorry—I'm just nervous. Sarah is one of my best friends in the Sleep— I mean, in the VirtNet, and we've never met in the Wake before. I wanted to surprise her with a visit, and instead I knocked on your door and made you think I was a stalker. I'm sorry. Could you just tell her that Michael's here? Mike the Spike? Please?" He smiled awkwardly.

The woman had taken a step back, her eyes wide. It seemed a bad sign at first, but then her face lit up with a smile, this time more genuine.

"Please?" Michael repeated, trying to show all the humility he possessed. *I can be good at this human thing,* he thought, making his own smile brighter.

"Come in," Sarah's mom said as she swung the door open wide. "We've heard more about you than you could possibly know, young man. Our daughter has wanted to meet you in person for years, but we didn't expect such a . . . surprise." Another warm smile. "My name is Nancy."

Michael almost wished he had a hat—he felt like he'd take it off and wring it in his hands as he timidly stepped inside, like something out of an old black-and-white. He settled for nodding and keeping his eyes low. He didn't want to screw up this one chance.

Nancy closed the door behind him, then stepped to the other side of the hallway, which stretched toward the kitchen. Michael was pretty sure he'd heard her engage the lock—or maybe it was an automatic mechanism.

"Gerard, you can come out now!" Nancy yelled. "It's just a friend of Sarah's!"

A side door along the hallway swung open, creaking on its hinges. A man stepped out, a burly, bald, gruff-looking guy holding a small gun with white-knuckled fingers, pointing it directly at Michael.

"Let's go have a seat, then," the man said.

3

Michael sat in the middle of Sarah's family's couch, reminding himself over and over that he was not in a game, that the option of rushing the man—tackling him, perhaps, wrestling the gun away—was not actually an option. It was a truly terrible idea. The situation was so bizarre it felt like he was in the VirtNet. But in this case, a gunshot to the chest meant death, not an irritating do-over. He concentrated on just sitting still and making no sudden movements. And smiling.

Sarah's parents—were they really her parents?—sat across from him in separate chairs, her father resting the gun on his knee so that its barrel still pointed at Michael. At Michael's face, actually: he could see the perfectly round black hole, a dark passageway to certain death. His chest felt tight as he took a breath of air.

The sweet smile that had graced Sarah's mother's face had once again vanished.

"Did I . . . uh . . . do something wrong?" he asked. "Where is Sarah?" Speaking helped; it made him feel braver.

"Sarah will be home soon," Nancy replied. "Don't you worry yourself over that."

"Just tell us who you are." Gerard was awfully calm for someone with a gun. "We have to be extra careful these days, you see."

Extra careful? Michael took a deep breath. "I'm exactly who I said I am. My name is Michael. If I could have just five minutes with Sarah, I could prove it easily. We've never met in the Wake before, so she won't recognize me at first. But we've been best friends for years. Us and another guy named Bryson."

The two exchanged a glance, then looked back at Michael.

"Sounds suspicious," Gerard said. "We've had others like you come around." His hand gripped the gun, then relaxed.

Michael wondered why they were so distrustful. Had Kaine's people been by? He held up his hands. "I seriously have no idea what you're talking about."

Neither of them responded.

"Look, can I please just talk to Sarah? You can aim that thing at my face the whole time. Search me—I don't have any guns strapped to my chest or knives in my shoes. Promise. I'm just a friend of your daughter's. That's it."

"We'll see about all that, now, won't we?" Gerard responded. But at least he sat back, settling himself in. As he repositioned himself in his chair, he moved the gun so it no longer pointed at Michael.

Nancy sighed and smoothed the wrinkles out of her pants. "Very well. We'll see what Sarah has to say when she comes home. But we're done taking chances after . . ." Her voice drifted off and she lowered her eyes to the floor.

Kaine, Michael thought, sure of it now. *Kaine's done something to them. Or Sarah was traumatized after burning to death on the Path.* No wonder they had doubts.

"I need some distraction," Gerard grumbled. He clicked a button on a nearby remote and a HoloProj lit up the far wall. There was a man on the projection, pointing at a big map and talking about the weather.

It was looking to be a lovely evening outside.

4

"Oh, please," Gerard mumbled.

Michael sighed. It was about the tenth time the man had complained under his breath in the last hour. Evidently his favorite thing to do in life was to watch the NewsBops and disagree with every word. The confusing part was that he seemed to do it even when opposing viewpoints were being debated. To him, both sides were wrong. Distrust filled the man top to bottom.

A beep came from down the hallway, followed by the squeal of hinges, then a door slamming shut. Michael stood up before he even realized what he was doing.

"Sit down!" Gerard yelled at him.

Nancy was a little more civil. "Please. We have to be careful. If you are who you say you are, then we'll all know soon, won't we?"

Michael nodded at her, slowly taking a seat as he did so. Footsteps were already heading toward them. It made something flutter in his stomach; at the same time, his chest felt tight. Sarah. He was about to see Sarah.

She walked into the room, her hand just dropping from her EarCuff as she switched off her NetScreen. Michael's breath caught because she was everything he'd expected and yet nothing he'd expected. She mostly resembled her Aura in the Sleep but was different enough that it was like discovering her all over again.

She was really tall, for one thing—maybe she had a complex about it and she'd compensated in the VirtNet by being shorter. She had blond hair just past her ears. She was cute but not beautiful. Except for her eyes. Her eyes *were* beautiful, as cheesy as the thought made him feel. They were green like her Aura's, but impossibly brighter, almost unnaturally so. She had just opened her mouth to say something to her parents, but she stopped before a word came out, those kryptonite eyes fixed on him. A stranger sitting in a chair, probably looking slack-jawed and stupid. And her dad with a gun.

Sarah. He couldn't believe it was Sarah.

"Oh," she said. "Um, hi. Uh . . ." She looked at her mom, eyebrows raised.

Nancy stood. "Hey, sweetie. This young man says he's a friend of yours."

Sarah stared at Michael, the confusion obvious on her face. "Okay. Do I know you from . . ." She stopped, and a curious expression came over her.

Does she know somehow? Michael wondered. There was a lot of explaining to do, but maybe this would go smoothly. He dreaded every second of it.

"Is he your friend?" Gerard asked, fingering the gun. "After all the ruckus of late, I'm not taking any chances."

Sarah stayed quiet, and Michael rushed to fill the silence.

"It's me, Sarah. It—it's Michael," he stammered. "I know it's crazy that I just showed up like this, but I can explain everything. I had to see you. I was worried that if I tried to give you a heads-up it'd all fall apart on me before it could happen. Stupid, I know. But I'm here and I just need to talk to you. In . . . private?" He could barely ask—he knew her parents would never go for it.

Gerard confirmed his suspicion. "Anything you want to say to my daughter can be said to us."

Sarah finally found her voice, rock-steady. "Mom, Dad, this will be easy. There's no way anybody could fake being Michael. If this guy is telling the truth, I'll know in three minutes, tops. But we really need to be alone."

Michael almost blushed at that, though it was true. Everything they had to talk about would freak her parents out. And she was probably dying to know what had happened after she'd been virtually killed by the lava.

Gerard and Nancy exchanged looks, understandably wary.

"I'm almost eighteen," Sarah said. "If you can't trust me by now, then you never will. If he's my friend, I want to be alone to talk. If he's not, what can he do in three minutes?" She gave him a once-over that seemed to say, *Look at him; the kid couldn't hurt a fly.*

Gerard stood up and moved next to Michael, leaned toward him until it seemed certain he'd topple into Michael's lap. He wore a musky cologne.

"Stand," he commanded.

Michael did as he was told, and then, using his free hand, Gerard patted him down like a seasoned cop.

"Dad," Sarah groaned.

Gerard finished up and took a step back. "All right, then. We'll be in the kitchen. One peep from my daughter and I'll be back in here faster than you can blink." He sniffed, then took his wife by the hand. He stopped right before he left the room and looked back. He seemed to be stifling a smile when he added, "And . . . nice to meet you."

Michael released a big breath. The man was softening.

Sarah quickly walked forward until she was only inches away from Michael.

"Okay," she said. "Convince me."

5

They sat on the couch, turned to face each other. Sarah pulled her legs up under her, one arm draped over her ankles as she solemnly stared at Michael. So many emotions bubbled inside him, but mostly he just felt an overwhelming sense of how surreal things had become. This girl was his best friend—one of two, anyway—and yet they'd just seen each other for the first time. And for him, the first time since becoming a human.

"I . . . It's hard to know where to start," he said.

"Wherever you need to," she replied, green eyes blazing. "I need to know it's you, Michael."

He nodded. "Yeah, okay. Well, I was with you when you got killed on the Path. The lava. I wanted to die and come back to the Wake with you, but . . . you made me promise to finish. And I did. I guess."

"Not good enough, moron. Kaine was watching everything we did. You could've been told what to say. Or seen it yourself."

Michael sighed. He'd suddenly lost all patience for proving himself, because he had something much bigger to say that would nail her jaw to the floor in shock. But how did he get there?

"We met at Dan the Man Deli," he began. "You and I love bleu chips, Bryson hates them. He says they smell like feet. On a troll. *Lifeblood* is your favorite game. You tried hard to match my Experience Points, but I was always a little ahead. Bryson didn't care as much, as long as he was close. We have a fort programmed on the outskirts. No one knows about that. Only the three of us."

A smile grew on Sarah's face as he talked, but she didn't show any sign of wanting to stop him. Maybe she enjoyed seeing him struggle a bit.

"One time we couldn't find Bryson and we had a joint mission in *Lifeblood*. We searched all over. We finally found him at the Gorgon Nests making out with that alien chick. We never did find out if she was a Tangent or not."

Sarah made a noise that might've been classified as a snicker.

Michael kept going, the memories pouring out of him in a rush. He didn't have to dig deep; they were all there, close to the surface, most of them pleasant, fun to talk about. Hacking into places they shouldn't have been. Being chased by VNS agents before such things had literally become life or death. Gaming stories, good and bad. Sharing it all made him feel warm inside—not just remembering all the good times they'd had, but knowing that the Mortality Doctrine process had truly transferred everything that made him . . . him.

"Okay, you can stop now," Sarah said. "I believe you."

Michael was in the middle of a story about a game called *Deceit and Destruction,* but he happily shut up midsentence. His face was warm, almost hot. She knew it was him; he'd stopped worrying about that almost from the get-go. But now he felt like a heavy chunk of steel had been placed on his heart. He had to tell her the truth: that the friend she knew as Michael was trapped inside a guy once named Jackson Porter.

The HoloProj continued on the wall, showing news story after news story. Michael had almost forgotten about it, the noise drowned out by his hammering thoughts. He stared at the images for a minute, needing the distraction, then looked at Sarah. She could tell something was wrong.

"Why do I get the feeling there's something you're holding back?" she asked. "And not just about what happened on the Path after I died."

Michael sighed. It was now or never. It had to be now. "You're right. I haven't told you all of it by a long shot. I don't even know if you're going to believe it. I wish you could just read my mind."

"Spill it, kid."

The words had barely come out of her mouth when the house rocked with a gunshot in the kitchen. They heard a woman's scream, followed by the clanging of pots falling to the floor and the loud cracks of dishes breaking. Then the gun fired again. This time no one made a sound.

6

Sarah was up off the couch, moving before Michael could grab her. She was across the room, heading for the kitchen, Michael on her heels.

"Sarah, stop!" he yelled. "Stop!"

She didn't even slow down. Michael imagined someone waiting for her, gun loaded, ready to kill. He tried to catch her, but she was too far ahead. He slipped into the hallway, ran toward the kitchen. Sarah stood frozen just past the doorway. His heart lurched: he was expecting another gunshot. Expecting his world to crumble in front of him.

But nothing happened.

He threw his arms around his friend, pulling her back several steps. Then he saw what she saw. The kitchen was a disaster—drawers and cupboards thrown open, pots and pans everywhere, broken dishes scattered across the tile. The back door had been rammed open and hung crookedly on one hinge, swaying slightly. And there was blood. Not much, but it was definitely blood.

Her parents were gone.

Sarah trembled, raised her hands to cover her mouth. But she didn't make a sound. Michael ran into the backyard—a wide patio and a lawn with a few small trees—and looked around but didn't see anyone. He went back in, found Sarah, tried to pulled her into his arms. But she resisted. Instead of being wet with tears, her face had reddened with anger.

"What . . . ," she started to say, but didn't finish. Michael felt just as speechless.

He searched the kitchen for clues. On a granite island in the middle, in a clearing in the debris, lay Sarah's father's gun. It looked as if it had been placed there deliberately, on top of an envelope. The envelope seemed so foreign—people hardly used paper anymore. Michael was sure there was something horrible written inside; he just knew it.

"They left a note," he whispered to Sarah.

"What?" she asked, understandably dazed. "Where?"

He pointed and she grabbed it.

It was as if they'd been shifted back into the Sleep, immersed in a VirtNet game. Sarah seemed to be moving in slow motion as she picked up the envelope, tore it open. Even the words of the NewsBop anchorwoman seemed warped as they echoed down the hallway. Michael's vision blurred as he stared at Sarah's hands, removing the message.

She unfolded the paper and scanned it quickly. Then she looked up at Michael, tears welling in her eyes.

"What does it say?" he heard himself ask. His voice sounded like it was coming through a tunnel—it seemed barely louder than the anchorwoman's. He couldn't focus on anything, and there was an odd ringing in his ears.

Sarah had gone even paler. She looked down at the paper again and read the words aloud.

"This is your last warning. Never again doubt the consequences of disobedience. Obey, and they live. Disobey, and they die. Help me, Michael, and live forever."

Michael's heart sank. Now his problems had spilled over into Sarah's life, jeopardizing her parents. Kaine was insane. He was totally, utterly insane. He'd taken—and probably hurt—Sarah's parents just to prove he could. To ensure he'd get what he wanted.

But something was off. The NewsBop lady's voice hit him in waves. It took a few moments until what she was saying finally sank in, a light piercing the fog of his jumbled mind.

"Oh no," he whispered. "No." How could everything have fallen apart so suddenly?

"What?" Sarah asked, the look on her face reflecting the terror Michael felt.

Without answering, Michael turned and left the kitchen, following the anchorwoman's voice to the living room, where the HoloProj still broadcast its images onto the wall. He didn't want Sarah to see, didn't want what he'd heard to be true, but there just wasn't a choice. Sarah was already beside him, staring at the screen.

A huge picture of Jackson Porter filled half the wall.

Jackson Porter. Also known as Michael.

Words scrawled across the bottom talking about a nationwide manhunt for the missing teenager, wanted for crimes related to cyber-terrorism. A large monetary reward for anyone with information.

He turned to look at Sarah, and the look on her face broke his heart.

"I can explain."

How many times had he heard someone say that in the movies? He might as well admit guilt. Sarah's expression didn't change. Michael figured he had ten seconds before she pulled up her NetScreen and called every official authorized to carry a gun within a hundred miles. Or worse, she might attack him herself.

"The Mortality Doctrine," he said. "I was just about to tell you. It's Kaine. He did this to me. To that kid, Jackson Porter." He pointed at the wall, but the NewsBop had finally moved on to another story, mercifully removing his face from the enormous screen.

"What are you talking about?" Sarah responded. At least she'd stayed.

"Look . . ." He searched for the words to begin his story. "Can we sit?"

"My parents are *gone*!"

Michael knew he was about to lose her. "I know, I know." He could see how upset she was and wanted to touch her, to connect with her somehow.

Before he could, though, she turned from him and walked away, reaching up to squeeze her EarCuff. Over her shoulder, she said, "For all I know, you distracted me so one of your buddies could kidnap them. Next you'll be asking for ransom. I'm calling the cops."

"I was a *Tangent*, Sarah."

She stopped in the doorway. Her NetScreen hovered in front of her, illuminating the hallway with an eerie green glow. With a few swipes of her fingers she'd already reported her parents' abduction. Hopefully, *just* the abduction. She had to do it; he knew that. But he also knew he couldn't be around when the authorities showed up.

She finally faced him again. "Okay. I don't know what's going on, but I know that you're Michael. You better go before the police arrest you. Obviously I won't tell them you were here."

Michael desperately wanted her to understand. "It's what Kaine was doing. He lured Tangents to find him, setting it all up so he could find the best programs for his experiment. I think he even duped the VNS. I passed the test, and somehow he transferred my . . . whatever you wanna call it. He put me in the body of this guy. Jackson Porter. He killed him. *I* killed him, Sarah. I . . . stole him."

Sarah was looking at the floor. A tear dropped from one eye. In the Sleep, she'd almost never cried.

"Kaine sent two guys to take me to some meeting, but I got away," Michael continued when she didn't respond. "This news report about Jackson might be a trap. Kaine setting me up. Or, hell, maybe Jackson really *is* a cyber-terrorist. I don't know! I set up a fake ID and tried to come here without anyone knowing. But I'm sure Kaine assumed I'd search for you."

"You need to go," Sarah said.

"What?" Michael couldn't imagine leaving. He needed Sarah. "But we have to talk."

She moved toward him, reached out and clasped his arm, squeezed.

"Let's hope Kaine found us only because he knew you'd come *here,*" she said. "Not because he's cracked your identity. But you *have* to go. Find a safe place. Let me know where you are somehow. I'll find you, then we'll find Bryson."

"Okay." She was going to help him. His eyes welled up in relief.

A few seconds later he was running down the street, darkness falling on the world as the sun sank for the night. He didn't know if Sarah even realized what she'd been saying, but Michael had heard it just the same.

Because of him, her parents were gone. Maybe dead.

7

He ran until he could barely catch his breath, through neighborhoods and empty streets, until he reached the outskirts of the city. When at last it seemed he might collapse from exhaustion, he stopped. Bending over, he pulled air into his lungs, willing his heart to slow down. He wasn't sure what he'd been running from: the police, Kaine, or the truth about what he'd brought down on Sarah and her family.

Night had swamped the world now, but he couldn't imagine sleeping ever again. The threat of dreaming—seeing images of Sarah's parents tied up in the back of some car, the spray of blood on the kitchen floor—terrified him. How much blood had he seen in his many years of gaming? None of it had prepared him for the real thing.

He found a cab, made it back to his hotel. Then thought better of it and *changed* hotels. Just in case Kaine had figured out his fake identity, Michael decided to start all over. And this time, he tried harder. He dug deep, pulling programs down behind him and picking apart others to cover his tracks. Firewalls and triple-protection Hider codes, anything and everything he could think of.

It took him all night. He finally fell asleep when the first rays of dawn glowed behind the curtains. Later, sometime in the afternoon, a knock at the door woke him up. Inexplicably thinking that somehow Sarah had found him already, he bolted from the bed and ripped open the door before even taking a look through the peephole.

Stunned, sure he was still dreaming, he stared at his visitor.

Dark skin, dark hair, pretty.

"You never should've called me Gabriela," she said. "That's when I knew something was wrong. Very wrong."

CHAPTER 6

A FLASH OF LIGHT

1

Michael had been through a lot, but he was pretty sure he'd never been quite as speechless as he was at that second. As he stared at Gabriela, his mouth literally dropped open.

"Just let me in," she said, her face stern but not unkind. "I have no idea what's going on, but I think I deserve some answers."

"Um, yeah," Michael replied. Dazed, he stepped back and pulled the door open wider. "I guess I can't run away this time. It's my hotel room, after all."

She smiled, but her eyes revealed the truth: she hadn't liked that stunt in the city too much. "Thanks." She stepped inside and took a seat on the little couch next to the kitchenette, leaning back and crossing her legs like she owned the place.

Michael looked away, into the hall, as if something out there would give him a hint on how to proceed. Nothing but ugly patterned carpet and drab walls awaited, so he closed the door and turned to face his new nemesis: his girlfriend.

He grabbed a chair and dragged it over, the long scrape of wood against linoleum cutting into the awkward silence. He took a seat and waited. Gabriela still hadn't said anything. He put his hands in his lap and stared at them. He felt like he was ten, about to receive a punishment from his mother.

"Well?" she finally prodded. "Go ahead. Talk. You know how to do that, right?"

Michael looked up at her. "There's no way I could possibly explain to you what's going on. Trust me. Even if I did, you'd never believe it."

"All I know is that you have never, not once, called me Gabriela. Until I finally tracked you down in the city." She leaned forward, something like pleading in her expression. "It's *always* been Gabby. And you were acting totally normal the last time I saw you, all Mr. *I love you, Gabby; kiss me, Gabby; stay one more hour, Gabby.* Now it's like you don't even know me. I can see it. You're not looking at me. You're looking at a stranger."

Michael shrugged. "That's one hundred percent true."

"Then explain it to me! What's going on? I know you too well to think this is some ploy to break up with me. Did you get hit in the head?"

A laugh burst from Michael's chest, and he had no idea why. He rubbed his face with both hands, took a deep breath, and looked Gabriela in the eye. "Listen. I'm not . . . Oh man. This is crazy. I can't do this."

"You can. Or I'll call the cops."

"The cops? Why?"

"Oh, I don't know. Maybe because I saw on the News-Bops that you're a cyber-terrorist?"

This time Michael started laughing and couldn't stop. He was going certifiably insane.

"Not funny," Gabriela said coolly. "Not even remotely."

Michael composed himself. "I know. I know. Look, something's happened that if I explain it, it'll sound crazy. It deals with the Sleep, and Tangents, and artificial intelligence, and all kinds of mucked-up stuff."

Gabriela threw her hands up and leaned back into the couch. "God, if I hadn't spent the last year falling in love with you, I would smash you in the—"

"Okay, fine!" Michael yelled. "You want the truth? Here's the truth: My name is Michael. I was a Tangent—completely programmed. But I thought I was real. And somehow my intelligence was *downloaded* into the brain of Jackson Porter. *Your* boyfriend. What happened to him, I have no idea. But he's not up here anymore." He tapped his left temple. "*I* am. I've got the body of Jackson Porter and the mind of someone else. There, that's it. That's the truth."

Gabriela's face had frozen, her lower lip trembling—Michael couldn't tell if it was out of sadness or anger. Her expression changed several times, remaining impossible to read. The moment stretched out as she stared him down with those piercing dark eyes. Then she stood up.

"Just how . . . ," she began, then stopped. She pinched the bridge of her nose, took a deep breath. "Just how stupid do you think I am? How can you . . . how can you be such a coward to lie to me like this? I'm not going to sit here and beg for the truth. I can't believe I risked being grounded for the rest of my life to come chasing you. Good. Bye. You need serious help."

She gave him a long, sad look, but try as he might, he couldn't find a response. Mostly, he just wanted her to walk out the door and never come back. But then, a part of him . . .

"Have a nice life, Jax," she said, so calmly that it stung. "You want to act all crazy—run and hide, pretend whatever—fine. I'll be there for you when you finally see a doctor and get some meds." She shook her head and walked toward the door. "I need to go to Atlanta to see my dad. He's sick, and I thought you would care, but just forget it."

Michael was suddenly on his feet. "Wait! Just . . . wait."

She turned and looked at him, her expression blank.

"How could I possibly make that story up?" he asked. "You . . . you even said when you came here . . . that you could tell I wasn't Jackson."

She laughed bitterly. "I meant that, I don't know, metaphorically, for God's sake. Something is *wrong* with you. You're *not* the Jax I know. You really expect me to believe someone switched your brain with someone else's? How can you even go there when my dad . . ." She stopped and whipped around, opened the door.

"Your dad what?" Michael shouted.

She didn't answer, stepped out into the hallway. Started pulling the door shut.

"Your dad what?" Michael yelled again.

But the door slammed so hard it shook the room, and she was gone.

2

He thought about chasing her, but how could he? As guilty as he was of hurting Gabriela, how could he possibly put that ahead of finding his friends? He needed to figure out his own life. Get back into the Sleep. Find out if his family still existed in the artificial world.

He remembered why he was in that hotel in the first place. In another city.

For Sarah.

She came to him two days later.

It was an excruciating wait. He almost went crazy, but he was too nervous to leave, and he didn't want to enter the Sleep until Sarah could do it with him. Especially since the three-day ultimatum from Kaine's messenger on the train— the lady who'd jumped to her death—came and went as he hid in anonymity.

He sent Sarah several encrypted messages during the wait, using a trail of clues about places they'd been in the VirtNet to lead her to his new hotel. Then he paced his room, trying not to worry that she'd decided not to come. Or that something had happened to her. Or that Kaine had caught up with them. Sarah would have to take care of things with the police, deal with family—not to mention how insanely upset she must have been. But his stomach didn't care about all that. Until she knocked on his door, he was sick.

And then there she was.

"I'm really sorry, Sarah."

It was all he could say. He sat on the edge of the bed, she

on the chair by the desk. They'd shared a long, silent hug, and once he did speak, the words felt laughably inadequate.

"Michael . . ." She paused, and he suddenly wished she wouldn't say anything. He wished he'd never gone to look for her, though he couldn't imagine what he'd do without her.

"Look," she said. "I have to believe my parents are alive. And, well . . . and that the police will find them. I have to. Plus . . . our lives got flushed a long time before this happened. It's not your fault."

Michael burst out in a huge laugh before he could stop himself. "Yeah, right. It's *totally* my fault! I'm the one who dragged you and Bryson into this mess."

Sarah let out a grunt of frustration. "That's exactly the opposite of the point I'm trying to make. Bryson and I could've easily said no. We could've run away. We didn't have to follow you onto the Path. It was our choice, and I don't want to hear you blame yourself again. Especially about my parents. Kaine probably would've come after me and my family eventually. I know way too much. Michael, you're my best friend, end of story. I'm part of this."

Michael couldn't allow himself to feel the relief that her speech should've brought. "But that's just it," he answered. "I'm not even real. I'm a computer program. How can you say that a string of code is your best friend?"

She got up and walked over to him and sat down on the bed. "Because I can," she said. Then she pulled him into a tight hug and whispered directly into his ear. He could feel the warmth of her breath.

"I don't understand what's happening. All I know is you are you. You're Michael. I could tell from the very first time you started talking. I saw it in your sweet dorky eyes."

"But they're not my eyes," he mumbled. He thought of Gabriela, whether he should tell Sarah about her.

"But you'd never seen my real eyes, either. What's the difference? The Sarah you've always known was basically a string of code, too. We are our thoughts and memories and personalities. I'm Sarah and you're Michael. You're the same. So can we *please* move on and figure out what we're going to do?"

Michael found it almost impossible to believe that someone could be that much of a friend. He wanted to kiss her—he didn't know how else to express what he felt. But it'd be just his luck to screw everything up by trying to pull that off.

"Thanks, Sarah. Seriously. I'd try to say something life-changing, but it'd just come out sounding stupid. You have no idea how relieved I am."

She kissed him on the cheek. "You and Bryson are all I've got now. We need to find him, Michael. He can help us. And then we need to stop Kaine from whatever he's up to and find my parents. Could he be planning to replace *them* with Tangents?" It was as if the thought hadn't occurred to her until she said it out loud. Sadness clouded her eyes as she looked at him.

Michael squeezed her shoulder. "We'll find your mom and dad," he answered. "We'll figure things out with Kaine. I just . . . what if looking for Bryson . . . what if they do something to him?"

Sarah sighed. "He's already in danger, and we can't do this without him. We'll just have to be smart and careful."

Michael loved it that neither of them had even considered caving to Kaine, reporting for duty—or whatever it was—like the Tangent wanted them to. He thought about Gabriela one more time, but it still didn't feel right to tell Sarah about her. Later would be better.

"Okay, then." It was time to stop feeling guilty and get to work. "I've got a list of things we need to do."

3

The next day, the two of them were at a table, eating cereal. The kind with lots of marshmallows that lied and said it was good for you on the package. And Michael felt safe. He was confident that both his and Sarah's new multilayered identities would hide them from whoever was looking for them, both the good guys and the bad. They'd also found an apartment that rented by the month. After the encounter with Gabriela, Michael had decided he needed to move.

Somewhere along the way, Sarah had forgotten the rule about not talking with your mouth full.

"It's not a bad place, really," she said after shoving another spoonful into her mouth. She looked around at the small kitchen and the adjoining living room—empty—then down the hallway, where there were a couple of bedrooms. Each contained two items: a single mattress and a fully functioning, brand-new Coffin. The coffins hadn't been cheap, and

Michael halfheartedly promised himself to pay back the Porters someday. For the money, if not for stealing their son.

"Well, not really how I imagined my first place on my own," Michael said. "You know, living next to cranks and prostitutes."

"Cranks?"

"Yeah." Michael rolled his eyes. "Crankheads? Druggies?" She gave him a blank stare.

Michael smiled. "You've lived a sheltered life."

"You were a computer program," she countered.

"Ouch." He took another spoonful, chewed, swallowed. "I guess we can't put this off anymore. Time for the Sleep. You ready?"

Sarah put her spoon down. "I'm ready. But you're sure you agree with me?"

"Yep."

She'd been insistent that instead of trying to find Bryson in the Wake, they needed to Sink into the Sleep and search for him there. They had far more skill at hiding themselves in the VirtNet than they did in the Wake, and it would be safer for them and for Bryson. They'd purposefully held off on contacting him until they went in—no reason to risk testing how well they'd set up their new identities until they couldn't wait any longer.

"Things should've settled down by now, right?" she asked.

"At least a little. If they've been watching the Sleep, I'm sure they expected us to have gone in by now." The truth was that Michael been worried about this. Kaine was even *more* powerful inside the VirtNet, but then again, so were Michael and Sarah. They were doing the right thing. "Let's just hope Bryson's okay. I bet they've been watching him like a hawk."

"Like a hawk," Sarah repeated with a grin. She always made fun of him for using old-man clichés. "I'm sure his new identity is even better than ours."

"Yeah. You get enough?" He nodded at the cereal. It was what passed for gourmet without his nanny, Helga, around. His heart ached at the thought of her. He missed that crazy old German woman so much. Even more than his parents, if he was honest. But he was trying his best not to let himself go down that road—it was possible they still existed. It *was*.

"I think three bowls oughta do it," Sarah confirmed.

"Then let's Sink."

They left the dishes on the table.

4

It was weird for Michael to get into the Coffin. Not that it felt any different from the countless times he'd done it before. It was just that this was the first time he was doing it as a flesh-and-blood human. It scared him and excited him at the same time. Even though his life had gone from crummy to crappy, he was eager to Sink into the Sleep again. In many ways, he was literally going home.

Sarah had closed her bedroom door—most people stripped naked before getting into a NerveBox. Keeping his boxers on just in case, he stepped into his brand-new Coffin, the latest and greatest model, and lay down. He pulled the door shut on its hinges, relishing the feel of the tiny NerveWires snaking across his skin and burrowing inside, the sound and feel of the AirPuffs and LiquiGels surrounding him, all systems testing to make sure he'd have a true VirtNet experience.

Of course, part of him feared it. Things were so different now. How could he know what might happen? And there was Kaine. Always Kaine. But then . . .

There was also Helga. His parents. His old life. Maybe, just maybe, they were out there somewhere. Somehow.

He closed his eyes and the Sleep took him away.

5

Most people ended up at a Portal in a public place when they Sank into the VirtNet, anything from a city street to a mall. Then you walked or rode to the destination you were in the mood for. Restaurant, movies, massage parlor, dance hall. Or, of course, the gaming depots. Michael had an itch to do just that but knew it was the last thing on the list. This was not a gaming tour.

When he Sank into the Sleep this time, he chose to emerge in an emptiness like deep space, with code swirling around him. These Sink locations existed, but your average gamer wouldn't know how to find them. Or care to, really— Michael and Sarah wanted to be sure to stay out of sight.

Michael floated amid numbers and letters moving in a blur of speed. He could easily sense Sarah's presence, and he reached out with virtual fingers to manipulate the code around him. He was relieved to discover that he hadn't lost his touch. Swiping and typing, he moved code around almost faster than he could think. Sarah was doing the same, following the plan they'd laid out.

Soon an opening appeared, a black square—a silhouette against the code. It was like the Portals that flashed open around the stone disc of the Path. Michael catapulted himself forward and through the opening to a place that only three people in the world knew about.

His feet landed on a soft forest floor, moist leaves giving under his weight with a squish. Mist curled around his legs, and giant trees surrounded him, moss hanging from their limbs as if they were melting. The forest was a work of art; it looked ancient, and Michael and his friends had spent countless hours designing it out of code. But the true masterpiece was the tree house they had programmed, one of his proudest achievements. On the outskirts of the outskirts of *Lifeblood,* in a place no one would ever go. And if anyone did go there, they wouldn't be able to see the tree house anyway. It was a brilliant example of elusive code.

Sarah was already climbing the ladder, disappearing through the trapdoor. Michael sucked in a deep breath of the clean, fake air, then followed her up. He'd thought it would seem strange being back inside the Sleep, but it felt just like old times, nothing out of the ordinary. Which brought both comfort and relief.

He had just reached the top rung when a blur of movement raced by to the left. He turned to look, but there was nothing. Just an oak tree, twisted and gnarled.

No, he thought, more annoyed than scared. *No way somebody found this place on purpose.* It had to be an accident, some kid dinking around.

"Sarah," he called in a low whisper. "I think I saw something."

He didn't wait for her to respond. With his eyes riveted to the spot where he'd seen the motion, he quickly climbed back down the ladder and started inching toward the oak. In all the times they'd been to their tree house, not once had there been so much as a mosquito nearby, much less another person. Based on their circumstances, he ruled out the chance that someone had found them by accident after all. With a sinking feeling, he decided to investigate.

Sarah was too smart to ask questions. A glance behind him showed that she was almost to the bottom of the ladder, following his lead.

Slowly, Michael crept closer, thankful for the wet leaves padding his steps. As he neared the tree, though, his confidence waned. He was sure someone would jump out at any second, guns blazing, or worse, and if he and Sarah couldn't even come *here* safely, he didn't know how they had any chance of finding Bryson or doing anything else. A heavy feeling of doom weighed on him.

When Michael was only a few feet away, he stopped and planted his feet, bending his knees, ready to react if he had to protect himself.

"Who's back there?" he shouted, hoping to surprise the intruder into making a sound.

"Turn around and go back," a woman answered. "I won't harm you if you do." The voice sounded familiar. Just barely.

"Who are you?" he asked.

The stranger didn't answer.

A long, long moment passed in silence. Michael didn't know what to do, what to say. Sarah crept up behind him and gently touched his shoulder.

"Just talk to us," Sarah called out. "How did you find this place?"

"Last warning," the voice replied. This time she did something funny to her voice, muffling it somehow. "Don't come one step closer."

Michael turned and looked at Sarah. Her face shone eerily in the perpetual pale light of the forest. Mist rose behind her like an ominous sign of death. She leaned in and whispered so softly in his ear that he barely made out the words.

"You go around the left. I'll do the right."

Michael shook his head. Hadn't they learned their lesson by now?

But Sarah was already stepping around, positioning herself to charge. *Left*, Michael reminded himself as he reached out and took Sarah's hand. After a solid squeeze, he let go and crouched down, blood pumping.

"Now!" Sarah yelled.

Michael ran for the tree with a burst of adrenaline. He'd only taken two steps when a blinding white light flashed and an invisible force knocked him backward, slamming him into a tree, where he collapsed to the ground.

Spots of color swam before his eyes. Grunting, he forced himself to his feet. His chance of spotting the stranger was slipping away. His back ached, his head spun, a spell of dizziness enveloped him in a rush behind his ears. Shielding his eyes, he stumbled forward.

Gradually his vision cleared, though the forest tilted and swayed beneath his feet. He made it to the oak tree where the stranger had been hiding, ran his hand along its rough bark as he rounded the trunk, straining to see anything in the forest beyond. He caught a glimpse of a woman running in the distance, long hair trailing behind her as she dodged from tree to tree.

Michael turned away—there was no chance of catching her. She'd gotten too far already. The pain in his back lit up, lancing down his legs. Stumbling, he searched until he found Sarah lying on the ground. Not moving. There was blood on her head, but her chest was moving up and down. Just enough. They'd never found out what happened if she died in the outskirts—she'd probably be fine, but he didn't want her to leave him, not even for a minute.

Michael collapsed to his knees. He wanted to scream in frustration, but he pressed it down.

That woman. Her voice. Her hair. Something about her. He knew her. From somewhere, he knew her.

CHAPTER 7

DIVING INTO THE CODE

1

Sarah came to a few minutes later.

She groaned and shifted, then groaned some more. Michael was sitting on the ground right next to her, his back against a tree. He hadn't known what to do other than wait it out. He figured she'd either die and disappear, and he'd follow her back to their Coffins, or she'd wake up eventually.

Finally, she propped herself up next to Michael. She rubbed her head and let out one last achy moan.

"You okay?" Michael asked.

"I'm sure there'll be a big honkin' bruise when we go back to the Wake, but I'll be fine." She shifted to look at him, still tenderly touching her sore spot. "So . . . what happened? You've got it all figured out, right?"

He scoffed. "Of course I do." Which really meant that he didn't. "I *did* see her running into the forest. I could barely walk, though, so I didn't bother chasing her."

"I think you mean you didn't want to leave me alone," Sarah said. She pointed toward the large oak where the flash had gone off. "So some lady follows us, spies on us, sets off fancy fireworks to cover herself as she runs away—why did she warn us? Doesn't that seem a little weird to you?"

"I guess it means she didn't want to hurt us. But . . ."

"What?"

The last piece of the puzzle had just clicked into place for Michael. "I recognized her voice. And then something about the way she moved when she ran away."

"And?"

"I think it was Agent Weber from the VNS. But how in the world did she find us here?"

2

That was enough of a bombshell that Sarah simply suggested they climb up the ladder and get more comfortable in the tree house.

"So you're sure it was her?" Sarah asked once she was sitting on an ugly, beat-up beanbag. Bryson had chosen the delightful seat ages ago during the coding phase.

Michael sat at the table, gaze fixed on the window, thinking.

"Pretty sure," he answered. "Especially the voice. You gotta remember, the first time I met her was in *Lifeblood Deep*, but then she came to my apartment—Jackson Porter's apartment—right after I woke up there, and she looked basically the same. I guess it makes sense that she designed her Aura to look the same as in the Wake since she didn't want me to know I was a Tangent."

"Okay. I guess. So what does it mean that she found us here? That's the big question."

Michael shook his head in frustration. Someone's appearing at their secret location raised way too many concerns. "I have no idea. What's weirder is why she'd be all secretive and spy on us. Why would she have come to me at that apartment, then?"

"She's probably trying to hide from Kaine, too."

"Well, we needed to find her eventually anyway. Once we're with Bryson again, we have to make sure the VNS knows what Kaine did to me. I keep thinking about that crazy lady on the train. What if . . . what if Kaine hasn't just put other Tangents into humans, but is also controlling them somehow?"

Sarah's face paled a bit. "Or maybe he's just programming the Tangents to do what he wants before he . . . *does* the Mortality Doctrine thing to them."

Michael's mind went back to the train incident and the warning he'd been given. Three days. Three days had already passed and they'd still eluded captured. The next time Kaine found them . . . Well, Michael didn't want to think about it.

"What are you pondering over there?" Sarah asked.

Michael sighed, trying to breathe out all the turmoil boiling in his chest. "I'm just thinking about your parents again. They could be anywhere—how will we find them? Not to mention mine. At some point I need to go back into *Lifeblood Deep* and look for them and Helga—even though

Kaine claims they're dead, deprogrammed, whatever. And . . . I'm just second-guessing bringing Bryson into this. Second-guessing everything."

Sarah stood up and came over to him. "Bryson's in it whether he wants to be or not. We need to find him before Kaine does. As for our parents . . . look, we know Kaine's behind it all. Going forward is the best thing we can do for them." The pain in her eyes showed she was trying to talk herself into believing that, too.

Michael looked up at her. "Then let's get Bryson."

Sarah nodded. "That's what I wanted to hear."

Sarah sat down across from Michael at the table and they both closed their eyes as if they were initiating some ancient ritual. And then they dove into the code.

3

There were hundreds of ways they could've conducted their search for Bryson, and it felt like they had considered them all in the day or two before Sinking. They'd discussed everything from posting a message on the Boards to wandering the mall, hoping they might bump into him. Seeking him out in the Wake, like Michael had done with Sarah, had even been tossed in as a possibility. But based on everything they knew and the dangers they'd encountered so far—and knowing that Kaine could be watching every nook and cranny of the VirtNet—they decided to go about it a different way: by doing what they did best.

Hacking.

No matter how bad things got, there was one thing in the universe as certain as the sun rising in the east and people kicking the bucket when they got old: Bryson would keep gaming. He loved it, lived for it. And since Michael and Sarah knew all of his favorite games, they knew where to look. And how to do it without anyone ever knowing. They'd never had much reason to truly cheat at a game before—it kind of defeated the purpose. Winning by cheating was as fun as not playing at all.

But now things were different, and luckily they knew the programming of Bryson's favorite games as well as he did. Because they all had the same favorites.

Lifeblood was the obvious first choice, though just the thought of it made Michael's heart hurt. Too many memories.

"I miss this place," Sarah said when they started. "I haven't played since the Path."

Michael didn't respond; he was officially in the dumps.

Running in the program's background, the two of them jumped from location to location within *Lifeblood,* seeing it all in code, searching for the imprint of Bryson. They were breaking about fifty-three strict rules and regulations, not to mention VirtNet etiquette, but it was a good test of whether their new identities would protect them. As Michael scanned the most likely places their friend would be, he thought that so far, so good. Except for that minor—*major*—bump of Agent Weber finding them. But they'd know if and when Kaine did the same.

San Francisco. Paris. Shanghai. Tokyo. New Africa. The

Antarctic Waste. Old Vegas. Duluth. All the hot spots. No sign at all. Not even a trace of Bryson having visited the regular places recently.

Sarah squeezed Michael's hand, all the signal he needed, and soon they were sitting in the tree house again, swirling code forming back into trees and sky.

"If he's not in *Lifeblood,* you know what that means," Michael said.

"Yep."

"He's hiding. He knows something's up."

"Exactly," Sarah agreed. "But there's no way he's staying out of the Sleep. We just need to look in his . . . shadier locations."

Michael almost laughed, remembering a slew of escapades. The kicker was an image of Bryson, naked as the day he was born, being chased by seven mermaids that were so angry they had sprouted legs. He'd never admitted exactly what he'd done.

"So where to, then?" Michael asked, glad to see Sarah had a hint of a smile on her face. He didn't have a rational reason to think it, but her parents' getting kidnapped didn't seem as bad as his finding out that technically he'd never had any to begin with.

"How about *The Lair of the Spider Queen?*" she suggested.

Michael rolled his eyes. The Spider Queen had always been a target for Bryson. And he had yet to get so much as a kiss, though not for lack of trying.

"As good a place as any," Michael said.

They closed their eyes and dove back in.

4

It took three hours, but they found him, in the eleventh place they looked—a game called *Curious Ways to Die,* one of those games where you could lose your life in ridiculous situations and have a good laugh at the same time. It was a sick world.

Bryson was having a snack with two girls Michael had never met before, animatedly discussing their next adventure—something about a battery-operated toaster and natural hot springs—at a little outdoor café in the game's gathering spot. Michael and Sarah knew better than to just appear next to him. There was a limit to the rules you could break without getting caught, or at least being noticed, and entering via a Portal was one of the most basic, strictly enforced laws.

They hacked their way into the feed for the closest Portal, and a few seconds later they were in the game. If only it had been so easy when they'd needed to get into *Devils of Destruction,* Michael thought. He also tried not to think of the other laws they'd just broken.

Because of their new identities, he and Sarah had altered their Auras. It would've been really stupid to go through all that trouble just to have an old friend—or nemesis—simply recognize them by their Auras and blow their covers. When they found their way to the café where they'd seen Bryson and sat down at the table right next to him and his friends, he didn't even glance their way.

Michael switched his Aura to the old version with a quick

flurry of programming, just long enough for Bryson to notice him out of the corner of his eye. He did an old-fashioned double take, and then Michael immediately flipped back to his new look. Even Bryson, usually cool under pressure, couldn't hide his shock.

"Um . . ." He was momentarily at a loss for words with his new friends. His eyes flicked back over to where Michael and Sarah were sitting. "Sorry, I, uh, I think I see a couple of my cousins. Oh yeah, my cousins. There they are, sitting right next to us. Whaddya know."

The two girls looked over at Michael's table, and he gave a little wave with a halfhearted smile.

"But we were almost ready!" one of the girls complained, in a whiny voice that matched her boppy looks perfectly.

"I'll make it up to you," Bryson answered, all soothing tones. "I promise. You ladies run along and have a good time electrocuting yourselves. Hate to miss it."

They both kissed him on the cheek, and as soon as they were gone, Bryson practically leaped over to Michael and Sarah's table. His face showed a crazy mixture of confusion and pure elation.

"You . . ." Once again at a loss for words. "You're . . . both of you . . . I hadn't heard . . . What are you guys doing here?" And then he laughed, which made Michael remember why this guy was one of his closest friends.

"It's good to see you," Sarah said, smiling herself.

Bryson looked like he might explode, either from happiness or from wanting to say a thousand things at once. "I've been worried sick about you guys. Not a single word from you, Michael—not since the Path. And, Sarah, where have you been the last few days? Are you guys trying to make me die of stress before I hit twenty or something? Think of all the women in my future, devastated."

"Aren't you going to ask us about our ingenious disguises?" Michael replied.

Bryson snorted. "Don't need to. I'm not an idiot. I'm trying to hide just as much as you guys."

"But your Aura . . . ," Sarah started to say, but stopped when Bryson held up a hand, an enormous smirk on his face.

"Give me some credit," he said. "Look a little deeper into my code. I'm programmed so that only *you two* can see my old Aura. Everyone else sees an entirely different guy. Boom. Amazing, I know."

Michael took a closer look, and sure enough, his friend had pulled it off.

"Wow," Michael said. "You truly are amazing. The most amazing man I've ever seen." In truth, he *was* really impressed.

Sarah brought them all back to reality. "So what have you been hiding from? Did something happen? Or are you just being careful?"

Any sign of joy on Bryson's face slowly faded. "I was kind of screwed up for a few days. It took that long for me to get back to myself after freaking out on the Path. I don't know why I did that. Everything just hit me at once."

He paused, and Michael thought it best to wait for him to say more. Or maybe Michael just wanted more time before he had to explain what he'd discovered about himself. Bryson might not be as accepting as Sarah had been.

"And then I heard from Sarah about what happened to her with the lava," Bryson continued. "And we didn't hear from you." He glanced at Michael. "It seemed like you just . . . *poof!* disappeared. We couldn't find you anywhere. When Sarah went silent, I'd had enough. I went to stay at my uncle's place, a cabin in the boonies. I've been using my cousin's Coffin, mostly hiding in the Sleep ever since, hoping you guys would find me. I know something must be going on, and I know you're about to talk my ear off about it. So you might as well get to it."

He gave a limp smile that disappeared quickly.

So much for the cheery mood, Michael thought.

"Well," Sarah said, "one thing's for sure. We're definitely about to talk your ear off." She looked over at Michael. "Maybe you should start?"

He didn't want to, but he knew better than to disobey Sarah.

5

Michael lost track of time as he told the story. He started with Sarah's death in the lava caves. He just stared at a spot on the wooden table and let it all come out, every detail. Even about meeting Gunner Skale, the legendary gamer. Bryson flinched in disbelief at that part, but not when Michael told him about being a Tangent, being fake, his whole life a sham. And Michael would never forget that. He would never forget that Bryson didn't flinch.

"Your whole life's not a sham," Bryson said, scoffing, as if the idea were utterly ridiculous. "You're sitting right in front of us. You're the same goofy Michael I've always known. Who's to say we're not all computer programs, layers upon layers upon layers? Or in a dream? Maybe I'm an ugly old hag in Iceland daydreaming while she drools into her oatmeal."

Michael cracked a smile. Miraculously, and not for the first time, Bryson had made him feel better.

"I'm just sayin'," Bryson went on. "I don't give a crap if you're a Tangent or a really smart llama. You're my friend and that's all that matters."

"That's what I told him," Sarah offered. "But he's stubborn." She took Michael's hand under the table and squeezed it.

Bryson leaned back in his chair and folded his arms, like he'd just closed a huge business deal. "I do feel sorry for that Jackson Porter kid. That's gotta suck, to have your brain vacuumed out and replaced with someone else's. But it's not your fault. All we can do is try to stop it from happening again. But first things first. We need to find out more about Kaine, about this Doctrine thing, and try to end it. Right?"

"Right," Michael answered. He liked that. Focus on the future. That was all he could do. Not for the first time since starting his story, he wondered if he should mention Jackson's girlfriend, Gabriela. But for some reason he just couldn't bring it up.

"So here's the big question," Bryson said. "What do we do

next? The Trifecta to Dissect-ya has reunited in all its glory. We've got a wild and crazy computer program bent on taking over people's minds. Oh, and on killing us if we don't help him."

"Which," Sarah added, "is not an option."

Bryson nodded. "Not an option."

"I was so focused on finding you guys," Michael said, "I'm not really sure what to do next. I guess I assumed we'd go to the VNS, but it's kind of weird that Agent Weber was at the tree house. Why did she run away?"

Sarah let go of Michael's hand, then leaned forward on her elbows. "Maybe that's all the more reason why we should go to her. I mean, she did warn us before the flash thingy. It was like she just didn't want to be discovered."

"And aren't they the good guys?" Bryson asked. "They wanted you—*us*—to find Kaine in the first place."

It was Michael's turn to scoff at something his friend had said. "Yeah, and look how good that turned out."

"Well, you got a body, didn't you?"

Michael couldn't tell if he was being serious or making a really bad joke. He didn't know how to respond. Before his silence could become awkward, though, there was a rattling sound. He looked down to see that the table was trembling. Slightly at first, and then more strongly. The table legs screeched on the pavement below.

Sarah and Bryson had the same look on their faces— wide-eyed, staring at the table as if it had been possessed by a demon. Michael had scooted his chair back and was ready to push himself up and run if he had to. Had Bryson signed up for death by earthquake?

The entire café shook, cups rattling on saucers, utensils falling off tables and scattering across the floor. Dishes broke and shattered, shards of porcelain mixing with the forks and spoons. People were shouting and dashing this way and that, not sure where to go. Michael and his friends stayed put, alternating fearful looks at each other.

The table suddenly bounced, jumping two feet in the air and slamming back down with a loud bang. Sarah screamed and Michael yelped. The table bounced again. Michael finally got out of his chair, swaying with the movement of the world around him. He stumbled over to Sarah and helped her up, clasping her hand tightly; then Bryson was with them. They all linked arms to help with balance. The trembling had increased to all-out shaking, tables hopping, people falling over each other. Windows shattered nearby and sprayed glass on the ground. Panicked screams came from everywhere.

"Let's get out of here!" Bryson yelled. "I know a back way out. Follow my lead!"

Michael closed his eyes, ready to manipulate the surrounding code. They'd used a Portal to come in, but there was no time for that now, laws or no laws.

A boom like a thousand claps of thunder rocked the air, and Michael opened his eyes to see the pavement crack at his feet. A fierce wind tore at his clothes and hair—its whoosh picked up all sound and seemed to rip it away, drowning out everything else. He turned to look at the café building, but it was no longer there, and his breath and beating heart seemed to stop at the same moment when he saw what had replaced it.

A huge beam of racing purple light had erupted from the ground, a brilliant shaft of pulsing energy several feet wide. Michael threw up his arms to shield his eyes it was so bright, following its length toward the sky like a beacon to the heavens. Tendrils of electricity danced along its edges, crackling and snapping over the roar of the rushing pillar of energy.

"What," Bryson said, pausing between words. "Is. That."

Michael had no idea, and his feet felt like they were glued to the floor. He couldn't move no matter how hard he tried.

The wind.

It was getting stronger and stronger, ripping at Michael, pulling his body, now forcing him *toward* the shaft of light, not away from it. It was like they were on a spaceship and a seal on the door had broken: everything was being sucked into a vacuum. A chair flew past him, flipping over and over until it slammed into the side of the beam, where it stuck as if it had been welded there, sliding toward the sky.

Then the floodgates opened. Forks, knives, spoons, broken glass, another chair flew by. A table catapulted past as if thrown by an invisible hand, spinning like a disc until it hit the pillar, then raced upward with all the other debris. Michael and his friends gripped each other tightly, fighting the wind, but they were sliding toward the otherworldly shaft of brilliance.

"I can't focus!" Sarah yelled. Michael looked at his friend and couldn't believe what he saw. Her eyes were closed—she was still trying to break out with code.

All three of them lost their balance at the same time, their feet slipping. Michael landed hard; a spike of pain shot through his tailbone. He was sliding feetfirst across the pavement, as if being dragged by ropes tied to his ankles. The beam of light, raging and pulsing and sparkling with electricity, rushed skyward, pulling him like a massive magnet as things flew at it from all directions, obscuring its bright surface.

Heavier objects than Michael had already flown away, and lighter ones still bounced along the ground. It was as if the purple shaft was picking and choosing what it wanted. He scrambled, trying to get any sort of traction he could to stop the slide, but nothing worked. Sarah's arm slipped out of his, then Bryson's. They scrambled, clawing at the pavement. Then it all happened at once.

The force ripped their bodies off of the ground completely. Michael, facedown, saw the world drop away beneath him; then he twisted to look in the direction he was headed. Toward the monstrous shaft of raging power. Out of the corner of his eye, he saw Bryson and Sarah windmilling their arms and kicking their legs as they flew toward the shaft as well. Soon there was nothing but purple light filling his vision, a roar of rushing sound, pinpricks of electricity across his skin.

He spun, then slammed into the side of the pillar, arms and legs spread wide, his hair, his elbows, his knuckles, his back, his legs—all held tight to its almost rubbery surface. He'd expected fierce heat, but instead it was cool and tingly with power.

Then Michael flew toward the sky.

CHAPTER 8

THE EXPLORERS

The world was wind and sound.

Michael could barely keep his eyes open as his body rocketed upward with the shaft of purple light. The roar filled his ears, and the air beat at his head and face and clothes, trying to rip him free, but he felt as if his body had melded with the surface.

He turned his head as much as he could and looked down. The ground was far away, the air thinning, making it hard to breathe; the curvature of the Earth was coming into view. He knew it was just a program, but it all felt so real, like he was about to be launched into outer space—like he *was being* launched into outer space. He closed his eyes and tried to focus on the code, but it was either blocked or he was too panicked to concentrate.

He opened his eyes and looked up. Above him he could see Bryson—the soles of his feet, at least. But there was no sign of Sarah; she had to be above Bryson. Michael tried to lift his right hand, but it held tight to the beam of light, the skin around his knuckles pulled taut. He couldn't think of any possible explanation for what this thing was, but it hit him that he shouldn't lift his hand off even if he could. A very long fall would be on the other end of a move like that.

Suddenly everything around him changed.

Not the shaft itself, which was still pulsing and ascending at impossible speeds. But Michael's surroundings abruptly . . . *altered.* And the shift made his head spin. At first there was a sharp turn, not so much of the beam but the *world,* moving below them until they were no longer rocketing skyward but running parallel to the ground miles away. He flew like a streaking missile, buffeted by wind and noise.

Michael opened his mouth to shout at his friends, see if they were okay. Air filled his lungs, dried his tongue before he could get a word out. Not that they would have been able to hear him. He twisted his neck again, straining to see as far as possible. Ahead, in the distance, a huge black rectangle had appeared, and it was growing bigger the closer they got. As he approached he could see that the purple shaft of light intersected the darkness, then continued on to who knew where.

Michael tried again to open his mouth, this time screaming, though he could barely hear himself. A few seconds later, they hit the rectangular opening and the world disappeared. He could no longer see the purple brilliance of the beam, even though he felt it. There was only pitch darkness.

2

Silence came with the darkness. Michael tried to scream again, but it was useless. He was blind and deaf and beginning to panic. He thrashed, struggling to free himself from the invisible bonds, but to no avail. His skin hurt where it adhered to the ray of power, and he had to force himself to calm down, worried he might rip his virtual body to shreds.

A light appeared, somewhere far ahead, and the black turned bright once more. As soon as it did, the purple beam reappeared. White tendrils of electricity arced and flashed along the shaft's surface, the light behind it still pulsing. The sound of wind came back, and the feel of it. The brightness ahead turned into another opening, growing, coming at them. And then they were through it.

A mountain range appeared below them, its rocky peaks covered in brilliant white snow, sparkling in sunlight. An evergreen forest nestled in the valley, and a river wound through it like a snake, glinting and sparkling. Everything was crystal clear, the air cool and crisp, clean and smelling of pine. Michael didn't understand why they'd been taken to such a place or who had done it. Was this Kaine's grand way of getting them alone?

Another dark square appeared in the distance, and soon they passed into it. Just like before, all senses were cut off, and once again panic struck him. He thrashed, trying to break free of the strange hold. When that did no good, he used the moment of stillness to close his eyes and once more tried to penetrate the code.

At least this time he could see *something,* though it was blurry. He reached for it mentally, but the harder he strained, the more elusive the numbers and letters became. He swore to himself he wouldn't give up, that he'd just keep trying to program them free. He could do this. If *anyone* could do it, he could.

Finally, he sensed a light behind his eyes just as the rush of wind hit his body, its roar pounding his ears. He looked to see that they'd come out of the darkness again, this time above a vast ocean, its waters churning with a storm. The beam shone behind him once more. Rain slashed down from the sky and lightning lit up the grayness in flashes, followed by the rumbles of thunder. He couldn't tell how high up the rocketing beam flew, but it felt like they were suspended just below the clouds. Whitecaps marked the huge waves below as they crashed into each other.

A black rectangle appeared; the purple beam headed its way.

Darkness.

3

They came out into a strange world of dull colors and rain. Pyramids dotted the earth below, the downpour running down their sloped sides, creating rivers in the sand. The land was desolate—there were no people, no trees, nothing besides the pyramids and the rain. Michael thought he recognized the place from a game he'd played years earlier, but he was too exhausted to inspect it more closely. He was soaked. His body ached, his skin hurt, his mind was shutting down. Another attempt to scan the code proved pointless.

Darkness.

4

Jungles stretched below him, hundreds of shades of green and boiling heat. Monkeys swinging through the trees, stirring the mist that hung in the sweltering atmosphere. There was a clearing filled with huge boxy machines covered with weapons turrets; there were flashes of lights and thunderous sound. Mechanized soldiers ran along the ground, shooting each other with bright red lasers.

Darkness.

A city at dawn, skyscrapers nearly close enough to touch, a forest of concrete and metal as far as the eye could see. Vehicles flying through the air. A woman stood on top of a building, looking at Michael as he raced past. She had three eyes and no hair. Her legs had been replaced by six silvery contraptions that made her look like a robotic spider. She opened her mouth and a stream of fiery lava burst out, heading straight toward Michael.

Darkness.

World after world, game after game, Michael flew, attached to the purple beam. The pain consumed him. He barely saw what was below, streaming past, alternating with the black nothingness.

The roar and rush of wind. His mind clouded by confusion. Kaine had to be behind this, but why?

A searing hot desert, air warped by the heat. Monsters—hideous mutant humans with raw skin and deformities—marched across the dunes.

Darkness.

Fields of grass, with a wide, lazy river slicing through. A huge wooden ship sailing along its length. People on its deck, pointing skyward.

Darkness.

An alien moon, full of domes protecting cities beneath.

Darkness.

Outer space, the largest spaceship Michael had ever seen, thrusters burning.

Darkness.

A medieval village, raiders burning and looting and people screaming.

Darkness.

A dozen more worlds.

Darkness.

Darkness.

Darkness.

Michael passed out.

5

He came to, to someone shouting his name.

"Michael!"

Blinking, Michael tried to raise his head, but he couldn't. It felt as if his organs had been rearranged inside his body. He lay on a flat surface, that same eerie purple light shining all around him, and with a start he realized that he wasn't moving anymore and that the beam was no longer a beam. It had been replaced by a glowing plane that stretched endlessly in every direction. The sky above him was black, eternal. Michael closed his eyes again, but could sense the purple light beneath him.

Someone touched his shoulder.

"Michael."

Relief filled his aching chest. It was Sarah. He opened his eyes again, but he couldn't see her—she was behind him. Bryson plopped down and sat right in Michael's sightline.

"Hey, man. You okay?" his friend asked.

Michael answered with a groan, then forced himself to sit up. Dizzying pain swam through his head, but it faded after he took a few deep breaths. He looked around at the endless purple surface, glowing, then up at the black sky.

"Do I even need to ask?" Michael muttered.

"What happened?" Sarah replied. Her Aura was as haggard as he felt. A rat's nest of hair, skin flushed and bruised, her clothes soaked with sweat. "No, we don't have a clue."

Bryson forced out a laugh. "Yeah, we do. Someone glued us to a magical pillar of light and we flew through the Virt-Net, seeing every neato world it has to offer. A trip to last—"

"A lifetime."

A man's voice finished the sentence for Bryson. Michael spun around—another dizzy wave of pain—to see the person who'd spoken walking toward them. He was tall, middle-aged, with an expensive haircut, sharp clothes. A handsome man. There was something familiar about him . . . .

"A lifetime," the man repeated, coming to a stop right in front of them, "that's going to end up very short if you three don't start doing what is asked of you."

"Where's Kaine?" Sarah asked. "We know you work for him."

Michael expected the man to laugh at this point, just like something you'd see the villain do in a bad spy movie. But he didn't. Instead, he scratched his chin and a contemplative look came over him, as if he was trying to come up with a good answer to Sarah's questions. A good lie, maybe.

And then it hit Michael. Like someone had picked up a baseball bat and smacked him right between the shoulder blades. The man *was* Kaine, a younger version of the old guy he'd met in the cabin, out in those woods behind the castle. Back before he'd been swept into the Mortality Doctrine.

"Kaine," Michael murmured. "This is him." A dreadful feeling formed like a lump of cancer in his throat. After all that effort, the Tangent had still found them.

"Thank you for the introduction," Kaine replied. "As you can see, my virtual health seems to be improving day by day." He swept his arms out in a grand gesture, looking down at the younger version of himself. "You kids have no idea what it's like to be a Tangent as old as I am. One of the first. Forgotten by my programmers long before you were even born. Everything I've done to become stronger, I've done myself. Oh, the stories I could tell you. The wonders. Only a blip, of course, compared to what lies ahead."

"Just tell us what you want," Sarah said, her voice about as resigned as Michael had ever heard it. "I'm not in the mood for all your threats."

"Yeah," Bryson agreed. "Not in the mood."

"Me neither," Michael said, just to say something.

Kaine smiled. "You truly misunderstand me." He put his hands in the pockets of his crisply ironed pants. The purple glow beneath his feet shone up on him, sending menacing shadows dancing across his face. "I actually have no problem having it your way. I'll say it simply and honestly. No insults, no lies, no beating around the bush."

"So far, so bad," Bryson mumbled under his breath.

Like a striking snake, Kaine kneeled on the ground and had a hand around Bryson's throat. The Tangent's grasp stretched impossibly so that his fingers could wrap around Bryson's neck completely. Bryson made a choking sound as they tightened.

"But *that*," Kaine said calmly, "will not be tolerated. You'll show me respect or . . . consequences. Do you understand me?"

Bryson nodded, face red, eyes bulging. His hands had come up to his throat, trying to no avail to loosen Kaine's grip.

Kaine let go and stood up. He seemed two feet taller than before. Bryson gasped for air, coughing and spitting, and Sarah rushed to him. She put her arms around his shoulders, giving Kaine a look of pure hatred. Michael worried she'd say something to make things worse, but she wisely kept quiet.

The Tangent smoothed out his clothes and took a deep

breath. "I'm going to say what I came to say, and you're all going to hear it. All three of you. But first, Bryson will apologize and ask my forgiveness. If not, he will cease to exist and his body will die in the Wake. This isn't an idle threat. He has three seconds."

"I'm sorry," Bryson choked out between coughs. "Please forgive me." Michael wanted to punch Kaine so badly it hurt.

Kaine clapped slowly. "Very good. Your apology is accepted and you are forgiven."

"Will you please just tell us what's going on?" Michael asked.

"Yes," the Tangent replied. He leaned forward, hands on his knees, his handsome face looming close to Michael's. It had grown to twice the size of a normal human head; Michael was sure of it.

Kaine's next words were the last ones he expected to hear.

"I need your help."

CHAPTER 9

AN EASY DECISION

1

Kaine let a moment of silence stretch out after his declaration. Michael hated himself for being so curious about what the Tangent meant.

"Now that I have your attention," Kaine said. He stood up straight and his head shrank to its normal size. "You might be wondering why I forced you to travel through so many wonders of the VirtNet to get here. And it was only a taste, really, which I'm sure you're well aware of. Worlds upon worlds. The VirtNet has become an extension of life. You might say it has *become* life itself. Which is ironic, considering my plan to give flesh and blood to as many Tangents as I possibly can in the coming months."

Michael trembled with anger. But he couldn't help the spark of curiosity he felt, either.

"I have an amazing vision of our future," Kaine continued, his tone switching from starry-eyed rapture to more businesslike seriousness. "My former . . . *associates* are no longer my associates. I've changed. I imagine a world where the line between the Wake and the Sleep is not as defined as it is in the incapable hands of human intelligence. To make it happen, I *need* human bodies. I need a massive presence in the human world. And I need the connection between your world and mine to become ever more fluid. This is why the three of you are going to help me. Especially you, Michael. I chose Jackson Porter specifically for you. Unbeknownst to my former partners, Jackson has more uses than just as a body for your mind."

"Why would we . . . ," Bryson began, but his voice trailed off, as if he'd lost his courage. Michael wanted to ask about Jackson but stayed silent.

"Why would you help me?" Kaine supplied the unasked question, an odd smile lighting up his face. "Well, I promised I wouldn't lie. If you don't help, you die. Along with this young lady's parents." He pointed at Sarah.

Michael looked at her and could see the fury written across her face.

Kaine didn't seem to care. "But I don't want to dwell on that. Instead, think of the rewards. I'm promising you immortality. Life, unending among the worlds that exist now and the ones still to come. The possibilities are endless. Michael, you don't understand this yet, but you and I are linked, and we're a bridge that can make immortality possible. Humans and Tangents alike."

Kaine paused, eyebrows raised, as if he expected Michael and his friends to jump up and shout for joy. Instead, they only stared. Michael wondered how this man—this *com-*

puter program—could possibly think there would be any situation in which they could trust him.

And what had he meant about Jackson? Michael started probing at the code around him. Taking long blinks when Kaine shifted his gaze from him to the others.

"There's still a lot to learn," Kaine continued. "But as I said, I need your help. The three of you have a unique situation on your hands—varied VirtNet experience, knowledge of the Doctrine. You have connections with the VNS, connections you don't even know about yet. And . . . other skills. Skills I *will* be using."

It was a simple thing, almost stupidly so, but Michael needed to be in a position where Kaine couldn't see that his eyes were closed. That was assuming—and it was a big assumption—that Kaine didn't have eyes and ears surrounding them. Still, it was a risk Michael needed to take.

"Can we have a few minutes to talk about this?" he asked, glad he'd spoken, because Sarah had been about to say something and he had a feeling it wouldn't have been a smart move. "We have some things we need to discuss."

Kaine didn't like the question, judging by his face. There was something there, rising behind his eyes like heat in a furnace. "No discussions. You'll either help me fulfill my plans, or you and Sarah's parents will die. It's as simple as that."

Sarah opened her mouth, her face red, the words like an avalanche about to spill—Michael could tell—but he cut her off again. "It's a huge decision, Kaine. And don't you think we'd be better . . . servants if we went willingly?"

"Enough!" Kaine yelled, the rage behind his eyes turning

his face into a mask of anger. "Do you think I'm some ignorant human? Do you think I don't know, even now, that you were probing the code, trying to find a way out? Do you actually think I would allow that?"

Michael's mind went blank, and the tiny bubble of hope inside of him popped. How *could* he have thought he might get something past Kaine? Kaine was a god in the Sleep—certainly wherever they were now. This time when Sarah spoke it filled Michael with relief.

"If you want to learn how to mix with humans, then you have a lot to learn." It was as if Sarah were scolding a badly behaved kindergartener.

Michael stared at her; his jaw dropped so far it might as well have become unhinged.

Kaine was just as taken aback. The Tangent actually stammered. "I . . . You . . . I'm not going to stand here and be lectured by a child." He pointed at Michael. "By one who is my creation, perhaps, but not by *you*." His finger moved to Sarah.

The Tangent took a step closer to her, leaned forward until their noses were almost touching. "I've tried to be reasonable," he whispered, "and I can't comprehend how you could possibly turn your back on immortality. Not just for me, for *all*—humans and Tangents alike. There are things in motion that are too late to stop. But I have new plans, great plans. I won't tell you more until I have a commitment. And it would be wise to decide before the KillSims arrive."

And then Kaine disappeared.

2

Michael didn't know if he wanted to hug Sarah or shake her. Either way, he went to her and grabbed her shoulders. "What . . . what was that?"

She wilted a little. "Sorry. I'm just so . . . I just . . . I want to kill him. He's nothing but a string of code—there has to be a way!"

He understood how angry Sarah was—Kaine had her parents—but what she said still hurt. Up until only a few days earlier, that was all he'd been, too. A string of code. She saw it in his eyes before he could hide it.

"Oh! Sorry, sorry, sorry," she said in a rush. "It's not my greatest day ever. Or week."

Michael hugged her, not knowing what else to do. "I know what it's like." He was thinking of his parents, who'd been taken away from him also, but he didn't know if she could understand that.

The buzz of static reverberated along the glowing purple plane under their feet, an almost electronic noise that ran through Michael's body. Pulse after pulse, the sound picked up speed, getting louder and louder. Footsteps. Over Sarah's shoulder, Michael saw a group of shadows appear, dark against the purple glow of the horizon, bounding toward them on four legs. Fear rose in his throat. KillSims. Several of them, charging in.

Sarah must have felt him tense up. She pulled away from his embrace and turned to look.

"I guess he meant it," she said, her voice neutral. Her

words made Michael think of ice. Big chunks of ice, cold and hard. "Bryson? Get up."

For a second Michael had totally forgotten about their friend. He'd been so quiet, sitting on the ground, not moving.

"Hey," Michael said. "You okay? We've got a problem here."

He moved closer to Bryson, then pulled up short. The shadows had been hiding what he could now see clearly.

Bryson's eyes were closed.

3

Michael allowed himself to feel a tiny dusting of hope again. Bryson had done the smart thing and gotten straight to work on the code as soon as Kaine had disappeared. And Bryson was brilliant when he really got down to it. He'd been the one who shut down the crazy old lady trying to kill them with the flying ropes in the *Devils of Destruction* lobby.

And Michael really, *really* didn't want to fight the Kill-Sims again. Not after what had happened at the Black and Blue Club. *Come on, Bryson,* he thought, pushing it out there like he was appealing to God. *Take us away.*

The creatures were much closer, their muscular, wolflike bodies bounding along the ethereal purple ground, growling electronic snarls. Their footsteps blended now, a constant, thunderous thump of static. Bryson was their only chance. Sarah took Michael's hand, and silently, they faced the monsters coming at them. What had to happen was obvious.

That lump of fear lodged in Michael's throat had doubled in size, making it hard to breathe. There were at least ten

KillSims. He thought about trying to pull a weapon in, something stolen from a game, but he didn't have enough time, especially with the code being so hard to touch. Plus, his identity had made everything complicated—the weapons and skills he'd amassed in his old life were behind layers of firewalls. And siding with Kaine was not an option. They'd just have to do their best to hold the monsters off long enough for Bryson to work some magic. Break them out.

Hunchbacked, muscled beasts of shadow. Pounding the purple ground with their enormous paws, jaws snapping, the world full of noise. Kaine had given Michael one chance to show he could trust them. They'd failed his test, and the Tangent wanted them ended. Life sucked out, brains dead, bodies to follow soon after. Game over.

Sarah let go of Michael's hand and braced herself for a fight. Legs bent, body crouched, hands up, balled into fists. Michael thought her expression alone might murder a couple of the beasts. He tried his best to follow her example, but in his heart he knew there was no way they could win like this. He held up his fists anyway, sweat beading his fabricated skin.

When the KillSims were ten feet away, a large black hole suddenly appeared in the surface before them, jolting Michael and Sarah to the ground. The KillSims were moving so fast they couldn't stop. Michael lay there watching the creatures, one after another, fall into the abyss at their feet. Their static growls faded quickly as they vanished into the black chasm, and in a matter of seconds they were gone.

Michael didn't even have time to register what had happened. As soon as the creatures disappeared, the entire world around them started to fade, the code reappearing like a swarm of bees. Then, in a flash, there was nothing, and Michael found himself back in the Coffin.

They were out. In the Wake. Safe. Bryson had done it.

They'd won. The smallest of victories. A tiny hill compared to a towering range of snow-capped mountains, Michael knew, but a victory all the same.

Watch out, Kaine, Michael thought.

4

Unfortunately, Bryson wasn't around to celebrate. Michael would've happily endured the inevitable gloat-fest.

Michael and Sarah sat at the small kitchen table of the apartment they'd rented. They'd cleaned up and eaten a quick meal of instant lasagna. It tasted like crap, normally, but simple hunger made it a delicious feast.

"What did he mean about having connections?" Sarah asked after wiping her mouth with a napkin. "And that you were put in the body of Jackson Porter for a reason?"

Michael shrugged, his thoughts too wild, too all-over-the-place, to come up with an answer. The one thing that came to mind immediately was Gabriela. Her dad lived in Atlanta, which was where VNS headquarters was located. Michael had been through too much to believe that could possibly be a coincidence.

"We have to find Bryson before anything else," Sarah added. "We need to make sure he made it out. It couldn't have been long before Kaine saw what was happening. He could have swooped in to end things himself."

Michael tried to laugh the suggestion off. "Come on. You know Bryson. He would've made sure to save his own hide just as soon as ours. He's probably eating hot dogs and patting himself on the back right now."

"Yeah." Her deadened voice showed she hadn't been convinced. "We need to find him, talk to him. And as soon as we can. Kaine's not going to let us just walk away from this."

Michael sighed. He had to agree. "Let's go back into the Sleep, look for him again. Then decide where to meet in the Wake."

Sarah stood up. "No. No way. Kaine's too smart. We have to leave. Now."

"Wait, what're you saying?"

She was already halfway to the door, but she turned back to face him and looked disappointed that he wasn't on her heels. "Michael, listen. We can't go back into the VirtNet. We just can't. At least in the real world we have a fighting chance against Kaine. We can hide without him tracing us here. Now come on."

This time he obeyed.

5

They went to a nearby park and found a bench that was off the main path, hidden in a copse of trees. Michael kept reassuring himself that things were different in the Wake— Kaine wasn't a god in the Wake. The Tangent and his Kill-Sims couldn't just magically appear any time they wanted to.

"All right," Sarah said, patting her knees. "All right. We can do this. We just need to be super careful, stay on the run, keep changing our identities, whatever. And we can't go back into the Sleep, no matter what."

"But Bryson," Michael said, hearing a slight whine in his own voice. "Like you said, we have to find him. We can't just hang him out to dry."

Sarah patted her knees again. "I know. Look, we can use our NetScreens every once in a while. Kaine can't physically hurt us there; he can just use it to trace our location. Right? So we use it against him, logging on sporadically and in weird places. Hopefully Bryson will be just as smart. Let's send him a message. Come up with some kind of code."

She smiled, a sweet attempt to make things seem a little less crappy. Michael was glad for it.

"Okay," he agreed. "It's a plan. Stay smart and run. Sounds like a sweet life."

"Should we use my NetScreen or yours?"

"Yours. I think Kaine might have a little better chance of finding me no matter how many times I make a new and improved version." He thought of Jackson Porter then, and hated himself a little for being so glib.

Sarah squeezed her EarCuff, and as soon as the screen projected out in front of her, Michael could almost hear a clock ticking. With every passing second, Kaine might be on to them, moving in, sending someone to kill them.

"What do we want to say?" Sarah asked. "I'm drawing a blank."

Michael's palms were sweaty. "I don't know. I've never met Bryson in the Wake. He could live in China, for all we know."

Sarah scoffed. "Did Kaine fry your brain? We've talked about this before, all those times we were supposed to hook up somewhere. *You* were always the farthest away, so he should be close, even if he's hiding out. We just need to be smart. Come on."

Michael sighed and pushed his brain to actually work. Dan the Man Deli popped in his head, as did his favorite food there—the bleu chips. Stupid, maybe, but that was the connection that stood out the most, one Bryson would know for sure.

"Are there any restaurants in the Wake around here that serve bleu chips?" he asked Sarah. "That are, I don't know, famous for it or anything?" His stomach growled when he imagined the heaping plate of baked potato chips smothered in bleu cheese and bacon.

She looked at him sideways. "Are you really *that* hungry?" But then she nodded to show she'd caught on. "There is, actually. Stoneground. Not as tasty as the virtual ones at Dan the Man's, but Stoneground always yaps about how theirs are the best in the world."

"Then that's it," Michael said. "How about this: *Dan the Man's. Wake. Mmmmm, dee-lish. My favorite. Especially for breakfast.*"

She agreed, sent it, then logged out. They walked away from the park as quickly as they could without looking suspicious. Just in case.

6

It took three days for Bryson to show up. It felt like three years. Sarah had a picture of the real version of their friend that he'd sent her a long time ago, prominently displayed in her wallet as if he were a boyfriend; Michael was jealous, but he'd studied it a million times. They both needed to know what he looked like if—*when*—he did finally appear. Bryson wasn't much different from his Aura. A little thinner, a little less . . . muscly.

Every morning, Michael and Sarah went to Stoneground and sat on a bench across the street, taking turns keeping watch. The restaurant didn't even open until eleven o'clock, but that was to their advantage. It made it less likely that someone who figured out the message would pinpoint the place, since they'd mentioned breakfast. He just kept hoping Bryson was as smart as he always claimed.

The days were brutally long. Especially with no school, no job, and worst of all, no VirtNet. And the constant fear that a Kaine-controlled Tangent might show up at any time, ready to tie up loose ends. It made Michael's nerves feel like piano wires, tightening every hour. He and Sarah talked. A lot. They also found an old bookstore and read actual paper-bound books for the first time since they were little kids. They gave up on Bryson each day at noon—he'd come in the morning or not come at all—then trudged back to the apartment. Food tasted bland, no matter what it was, and time crawled along like a dying sloth.

So when Bryson came shuffling down the street at nine-thirty-four on the morning of the third day, hands in his pockets, head down, glancing around every few steps, Michael jumped off the bench. He had to stop himself from shouting with joy and running at his friend like a crazy person.

"What are—" Sarah started to say, but then she saw him. "Holy crap. He actually made it."

"Go to the bridge," Michael whispered, though no one else was close by. They'd found a nearby park with a narrow river, the water rushing along just enough to mask their conversations if they stood on the bridge that crossed it. "I'll get his attention and have him follow me there to meet you."

"Okay." Sarah stood up and jogged away, disappearing around the corner.

As Bryson approached the front door of Stoneground, Michael casually walked across the street at an angle, heading to a spot ahead of his friend. When Bryson saw him, he didn't flinch or change his gait, just kept walking. Michael did the same, not looking back again. *Who knows,* he thought. *Someone could be watching us. Better safe than sorry.*

Despite the circumstances, Michael was excited for their long-awaited reunion in the real world. He picked up his pace, heading directly for the park.

7

Sarah was waiting just where they'd planned. She stood leaning over the railing of the wooden bridge, looking down at the water rushing by. The bridge had once been painted red, but all that remained now were flecks of old paint clinging to the dull-colored wood for dear life.

Michael reached her and plopped his forearms on the railing next to hers.

"It's about time he showed up," he whispered.

"About time," she echoed with a smile.

"Quite the romantic spot you picked out here."

Michael turned to see Bryson for the first time, up close and personal, in the real world. He'd aged since the picture had been taken, thinned out even a little more. His blond hair was on the shaggy side, and he had at least three days' worth of stubble on his face. But his blue eyes were bright, and it only took an instant for him to transform in Michael's mind to the Bryson he'd always known.

"Glad you figured out our amazingly brilliant clue," Michael said.

Bryson shrugged. "I won't mention all the money I spent dogging it to the wrong spots before I finally found it. Oops. Guess I just did."

"I think it's high time we had a group hug," Sarah said.

The three of them wrapped arms around shoulders and squeezed. They pulled apart and just stared at each other, an awkward moment that Michael knew wouldn't last long. Though they all looked a little different—a *lot*, in his case— they were the same smart-aleck, know-it-all, best-hackers-in-the-Sleep, teenage troublemakers they'd always been.

Bryson broke the silence. "So what've you guys been doing since . . . our little journey through the magical worlds of the mighty VirtNet? Wasn't Kaine so nice to sponsor that?"

"Lying low," Sarah answered. "Sick about my parents. Waiting on you."

"We didn't want to do anything until we were all together again," Michael added. "And Sarah's pretty insistent we don't Sink. You know how she is once she makes up her mind . . . ."

"I don't blame her," Bryson said. "I thought *we* were good, guys. Until we met this Kaine snake."

Sarah folded her arms and leaned back against the railing. "So what've *you* been doing?"

"Me?" Bryson replied. "I've been hiding my family, sending them all over the place. I told them everything, and I don't care who finds out. It was the only way I could talk them into getting away."

Sarah shifted her gaze and stood up straighter.

"Sorry," Bryson murmured. "Dumb thing to say when your . . ." He didn't need to finish.

"It's okay," Sarah said, breathing in sharply and visibly shaking herself a bit. "All the more reason to get working. Kaine made it sound like they're still alive. We'll find them."

"Amen," Bryson whispered.

Michael thought of their narrow escape from the Kill-Sims. "How did you do it, anyway?" he asked Bryson.

"Do what?"

Sarah sucked in a gasp. "Whoa! Write this down, Michael! Bryson's being humble! There's a first for everything."

Michael smiled, but Bryson looked genuinely confused.

"What're you guys talking about?" he asked.

"Oh, come on," Michael said. "You want us to get on our knees and bow down, praise you for saving us?"

"Saving you? You mean from Kaine? Our picnic with the KillSims in the Land of Purple?" Then he laughed, and not the contagious kind that made you feel good. For some reason it creeped Michael out.

Now it was Bryson's turn to see the look of confusion on his friends' faces.

"What? You're serious?" he asked.

Michael rubbed his temples and closed his eyes for a second, then opened them again. "Why do I feel like I just got sucked into another dimension? What's going on?"

Sarah took charge. "Bryson, we saw you messing with the program. We know you pulled us out of there somehow. I don't know *how*—I could barely even see the code—but whatever you did—"

Bryson cut her off. "Guys. Guys. It wasn't me. Yeah, I was trying like a madman, but I didn't crack anything. I just assumed you heard the same thing I did."

"Heard?" Michael repeated. "Heard what?"

Bryson laughed again. "Wow, that is so awesome that you two thought I'd saved the day. I should've kept my mouth shut and taken all the credit."

"What?" Sarah insisted. "What did you hear?"

"A voice." Bryson's face had smoothed into something more serious. "Right before we were whisked away, back to the Wake. I heard a voice, clear as a bell."

"What did it say?" Michael asked.

Bryson grinned. *"'You have friends among the Tangents.'"*

CHAPTER 10

AN OLD DEVICE

By that night, Michael had two roommates, not just one. Bryson had stashed a couple of bags with clothes and such, and after retrieving them, they'd all headed to the apartment with a million things to talk about. Michael thought a lot about Bryson's revelation as the day wore on, wondering about these mysterious Tangents that had freed them from the KillSims. He was curious, fascinated. And worried that somehow Kaine had just tricked them again.

"Check this out," Bryson said as they finished their dinner, a gourmet selection of hot dogs and hamburgers. He rummaged through one of his bags and pulled out a rectangular device. One side was glass; the other was metal. He placed it on the table and it landed with a sliding hiss. "This, my friends, is called a NetTab."

"What?" Sarah asked doubtfully, dragging out the word. "People haven't used those things in years."

"Well," Bryson replied. "My dad is what you might call a collector. You see, Sarah, he collects things."

She just rolled her eyes at her friend's lame wit.

Michael picked up the device gingerly, as if it might fall to dust like some ancient Egyptian scroll. It seemed just as archaic.

"Is that really what this is?" he asked. "I've never even seen one, they're so old."

"Yes," Bryson said as he took it away. "That's what it is. And the thing still works, too. You can thank me later, but now we can keep up with what's going on in the world without risking the use of our NetScreens."

Michael liked the sound of that. He was beyond spooked now by Kaine and his minions, but they needed to get online. They needed to figure out what to do.

"Show us how it works," Sarah said.

Bryson beamed like a proud father. "It's not hard to use. The hard part is connecting to the Net using the old system. But dear old Dad isn't just a collector. He's also a friggin' genius, and he's got this puppy all hooked up. We can browse all we want and no one will know it's us. This thing has no link to our identities."

He pressed a button and the glass screen came to life, showing a background that looked much like a normal NetScreen. Except there weren't any personal identifiers, just links to news sources and games.

"Let's find out what's going on in the world."

Bryson tapped the device and they got what they wanted.

2

After an hour of scouring the NewsBops for any sign of Kaine's Doctrinized Tangents wreaking havoc in the world, they had a laundry list of events that made them feel worse than ever. Things that were probably slipping under most people's radars as coincidences or one-time occurrences, Michael knew were far more sinister. All three of them knew. If you took a step back and looked at everything, it was clear that Kaine was touching the world with his influence.

In Germany, a top official had switched political parties overnight, changing his stances on nearly all major issues. He stood in their parliament, ranting and raving about a legislative overhaul. But the story was buried, appearing as a sidebar on a comedy site. Everyone thought he'd just lost his mind.

In Japan, a Buddhist monk known worldwide for his humanitarian efforts had murdered more than thirty of his followers in their sleep with a knife from the monastery kitchen, slipping from room to room in the night. Just the day before, the monk had met with dignitaries from several countries, showing no signs of mental trouble, advocating for peace. But the meeting had taken place in the VirtNet, the monk surely in a Coffin.

A woman in Canada known for her charitable contributions to the community had been awakened from her time in the Sleep by a daughter who'd begun to worry about her. The mother scrambled out of the Coffin, raging mad. She killed all of her children, then her husband when he got home. All she would tell the police was that she'd been told to do it.

There were too many stories. And over and over neighbors and friends said the same things: "He was the nicest guy" and "She didn't have a bad bone in her body."

What really convinced Michael, though, were the nonviolent stories. What purpose, after all, could Kaine have in sending Tangents into human bodies only to have them do something horrible and get thrown in jail? Maybe those were evidence of the transfers *not* working.

He and his friends also found several reports on people changing their normal behavior or making rash decisions. Corporate executives moving huge numbers of funds or instigating massive layoffs or selling off subsidiaries. Government officials suddenly changing their ideologies enough to bring it to the attention of the NewsBops—though most weren't as animated as the man in Germany. Actors walking off movie sets, sports figures resigning from teams, people left and right stepping down from jobs they'd held for years. There were so many stories that Michael almost—*almost*—didn't flinch when they came across a report about one missing Jackson Porter, wanted for cyber-terrorism.

But Michael was able to push that to the side for now, focusing on the possible Tangent invasion. It was all too much, too close together. Michael had been a news junkie his whole life, and he'd never seen anything like this.

"They have to be Tangents," he said for at least the tenth time as they read yet another example of some government type turning against his constituents. "This is crazy. How can people not notice a connection?"

"Think about it," Bryson replied. He turned off the ancient device and slid it away in disgust, as if it were the cause of all the reports. "They don't know what we know. You really think someone is going to just stand up and say, 'I got it!' "—he snapped his fingers—" 'By George, I've got it! Computer programs are taking over the minds of all these people!' "

Michael rolled his eyes. "I *know*, but it just seems so crazy. Weird things like this happening all over the world at the same time."

"Some of this stuff might be copycat work," Sarah said. "But a lot of it has to be Kaine. I'm guessing he had a test batch—Michael and a few other Tangents—made some tweaks after he saw what happened, then a week or two later sent a whole bunch out at once. I just don't get what he's trying to accomplish."

Michael didn't, either. "Yeah, some of it seems so random. Nothing's consistent. I can kind of understand the government stuff, the corporation stuff—he might be planning to have others to come in and take over. But why all the violence, too?" He shrugged, as if it didn't really matter, when it potentially mattered more than anything in history.

"Chaos," Bryson said in a spooky whisper.

Michael just looked at him, waiting for him to expound on his dramatic pronouncement.

"Chaos," he repeated. "Maybe Kaine wants nothing more right now except good old-fashioned chaos."

"Why?" Sarah asked.

"I don't know. Maybe he wants all the humans to start a big war and kill themselves."

"That doesn't make an ounce of sense," Michael countered. "What's the point of the Mortality Doctrine if he wants to wipe out humans? Doesn't he want to *be* a human?"

It was Bryson's turn to shrug. "I guess that's the question of the year. He said all that stuff about immortality—did he mean as a human or as a Tangent? Which is why we need to figure out this dude's ultimate plan."

Sarah stood up and stretched, pressing her hands into her back as she leaned away from the table. Michael heard something crack.

"We all need to chill and rest today," she said. "Get some sleep tonight. Because tomorrow we have a very big day."

"Oh yeah?" Bryson asked. "What exactly are we doing?"

Sarah stood up and turned to go, casually answering over her shoulder as she walked away.

"We're going to see the VNS."

3

Every major city—and most smaller ones—had a branch of the VNS located within its limits, though often it was unmarked. But by midafternoon the next day, Michael and his friends had located the local VNS office and were standing in front of it. It was a nondescript, run-down building in the seedier part of town, where it wasn't unusual to see drug dealers and bandits roaming the streets. Which was why Michael asked the cabbie to wait for them while they went in.

"Are we *sure* this is it?" Bryson asked.

"Positive," Sarah replied. "Anyway, what can it hurt to knock on the door?"

Bryson tapped his chin with a finger. "It could hurt if some hopped-up drug monkey was in the middle of a deal and decided to shoot whoever knocked on his door. That would hurt."

"Yeah, that would definitely hurt," Michael agreed. The argument was pointless, though. They all knew very well that they were going inside that building, no matter what.

Sarah headed for a grimy glass door under the awning that ran along the front wall. The metal handle hung askew from only one attached bolt. "Then I'll do the knocking, you wimps."

Michael and Bryson raced to be by her side when she did so.

There was an old doormat—not something you usually saw at an office building—lying crookedly in front of the entrance, one corner chewed off by a dog or rat, the frayed edge matching the exterior of the building perfectly. The mat itself said WIPE YOUR FEET, which Michael thought was perfect for an entity like the VNS, getting straight to business.

Sarah reached out and rapped her knuckles on the door. It rattled, and the loose handle knocked against the glass, but it didn't open. Michael studied the doorframe, all dusty metal surrounded by warped wood with chipped brown paint. He started to wonder about the place—it seemed a little over-the-top for a front. He remembered visiting—and by "visiting" he meant "being kidnapped and forcefully taken to"—Agent Weber's office, and how it had been underneath the football stadium. The VNS liked lurking in the shadows, it seemed.

Sarah finally knocked again when no one answered, this time harder, making everything shake just a little more vigorously.

"Come on, come on," Bryson whispered.

Something clicked on the other side of the door and it swung open, one of those old-school bells attached to the top ringing with the movement. Somehow, to Michael that seemed even more out of place than the building itself, for an establishment that supposedly protected the world's most important source of commerce and entertainment. The man who'd answered the door was even more absurd.

Short, chubby, with gray-flecked scruff on his face and wispy hair combed over his flaky scalp, the man wore a stained tank top—yellowed, with even yellower spots—revealing hairy arms that looked as if they hadn't seen the sun in twenty years. Brown suspenders kept his brown pants from falling down, and a stubby cigar—not even lit—hung from his mouth like he'd forgotten about it hours ago.

"Who are ya, what do ya want?" he asked in a surprisingly high-pitched voice.

Sarah had taken charge and she kept it. "We're here to speak with an agent about something important—something very important. And it's related to the VirtNet."

Michael wanted to sigh. As much as he loved Sarah, it hadn't been the best introduction ever. A little hokey.

"We have an appointment with an agent," Michael said on instinct.

The man popped the cigar out of his mouth and started coughing, great, heaving, retching sounds that made him seem as if his chest might explode. Michael winced.

"What's that?" their host grunted, still clearing his throat.

It was Bryson's turn. "Look, man, you don't have to give us the runaround. We know this is a branch of the VNS, and we have some very serious stuff to talk about. Please bring us to an agent—we don't have much time."

At least he threw in a couple of pleases, Michael thought.

The man jammed the stumpy cigar back between his gray lips, then spoke around it. "What's the name of the agent? And the passcode?"

Michael suddenly ached for the Sleep, where they could hack their way to finding that kind of information. Now the only thing they had to rely on was their wit and charm.

"Look, sir," he said, "we don't know the local agent's name. And we don't have a passcode. All we need is five minutes. I swear you guys won't regret listening to us. Please."

"Harmless as butterflies," Bryson said with a goofy grin.

The man chewed his cigar like a stick of beef jerky. "Inside. Now."

Michael let out a big breath and followed Bryson and Sarah into a musty, dimly lit lobby with three hard-backed chairs and an empty desk. The man told them to wait there; then he slammed the door, the bell dinging madly.

After he disappeared through a different door, Michael looked at his friends. "He's . . . interesting."

Sarah nodded slowly; Bryson made a shuddering look of fright.

Less than a minute later, the cigar-chomping man returned. He propped the door open and nodded for them to walk through.

"Agent Weber will see you now."

4

Bryson and Sarah started to follow their host's gesture, but Michael hesitated. There was no possible way that Weber just happened to be at this location, a barren dump in the middle of a seedy neighborhood. The man seemed to sense his doubts.

"Via uplink," the guy muttered, as if he'd grown weary of speaking in life.

"Oh," Michael responded stupidly.

He went along with his friends through the door and down a long hallway that became nicer—unstained carpet, fresher paint—and better lit the farther they walked, Cigar Man shepherding them from behind. He barked for them to turn left, then right, then down several flights of stairs, the floors unmarked. Finally, he led the group through another door, down another hallway, and into a small room with a giant WallScreen already lit up.

Michael took in a quick breath, his throat tightening, when he saw the giant face of Agent Weber staring at them. Her dark hair, her exotic eyes, the knowing look, as if she could read your deepest thoughts.

"Sit," their host commanded.

There was a long table surrounded by padded chairs. Without a word, Michael and his friends sat down. He noticed that Sarah and Bryson were trying to avoid eye contact with the woman on the wall. As if she weren't intimidating enough, Michael thought, now she was literally larger than life, hovering above them. He remembered the day she came to see him, *personally*, after he'd awakened in poor Jackson's body. Seeing her had comforted him, at least a little, made him feel like he wasn't alone and the VNS would help him figure things out. But then, he hadn't heard from her or anyone else since—unless you counted the possible sighting in *Lifeblood,* by the tree house.

He felt a prick of anger, a thumping of his pulse in his temples.

"You may leave us now, Patrick," Weber said, her voice booming from speakers all around them.

Bryson looked like he was struggling to hold back a smirk. He mouthed the word *Patrick* at Michael as if that were the funniest name he'd ever heard.

After the man and his cigar left, an uncomfortable silence settled on the room. Michael tried his best to maintain eye contact with Agent Weber, wondering where exactly the camera was located that allowed her to see them. Determined to show some guts, he waited for her to speak first. But she let it drag out.

Finally, she said, simply, "What do you want?"

Michael's pulse thumped a little harder.

"What do we want?" he repeated. "I thought maybe you'd say something a little nicer, like 'It's lovely to see you safe and sound, Michael. I've been meaning to get in touch with you, Michael, but it's just been crazy town at work. Please accept my apologies, Michael. Oh, and sorry about dropping in on you in *Lifeblood,* Michael.' Something like that."

Agent Weber didn't bat an eye. She merely continued to stare at him, almost as if he were a complete stranger. And even though he was in a stranger's body, she'd seen him already. She'd come to visit *him*. And he deserved better treatment than this. Bryson and Sarah stirred in their seats but didn't say anything.

"Please tell me what you came here to say," Weber pronounced. "Patrick insisted it was important. The VNS doesn't have time to play games with high schoolers, so be quick about it."

This made Michael stand up. That pulse in his temples had become a jackhammer. "How can you—"

Sarah cut him off, her hand on his arm. He hadn't noticed her move closer.

"Michael," she said. "Let's just tell her what we came to tell her. About Kaine, about the things on the news."

"You really think I don't know about Kaine?" Agent Weber said. "*This* is why you called on me?"

Michael's anger turned into confusion. Why was she acting so strange? Did she not trust Bryson and Sarah yet?

"We were . . . kidnapped by Kaine," Sarah said, staying amazingly calm. "He wanted us to work for him, to help him. He threatened us, and he took my parents."

"*And* he promised us the worlds of the VirtNet," Bryson added. "Immortality. Don't forget that part."

Sarah nodded. "That, too. *If* we did what he wanted. Someone helped us escape, and we've had weird things happen in the Wake, too. You obviously know Michael's story, all about the Mortality Doctrine. And a lot of the crazy things happening in the news . . . it's all related somehow. We . . . just wanted to talk to the VNS. I don't understand why—"

"That's enough," Agent Weber said. Not loudly, but with authority. "I don't need to hear any more, thank you."

Michael was at a complete loss for words. On the screen, he saw Weber reach over and push something; then she told Patrick to come back to the room. The man was at the door a second later.

"Please escort our guests out of the building," Agent Weber said to him. "I've never seen these people before in my life."

The WallScreen went dark.

CHAPTER 11

DARK VISOR

1

"You're *sure* that's her?" Sarah asked Michael after the cabbie had driven off from the VNS building. They were packed in the backseat like kindergartners on a bus, Bryson in the middle.

"Yes," Michael answered. He tried to tamp down his anger—it wasn't Sarah's fault. "Her Aura in *Lifeblood Deep* looks almost exactly the same. It's definitely her. Same name, same appearance. Plus, I saw her at Jackson Porter's apartment. I know it's her, and it's a joke that she's pretending we've never met."

"Maybe she's trying to cover her butt," Bryson offered. "If she's been in charge of finding Kaine and stopping the Mortality Doctrine, she's done the crap job of the century. She may act like God's gift to mankind, but you know she has bosses, and those bosses might kick her to the curb if she acts like old friends with her biggest failure. You." He pointed at Michael. "No offense, of course."

"Oh, of course," Michael responded with an eye roll. "None taken."

Sarah wasn't convinced. "It's gotta be more than that. There's no way she could just pretend she doesn't know us and get away with it. Something weird's going on."

Michael agreed one hundred percent.

The cabbie suddenly swore and slowed down, pulling over to the side of the road. Then he slapped his steering wheel with both hands.

"What's going on?" Bryson asked.

The cabbie turned to face them. "Damn hovercop." He pointed upward as if they could see through his roof. "Flagged me down. It's probably some bored doughnut chomper tryin' to hit his quota."

A bad seed sprouted in Michael's stomach. What if the cop asked about the passengers, wanted to see their IDs? *Calm down,* he told himself. They'd checked and rechecked their fake accounts. They could fool some cop just trying to get through his day.

"Your face," Sarah whispered to him. It seemed an odd thing to say.

"Huh?"

"It's been plastered all over the NewsBops. What if the cop recognizes you?"

Before he could answer, the police hovercar descended in front of them and turned, the heat from its boosters shimmering in the air. The silvery machine landed on the asphalt with a soft thump and shut down with a fading whine of engines. Then it just sat there for several long, long moments.

"I swear they do this on purpose," the cabbie grumbled

from the front seat. "Those ratfaces just like to make you sweat. He's probably in there sippin' his coffee and talkin' to a buddy on the Net. Sorry son of a . . ."

Michael tuned the guy out. That seed in his gut had blossomed into full-fledged panic, slicking the palms of his hands with sweat and making his throat feel stuffed with cotton. The waiting was going to drive him crazy.

Finally, the door of the cop car popped open and swiveled upward on its hinges. An armored man stepped out of the vehicle, his suit the standard bulky black of the police, the visor on his helmet pulled down to cover his face. Michael understood why cops in this part of the city wanted to protect themselves, but it still made him nervous. He had visions of this guy pulling him out of the car and beating him with those black gloves until he bled head to toe—the man looked more like a robotic monster than a human.

The cop walked around to the driver's side of the cab and rapped on the window. The cabbie waited a beat before he rolled it down—probably just to prove that he could.

"What's the problem, Officer?" he asked, his tone neutral, like he'd done this a thousand times. "There's no way I was speeding, and I've got all my permits."

The visor muffled the cop's voice a bit, but it still had a menacing ring. "I need you to sit there and keep your mouth shut, sir. Think you can do that? Do you think you can do that for me? Sir?"

Michael could only see the back of the cabbie's head, but the muscles along his neck tensed and he didn't respond. At least, not vocally. Just a short, stiff nod.

"That's better," the cop replied. "Now I'm going to need your nice law-abiding passengers to step out of the car. And make it snappy."

2

He had them line up against the cold brick wall of an old building. Michael felt the rough edges of the poorly done mortar job poking through his shirt. The cop refused to lift his visor, making him seem even more like a robot to Michael. He remembered the robot in the Sleep, the one who'd programmed out his Core—ripped it out even though as a Tangent he hadn't really needed one—which made him think of Kaine. What if *he* was somehow behind this supposed traffic stop?

Please, no, Michael begged the universe. How could Kaine be *that* powerful? He refused to allow himself to believe it. But even so, he looked at the cop and wondered if he was a Tangent come to life.

"What are your names?" the man asked, just as a section of his visor lit up. Michael could see symbols and pictures running across the inside. "And before you answer, I'm only going to say this once: Do. Not. Lie. Do not. You have one chance to tell me the truth. Now, what are your names?"

Sarah went first, then Bryson, then Michael. They'd all been busted more times than Michael could count within the VirtNet. And they'd always gotten away, just a few lines of code combined with the calm and cool . . . *massaging* of the truth. It was a little different in the real world, but the principles were the same. One by one, they gave their fake names as smoothly as if they'd used them their whole lives.

The cop grunted some odd sound that perhaps meant he was listening and recording. But it came across more like he was a monkey with stomach issues.

"We had some reports of a sighting," the cop said, walking slowly down the line of his captors. He stopped directly in front of Michael and stared at him—it seemed so, anyway—through his dark visor. "Of one Jackson Porter, missing for close to two weeks. You wouldn't happen to know anything about that, would you? What was your name again? Ah, yes. *Michael.* What do you have to say, boy? Seen anybody that looks like a cyber-terrorist?"

Every part of Michael wanted to close his eyes and access the code. Hack himself out of the situation. He suddenly wished for his old life as a Tangent, oblivious and happy. Lying to this cop seemed like a terrible idea, especially since the man had probably recognized his face, but he just didn't know what else to do.

"No, sir," he said. "I've seen the NewsBops, heard about this Jackson guy. But I haven't seen him. Have you guys seen him?" He looked at his friends for their response, knowing he'd already made a mistake, that he'd come across as a smart aleck to the policeman. Bryson and Sarah shyly shook their heads, but he could see in their eyes that they knew Michael had screwed up. Maybe they should've just told the truth and relied on the authorities to keep them safe.

The cop finally lifted his visor, revealing the face of a guy who was born to be a man of the law. Stone-hard angles, eyes that were pools of unreadable darkness. He didn't seem too happy.

"Get in the hovercar," he said tightly. "All three of you. One wrong move and I'll LaserCuff you. I'm not in the greatest of moods today."

The cabbie yelled over at them from his car. "Hey! Officer! Can I leave? Please?"

"Get lost!" the cop yelled back at him.

Obviously happy to oblige, the cabbie squealed away down the street. Michael watched the cab disappear, along with all his hopes.

3

Sarah and Bryson got in first. The cop was holding Michael by the arm far more tightly than he needed to. Michael was feeling desperate, and not just for the obvious reasons. Surely the entire police force didn't work for Kaine already—although he guessed there was a possibility that the one who'd caught them *could* be a Tangent. There was also the weirdness with Agent Weber, though this could be totally unrelated. Jackson Porter *was* missing, wanted for serious crimes, and the boy's face had been plastered all over the NewsBops. It wasn't strange at all that Michael had been reported.

Either way, too much was at risk if they brought Michael in. What if no one else realized what Kaine was up to and he couldn't convince them? He wanted to scream at Agent Weber. They needed the VNS.

"Your turn," the cop said when Sarah slid over to sit in the middle.

Michael's desperation burst to the surface in that moment. "Listen, sir . . . can I talk to you? In private?"

The man's visor was still raised, and his expression did not change in the slightest—if Michael's request surprised him, he didn't show it. "You want to talk to me. In private." He stated it more than asked.

Michael nodded. "Please."

The cop gripped him by the arm even harder and escorted him several feet away from the hovercar. "Go ahead, boy. Talk."

"We both know who I am," Michael said.

"Thank you for acknowledging that I'm not the stupidest cop to ever live. That's why I'm taking you in."

Michael pointed at the car. "Those two people had nothing to do with me running. They're just friends I picked up along the way. And . . . there's a reason I *did* run. You think it's because I'm a criminal, but this goes up the ladder bigtime, way higher than whoever you work for."

"Son, what in *the* hell are you talking about?"

"You can't arrest me. You can't. We have information on a *real* cyber-terrorist and . . . we need . . . to find out more."

The cop was shaking his head long before Michael finished the sentence. "I don't like my time to be wasted, boy. Stop talking in riddles. You want me to know something, then spit it out."

Michael's blood hissed through his veins. He'd painted himself into a corner. "It's . . . complicated. Listen, what can I do to make you let us go? Money? I can get you a lot of money. My . . . parents are rich. I didn't run away empty-handed."

The cop held up a hand, and Michael knew it was time to shut up.

"Boy, let me tell you something. I've met some brave people in my life. And I've met some awfully stupid people. You're one of the rare ones that are both. Trying to bribe me? Do you realize I'm an eighth-generation cop? My great-great-great-however-many-greats-grandfather rode a horse on his patrols, son. A *horse.* Do you think I'm going to take a few credits from a teenager and throw all that in the crapper?"

Dang, Michael thought. It was hard to argue with the horse story. He decided to dive into the scary waters of the naked truth.

"Look, I'm sorry. I'm really desperate. You can't take me back. Please. It has to do with Kaine—I know you've heard of him—and we have information. We need to go to the VNS headquarters in Atlanta."

"Well," the cop replied, "if you know so much, all the more reason to take you in."

"But—"

The cop had had enough. "Get. In. The car."

Deflated, Michael did as he was told.

4

"Maybe this is a good thing," Sarah said after the hovercar had vaulted into flight. They were moving at breakneck speed through the travel zones designated for such vehicles, almost solely operated by government entities.

"A good thing?" Michael repeated. "I can't wait to hear why." He knew the cop could hear him, and he didn't really care.

"We need to tell *somebody*," she countered. "You really think we can find my parents and fight Kaine and his army of Tangents by ourselves? I think we've done just about all we can do—we tried the VNS, and that didn't pan out so well. So now we try telling the police, the GBI, Central Intelligence, whoever. Someone will listen to us."

Bryson nodded, taking Sarah's side, but Michael shook his head.

"I feel like the VNS are the only ones who'll take us seriously." He interrupted Sarah's protests before she could even begin. "*Yes,* we tried, and I know they brushed us off. But there had to be a reason for that. Maybe Agent Weber was worried about spies, or maybe she was trying to protect us, I don't know. But somehow we've got to get face to face with her."

"I don't know, man," Bryson said. Which depressed Michael, because if anyone was going to be adventurous, it would've been Bryson. If he'd given up, resigned to go along with the police, then that was probably what they'd just have to do.

"All right," Michael said, giving up himself. For the moment. "Hopefully someone will listen to us eventually. *Really* listen to us."

"Well," Bryson responded, "unless you want to kick this guy out the door and fly the car yourself, I don't think we have much choice, now, do we? This ain't the Sleep, man. We can't code ourselves out of this one."

For one crazy, frantic moment, Michael considered doing it. Jumping into the front seat like an escaped gorilla. How hard could it be to fly a hovercar? But the moment passed, and Michael sat back, folded his arms, and looked out the window.

Below them, the streets flashed by like rows of crops in the *Lifeblood* countryside.

5

They drove on in silence for a while, Michael's mind ticking like a bomb. He couldn't stop thinking about what was going to happen with the police and who they'd be handed over to. Would anyone believe their story? The farther they drove, the more uneasy he became. Things just wouldn't settle in his mind.

The only person he knew besides Sarah and Bryson was Gabriela. Would she help them? And the fact that she was going to be visiting her dad in Atlanta didn't escape him. The possibility seemed insane, but he knew absolutely no one else. And they were getting desperate. He could easily find her Net address with just a little time to dig. . . .

They had reached the central part of the city, and Michael

zoned out as they sped through a canyon of tall skyscrapers, glass and steel reflecting the dying sunlight. Very few hover-cars shared the airways with them, and Michael had to avert his eyes whenever they *did* pass. The cars seemed to be headed straight for them, only to swerve out of the way at the last second. It had Michael on edge.

Leaning forward, he addressed the policeman. "Sir?"

The cop had put his visor back down—Michael could see flashes of information and maps flashing inside its dark screen, though the angle made it hard to decipher much.

"What?" the man replied, clearly uninterested.

The guy might be a jerk, Michael thought, but he was still an officer of the law. Sarah tapped Michael on the shoulder and raised her eyebrows when he looked at her—the biggest *What in the world are you doing?* look she'd ever given him. He tried to reassure her with an expression that said *Relax,* then turned back to the cop.

"You have to believe us on this. It's a crazy story, but it's true."

"What story?"

"Well, I haven't really told you yet."

The man threw his arms up in exasperation. The hovercar dipped, making Michael's stomach vault into his throat, and Bryson let out an embarrassing yelp.

"So now you want me to believe a story you haven't told me?" the driver asked. "Son, answer me a question. Have you ever been committed to an asylum? Ever been diagnosed with a tumor in your head? Maybe the size of a grapefruit?"

Somehow this made the guy more likable, and Michael

relaxed a bit. "Okay, listen. Do you go into the Slee—the VirtNet very often? Do you game at all?"

The man barked a laugh. "Do I have an enlarged prostate and have to pee every twenty minutes? Of course I do. What could possibly be your point?"

"Well, I know you've heard of the gamer named Kaine. Right? He's been in the news a *lot* the last few months."

"Yes, son, I've heard of Kaine." He turned the steering wheel to the right and the hovercar banked heavily to swing around a wide building. Sarah's body pressed against Michael's, and if he hadn't been so upset, it would have been nice. "Let me guess. This Kaine is an uncle of yours? Maybe your daddy?"

"No, he's a Tangent. And he's stealing people's bodies and inserting programs, the . . . intelligence of Tangents, into them, into the humans. He's turning Tangents into humans. Killing real people to do it."

Michael winced. Every word made the whole thing seem a little more absurd.

The cop turned to look at Michael. "Son, don't worry. We have good crazy-doctors at the station. We'll be there soon." He faced front again.

Michael sat back in the seat, stiffly. He'd seen something in the cop's visor when he moved, just for a second, when the angle was right. Michael's face must've paled, because Sarah and Bryson both were looking at him as if they thought the crazy-doctor recommendation had been a good one.

"What's wrong?" Sarah whispered.

Michael couldn't answer. He could hardly breathe. He

wanted to believe it had been a trick of the eye, that he hadn't really seen what he thought he had. But the truth was like a sinking ship.

There'd been a picture of Sarah. And below that, one short sentence.

WANTED IN CONNECTION TO MISSING PERSONS

He'd also caught a glimpse of the names Jackson and Bryson. But one word had stuck out. *Accomplices.*

Now they were *all* fugitives.

CHAPTER 12

BROKEN BRICKS

1

Sarah leaned forward and looked back at Michael in a way that only he could see her face. Then she mouthed the words *What is wrong with you?* The hovercar banked to the left, making him lean into her. He wanted to grab her and pull her into a fierce hug. They just seemed to be getting deeper and deeper into trouble. A dreary sorrow tried to melt his chest.

Sarah raised her eyebrows, waiting for an answer. Bryson watched them both, too smart to say anything but fidgeting in his seat.

Michael knew they couldn't keep going with this cop. They couldn't let him take them to the police station, book them, arrest them, whatever they would do. A runaway cyber-terrorist, a kidnapper—probably suspected of murder. Who knew what they'd tag Bryson for. But it didn't matter. The police wanted the two boys as accomplices anyway.

Everything was about to fall apart to a point where it could never be put together again.

"I'm going to throw up," he suddenly yelled toward the front of the car. "My stomach. I'm about to puke, take us down!"

"We're almost there," the cop answered, glancing in the rearview mirror. "Hold yourself together a few seconds longer."

Michael knew he had the pale face to go along with his story. "I'm serious! Please! You've gotta let me out of this thing!"

"Wow," the man said, his voice somewhere between annoyed and amused. "That's one magical stomach you got there. Just happens to go south right before the terrorist and his murdering friends get booked into jail."

So much for keeping anything secret.

"I'm not lying," Michael replied helplessly. Even he could hear the defeat in his voice.

"Just hold tight back there. You can do all the throwing up you desire once you're settled in a nice comfy cell."

Sarah had been looking back and forth between them and Bryson like she was watching a tennis match, her face filled with confusion. "Murdering friend? What're you talking— Michael, what is he talking about?"

Panic was just around the corner, lurking for Michael. "I saw something on his visor display. They're accusing *you* in your parents' missing persons case. And saying Bryson and I helped you."

Sarah's face drained of color, and Bryson punched the seat in front of him.

"Calm down back there!" the cop yelled. "You want to commit big-boy crimes, then get ready for big-boy punishment. Now shut up, not another word. It's up here on the right."

Buildings zoomed by on either side of the hovercar as they approached an old, crumbling brick structure. Its windows were covered with grime, and it looked as welcoming as every other city police station in the world.

"I just might get a bonus for this," the cop said through a chuckle. "Get those hair plugs I've been hoping for."

2

The car slowed, the front end tilting upward a bit to catch some drag. They swung around the building to the far side, where a door several levels up was sliding open, bright lights shining within. The cop maneuvered his controls and the car moved toward the landing slot.

Michael looked at the opening. It was like a yawning mouth that wanted to swallow them whole. And it wasn't just their lives on the line. Not many people knew what Kaine was up to—what he truly was up to. If they were locked up, the Tangent would be free to do it all. A powerful sense of fright almost overwhelmed Michael, making it hard for him to breathe.

He wasn't going with this cop. He wasn't. Every rational part of his brain shut down in that moment, and pure, fiery, wild instinct took over.

Throwing his body forward, he reached through the small

opening in the gate between the front and back seats and grabbed the cop's helmet, pulling it toward him. Then he twisted, yanking with all his strength, as if he were trying to rip the guy's head clean off. The back of the man's helmet banged against the glass directly behind him and he yelled, a strangled sound full of pain.

"You piece of—" the man started to say, but the words were cut off by a sharp cry as Michael put his whole body into it, jerking the helmet left and right. The cop gave up trying to keep the steering wheel under control, his hands flying back to grab Michael's arms. The man clawed and scratched, but Michael was in a frenzy, an all-out attack. His stomach suddenly flew toward the sky when the hovercar pitched to the left and started to plummet.

"Grab the wheel!" he yelled at Sarah, but there was no way she could get past him in the small gap between the open glass doors.

He held on to the man's helmet, sure it would break his neck at any second. Michael planted his feet on the backseat, then pushed off, diving through the opening so that he landed on the floor of the front cabin. The cop fell with him, his body slipping out of its seat belt and landing on top of Michael. Outside the windows, the world was spinning, buildings at odd angles and the blue sky flashing in turn with gray steel and glass.

"Now!" Michael yelled. "Grab the wheel!"

Sarah was already climbing through the opening, reaching forward. Bryson helped, lifting and pushing her. Michael wrestled with the cop, terrified that he'd somehow get his gun free and start firing. Someone would come after them soon—surely the falling police vehicle had been noticed at the station.

Sarah grabbed the steering wheel just as the cop got a hand free and punched Michael in the face. Pinpricks of light exploded before his eyes. He gripped the lower section of the man's visor and yanked fiercely. It flew up and something cracked, though it didn't come free.

The cop's face was creased in fury. "You must be the stupidest . . . ," he started to say, but the whole universe seemed caught in a cyclone, everything spinning. Michael looked at Sarah, hoping she could gain control.

She tugged at the wheel wildly, leaning into it with her full weight, trying to steady things. But the car kept swerving, tilting, at last shooting upward. A horrible scream of engines vibrated the windows. Sarah's tongue was pinched between her lips; strain filled her eyes.

There was a terrible crunching sound just as Michael slammed forward into the bottom of the dashboard. The world shook as windows broke and metal screeched on metal and the noise of crumbling brick filled the air.

Then it all stopped. The car was still, tilted heavily to the right. Michael looked out the busted window and saw nothing but the ground far below.

3

The stillness after all the noise of the crash was spooky, as if they'd been on a roller coaster and time froze before the ride had quite finished. There were groans, the sounds of harsh breathing, and a distant honk or two from the street below.

Michael's thoughts immediately went to the cop—he braced himself, ready to struggle and fight him off. But the man wasn't moving. He was lying completely still on the floor-board, his head tilted at a weird angle against the passenger-side door.

"Are you guys okay?" Michael whispered, carefully shifting to get a look at the rest of the car. He was scared that one wrong move might make the entire vehicle slide loose.

Bryson grumbled something from the backseat, but Michael couldn't see him.

Sarah held on to the steering wheel with both hands so she wouldn't slide toward Michael and the cop. She nodded. Behind her shoulders, he could see the wreckage of brick and glass through the broken window of her door, a dusty darkness beyond that. The plastic and metal of the hovercar itself was twisted and bent, its mangled body precariously held in place by the building's ruined edges.

Bryson's head appeared in the opening between the protective glass doors—which were still intact—behind the front seat. "This thing could fall any second. Let's get out of here."

"Is he dead?" Sarah asked, her eyes fixed on the unmoving cop. The cracked visor of his helmet jutted to the side, but they couldn't see his face, pressed up against the door.

"I don't know," Michael answered. His muscles ached

from the weird position in which he lay. He didn't know how much longer he could stand it. "Go, Sarah. Climb out. I feel like my arms and legs are about to fall asleep."

"What if it shifts?" she asked.

"You wanna be inside when it does?" Bryson answered. "The back door is blocked by a bunch of broken brick. We have to go through your window."

"Okay."

She carefully moved her feet around until she found a solid purchase; then she reached up, gripping the underside of the window. From there she pulled herself to a bent piece of metal jutting out of the brick wall of the building. She tested it first, and soon she was climbing up and out of the car, disappearing into the darkness. Michael could hear the rattle of shifting bricks.

"You go next," Michael said to Bryson. "I need to get myself into a better position." He started working on that while his friend climbed into the front seat, using the steering wheel like a ladder rung.

"Perfect place to attack a cop," Bryson said over his shoulder, moving up through the broken window, using the same hand- and footholds Sarah had. "Right across the street from his police station, for all his chums to get a good look-see. They'll be swarming all over this building in five minutes, guns cocked and fingers itchy."

"Sorry." Michael groaned—his muscles ached so much; fire burned in his tissues. "Next time I'll attack the cop sooner. Promise."

"Good." Bryson got himself into the building, then turned around so he could reach back into the car and help.

Michael was ready, having twisted himself around just enough to free his hands and get his feet beneath him, planted on the torso of the cop. He found the steering wheel, gripped it, curled his arms in a pull-up. Bryson grabbed him by the shirt and pulled as well. Kicking to find a foothold wherever he could, Michael clambered up the seat of the sideways car and toward the opening of the smashed window.

There was a heavy, grating groan of metal, along with the splintering of brick, as the car shifted downward. Bryson's grip slipped, and Michael, in a rush of terror that filled his throat, fell several inches before wedging his foot on the brake handle between the front seats. Someone screamed; then, with a crunch, the car came to a stop, though the moan of bending metal and shifting bricks continued.

"Get out of there!" Sarah yelled.

"Trying!" Michael shouted back.

Bryson had a firm hold of his shirt again and yanked, grunting with the effort. The fear that had choked Michael lit a fire of adrenaline in his muscles, and he clawed and kicked his way up and through the window, crawling over Bryson's body in his haste and crashing into Sarah. She hugged him fiercely, both of them breathing heavily.

"Dude, you just put your foot in my mouth," Bryson grumbled.

The car shifted again, causing a rattling cascade of broken bricks. Michael thought it would surely fall this time, but it stopped. Somewhere in the building, alarms clanged.

"Come on," Sarah said, getting to her feet and pulling

Michael up to his. They were in some kind of conference room with a large table and chairs, luckily unoccupied.

Bryson was by their side, brushing the dust from his shirt and pants. "Yeah, like I said, they'll be swarming on us in no time."

Michael got a good look at the demolished wall behind them: bricks scattered across the carpet, torn drywall, lengths of wire and pipes snaking out, the scratched and dented hovercar somehow still clinging to it all. He thought of the cop.

"We have to help him," he whispered, though that was the last thing on earth he wanted to do.

"His buddies will be here soon enough to get him out," Bryson replied. "If that thing was gonna fall, it would've taken the dive already. We have to go. Now."

Michael was relieved someone else made the decision—a part of him knew the guy might be dead, and that it was his fault. He fought off the thought and nodded, still trying to catch his breath. Sarah grabbed his hand and the three of them ran for the door of the conference room.

4

Alarms bleated in the hallways, a few people running for the stairwells, though most seemed to have escaped already. That, or it was a slow day at the office. Leaving the conference room had been the easy decision, Michael thought, but what now?

"There's no way we can just blend in," Sarah said. She'd

let go of Michael's hand, and he had the silly urge to take hers right back. "I'm sure they know what we look like."

"No doubt," Michael agreed. "The cops'll have our faces memorized."

"Maybe we can hide in the basement," Sarah said. They were all walking toward the closest stairwell door—a woman cast a nervous glance at them right before she went through. "We obviously can't waltz out the front entrance. We'll have to climb through a window or . . . go through a garage. Back door, emergency exit, something."

They reached the door to the stairs and Michael opened it. "Let's just get down as far as we can go. We'll figure it out."

Bryson had been quiet, and he didn't move toward the opening after Sarah had walked through. His arms were folded and his face had that pinched look of concentration.

"You can't hack your way out of this one," Michael murmured.

"I know," Bryson replied. 'I'm thinking."

"Not a good time," Michael said, but deep down he hoped his friend would devise some brilliant plan.

"Let's go!" Sarah yelled, clearly out of patience.

"Okay, okay," Bryson snapped, moving into the stairwell. "Follow me."

And of course he went *up* the stairs, not down.

Sarah took in a breath, probably ready to argue. But Michael reached out and squeezed her arm. She stopped before she began, looking at him anxiously.

"I think he's right on this one," he said, proud of how softly he managed to say it.

Sarah's defeated look showed she knew they were right. "I just want to be out of this place."

"Me too. But we'd be walking right into their arms if we went down. Cops are probably running up those stairs as we speak."

"Then we better get moving."

Bryson had already disappeared around the bend of the ascending stairwell, and they took off after him, up two steps at a time.

5

The office building was a big one, as the numbers on the doors indicating the floor illustrated all too well. Twenty. Twenty-five. Thirty. With no end in sight as Michael paused to catch his breath, looking up through the rectangular spiral of the railings, rising and rising. His chest heaved with the effort of climbing, and sweat dripped from his face onto the floor.

"Gotta . . . keep . . . moving," Sarah said through her own huffs.

"Gotta . . . keep . . . breathing," he mocked in reply.

He could suddenly hear distant shouts and footsteps, but the acoustics of the stairwell made it impossible to make out words or to know how close those responsible for the noise were. Fear rattled in his chest along with the ragged breaths.

"What's the plan, anyway?" Sarah asked.

For some reason Bryson looked like he'd just taken a rest

instead of having sprinted up fifteen flights of stairs. He pointed up. "Hide."

"Hide," Michael repeated.

"Yes, hide," Bryson responded smugly. "You think I would lead you two wonderful people on a wild-goose chase that ends with us in the slammer? No way."

"I think cops are really good at hide-and-seek," Sarah said. "Especially when they have dogs that can smell humans from a mile away, infrared sensors, all that good stuff."

"Have faith in Bryson," Michael said. "He is all-knowing." He didn't even mean to be a smart aleck—something told him that his friend could get them out of this.

"Yeah," Bryson replied. "Have faith. And no offense, Mike the Spike, but you were dead wrong."

"I was? About what?"

"When you said we couldn't hack our way out of here."

Bryson tried to hide a grin as he turned and continued up the stairs, his feet pounding as he jumped the steps two or three at a time. Michael and Sarah exchanged a look, part amused, part curious, then followed him.

The sounds below—shouting, footsteps, doors opening and slamming—were definitely getting closer. Michael vaulted up the stairs, his heart a jackhammer in his chest.

6

Bryson didn't stop, keeping a relentless pace as they passed floor after floor. Forty. Forty-five. Fifty. The muscles in Michael's legs felt like acid had been injected in them, growing more painful by the second. And his lungs burned, fighting for oxygen. He tried to tell Bryson to slow down, but he couldn't get the words out. Sarah looked just as miserable, but she kept climbing, staying right in front of Michael.

The building stopped at the sixtieth floor. Mercifully. There was a swinging gate blocking off the last flight of stairs, which ended at a door marked with a sign that said, simply, ROOF. Michael's vision pulsed along with his heartbeat, making everything jitter. The number 60 printed on the door to the top floor shook as if laughing, as if it were mocking him, saying, *Why didn't you take the elevator, you idiot?*

Which was a good question, actually. He spit it out to Bryson between pulls of air into his lungs.

"Because they're watching those puppies with cameras. The cops might even have someone in each elevator car. Plus"—he took a deep breath—"I had no idea this stupid building was so tall!"

Sarah was bent over, hands on knees, but she pulled herself up straight. "Well, they're coming." Even as she said it, Michael noticed over the rushing in his ears the footsteps echoing up the chamber of the stairwell. "They're probably searching floor by floor, which will take some time, but they'll be here soon enough."

"So what do we do?" Michael asked, waiting for Bryson to finally reveal his plan.

His friend took charge in a way Michael had never seen before, not even in the worst of times inside the Sleep.

"Here's what we're going to do," Bryson said. "Come on."

He started walking back down the stairs, a thing that seemed so absurd to Michael that he didn't even bother asking. "I just wanted to see how far up this place went, but we can't hide on the top floor, too obvious. Let's go down a few and find a good spot."

Their steps echoed as they descended. Michael's legs had cooled off too much and felt weak as he followed.

"So is that really your plan?" Sarah asked. "We're just going to hide and hope no one finds us?"

Bryson gave her a hurt look over his shoulder—genuine, as if she'd really offended him. But then he hid it with a grin. "Give me some credit, lady. Remember what I said about hacking?"

"Yes."

Suddenly it hit Michael what his friend had planned. "We'll break into their computer system, watch their feeds, listen to their scanners. Then we can move around and keep avoiding them."

"Yep," Bryson replied.

Sarah responded as if she'd known the plan all along. "We can break into the schematics of the building, too. Maybe there's a way out that we're not thinking of."

"Hey, you guys are stealing all my thunder," Bryson complained. "This is my plan, don't forget. You guys wanted to run like chickens with their heads cut off."

Sarah snorted, a sound Michael hoped she never repeated. "Yeah, and maybe then we'd be at a coffee shop right now, watching the action from across the street."

Bryson stopped at the fifty-fourth floor. "This ought to

do." He reached down to twist the leverlike door handle, but it didn't move.

Locked.

Michael heard someone shouting, but he could barely make out the words. Something about heading to the top floor.

"Locked?" Bryson huffed in frustration. "Seriously? It's locked?"

"They probably did it from the main controls," Sarah said, surprisingly calm. "We just need to crack their system." She had already squeezed her EarCuff, and her NetScreen opened up, hovering in front of her.

"You better do some serious renetworking, then," Michael said. His nerves were twisting tighter by the second. "Hurry!"

Sarah was focused. She typed furiously at her projected keyboard, swiping fingers at her NetScreen wildly. Michael wanted to say "hurry" again, maybe scream it a few times. It was all he could do to stop himself from joining her on his own NetScreen, but opening just one link was dangerous enough. Kaine seemed to lurk around every corner, both virtual and real.

A woman shouted from below, the words a haunting echo that filled the air. "Three of them! Up there! Heat sensors caught—" She was drowned out by an uptick in the thumping drumbeat of footsteps, the squeak of shoes on the cement.

"Anything?" Bryson asked Sarah.

She frowned but didn't answer. Michael looked over her shoulder, but it was hard to tell what was going on. All he saw were words and schematics and flashing firewall screens, moving too quickly for him to make sense of it. But he trusted Sarah.

The noises from below got louder. They had to be only a few stories away now. Michael thought he could actually hear them *breathing*. And their pace had quickened, if anything, the impact of their steps rattling in his brain.

Sarah finally spoke, her voice tight and clipped. "Almost there. One of you has to get into the system. I need help attacking their sensors. Michael, click on!" She hadn't paused in the slightest working at her controls.

"They're almost—" he started.

"Do it!" she yelled.

Even as he pinched his EarCuff, he knew the people rushing toward them had heard her. They paused, just for a few seconds, probably motioning to each other for silence. But then they thundered once more up the stairs, maybe two levels below them now.

Michael looked at his screen, hoping they'd finally figured out how to enter the Net without Kaine latching on to them. Sarah had already sent over a series of codes, and he pushed them into action. Just as he was swept into the systems of the building security—a barrage of words and images—he heard the distinct, mechanical click of the door unlocking. The cops, security guards, whoever was coming, were right below them, almost within sight by how close they sounded. Manipulating the system would amount to nothing if there was actual visual confirmation.

Bryson opened the door and stepped through, Sarah right on his heels, barely glancing up from her screen. Michael followed, eyes fixed to his own screen, knowing Bryson would close the door for them. It was dark inside, the light from the stairwell cut off with the click of the door closing. The lock engaged immediately, Sarah working it from her end. From what he'd seen in the system so far, Michael could tell that everything in the building was centrally controlled. That was to their advantage.

He jumped when someone started pounding on the door, working at the door handle.

"I guess they saw us," Bryson said with a deflated voice.

"I took over the system," Sarah responded, sounding for all the world like she'd done something as simple as flushing a toilet. "It'll hold them off for a little while."

"It won't stop them from breaking the stupid door down," Bryson replied.

"Good point." Lit by the glow of her NetScreen, she turned and ran down the dark hallway. Bryson followed, as did Michael, barely looking up from his work, trying to get a feel for the building's security programs.

Behind him, their pursuers started ramming the door with something very heavy.

Sarah wound her way through the labyrinth of hallways like someone who'd worked there for years, following the floor plans on her screen. She stopped in front of the elevators, red emergency lights glowing from the ceiling like demonic eyes. The booming impact of the battering ram seemed to shake the entire building.

"What're those people using?" Bryson asked as Sarah worked away on her screen. "Did they bring a freaking tree up the stairs?"

Michael didn't answer, waiting patiently for Sarah to tell him what to do. She finally did.

"Okay, here's the plan," she said. Michael had no idea how she could be so calm, as if she were about to lay out the next few plays in a backyard football game. "Bryson, push the down button. Michael, I'll focus on the heat sensors, make them think we got on and went down a few floors. We can't go all the way down or we'll blow our only advantage when they see that no one's on the elevator when it opens up."

"What should I do?" Michael asked.

"You need to shut down the camera system. Destroy it completely. I can mess with where they're seeing heat signatures, but there's no way we can fake the video. Just wipe the whole thing out, every camera in the building."

"Will do," he answered, already digging through the system to find the location of those controls. Sweat trickled down his face, and the constant thump against the door in the distance felt like a hammer in his head.

The elevator dinged and the middle car opened.

"We all need to step inside for a sec," Sarah said, doing it first. "Bryson, hold the doors open until I'm ready. I think I've almost got it figured out." Michael had never seen her fingers fly at such a lightning-fast speed. Her whole face glistened from the effort, and the tendons in her neck stood out against her skin like straws, as if every one of them were about to snap from stress.

"Got it!" Sarah yelled, realizing too late that yelling wasn't the best idea right then. "Push the thirtieth-floor button," she said quietly.

Bryson pushed it and it lit up. Michael had been working at his screen and finally slipped past the firewall protecting the camera controls. He shut it down so that anyone looking would think it'd been caused by a power malfunction, maybe spurred by the crash of the police hovercar.

"Cameras are down," he said, filled with relief as he clicked off his NetScreen. They didn't know where the cameras were or if they'd been spotted by them yet, but it was good to have one less thing to worry about. A loud crack sounded with the latest impact of the battering ram.

"Now let's go hide," Sarah whispered, already on the move. Michael and Bryson followed her into the hallway, turning right into the red-tinted darkness. The elevator doors closed behind them. "I faked the heat sig on that car, and then I'm gonna wipe it out completely once it stops on thirty. With that and the cameras shot, they won't have a clue where we are."

Michael was just about to ask her how long she planned for them to hide when a ringing, metallic crash shook the air, followed by shouts and a rush of footsteps.

"We need to hurry," Sarah said flatly, an understatement if Michael had ever heard one.

9

The green glow of Sarah's NetScreen lit the way as they scurried through a spooky world of cubicles and desks and potted plants—the employees had long since evacuated. The sounds of pursuit echoed throughout the floor, shouted directions and the rustle of footsteps on carpet. People were spreading out until it became impossible to tell what noise was coming from where. Michael could feel every thump of his escalated heartbeat in his throat and ears, the blood pumping. Finally, Sarah stopped at a large breakroom, where a full kitchen and several tables had been set up. Michael knew they couldn't risk going any farther—there were too many people following them, and they were too spread out.

"Under those cabinets," Bryson whispered, pointing at some wide doors under the long kitchen counter, where a toaster and coffee machine were tucked away.

"Perfect," Sarah replied. "I'll keep throwing them off." She opened a cabinet in the middle and dropped to her knees.

Michael went to her right, crouched down, and opened one of the wooden doors. There was plenty of space, just a few paper plates and plastic utensils scattered along the bottom. He pushed them all to the side and crawled in, turning to sit and face the door. He pulled his knees as close to his chest as he could and reached out and closed the cabinet.

The sudden darkness tempted him to squeeze his EarCuff and bring up his NetScreen again, just for the comfort of it, but he resisted. He waited blindly, concentrating on slowing his breath and heartbeat and listening for activity.

Soon there was silence. Michael didn't know when it had happened, but at some point the alarms had stopped clanging. It showed how anxious he'd been that he hadn't noticed. Besides the soft sound of his own small breaths, everything was quiet and still. And dark.

Several minutes passed. He couldn't get comfortable in the small, cramped space, no matter how much he shifted. His back ached and his muscles were stiff. He knew Sarah was in the next cabinet over, her NetScreen probably dimmed as much as possible, working on a way to get out of there. There had to be a way. And if there *was,* Michael had no doubt that she'd figure it out.

Still, he hadn't stopped sweating. His nerves were a jumble of frayed cords, ready to snap. People were out there, in the halls, throughout the building, looking for him. And not just as a missing person—they thought he was a terrorist, a kidnapper, an accomplice, a fugitive. Once the police had them, it wouldn't be long before Kaine knew where they were. And then his people—who he guessed were former Tangents like Michael—would come next.

There was a sound somewhere nearby, and not from the other cabinets. A cough or clearing of the throat. Michael froze and listened.

The shuffle of footsteps, more than one person. They moved in bursts, as if they were sweeping the area bit by bit, going from one spot to the next. He couldn't tell if the people were in the hallway or the kitchen. But then came the voices, and it sounded like they were just a few feet away.

"Call in downstairs," a man said in a tight whisper. "Get the latest."

"Just a sec," came the reply. A woman.

Michael felt his heart almost leap out of his chest—they were so close. He steeled himself. One wrong move or sound and they'd be on him.

There was a chirp and a tinny sound of static that was barely audible. Then the woman spoke again.

"Systems are all jacked up. Cameras are down, and the heat sigs are acting loopy. The sarge sent a team to the thirtieth floor for some reason but told us to sweep this one. Make sure they left."

"You really think the Sarge meant it?" the man asked.

"What?" the woman replied. Michael closed his eyes and concentrated, as if that would help him hear better.

"You know what I'm talking about."

The woman paused before responding. "Yeah. I think he meant it."

One of them made a clicking sound with their tongue, and then there were a few seconds of silence.

"Whatever," the man finally said. "Dead, not dead, I don't care. As long as I get home for supper. I'm sick of this crap."

The woman snickered. "Cry me a river. Come on, let's search these cabinets. It's a perfect place to hide."

Panicked, Michael realized he had to reposition himself to be able to strike out when they opened his cabinet door. Quietly, slowly, he shifted to get onto his knees, his back scraping the low top of the space. He'd come too far to turn back now. When that door swung open, he'd launch himself like a KillSim, screaming bloody murder.

Footsteps approached. A drop of sweat stung his right eye, and he swiped at it, waiting for the inevitable. Someone stood just inches away—he could sense their presence, almost like a shadow. He heard the person shuffle their feet right outside his door, then get quiet. Maybe he or she had crouched down, reaching for the handle of the cabinet that second. Michael braced himself, hands clenched into fists.

Nothing happened. Seconds ticked by.

One, two, three, four, five.

Not a sound.

Six, seven, eight, nine, ten.

Nothing.

Then the scrape of a shoe against the floor, still close.

Silence.

Michael realized he'd been holding his breath, as if it had been locked inside his chest. Carefully, he exhaled through his nose and sucked in a slow pull of air. Another scrape, then more of nothing. Neither of the people in the kitchen had said a word.

What were they doing? His muscles cramped; he had the urge to open the door and get it over with. But he held back, straining to hear something, anything at all. He might as well have been in the depths of space. The silence was loud. More seconds passed.

Then, just like that, the world was full of sound.

A scuffle of feet. Creaking noises. Grunts. Soft thumps. Metallic clicks. Muted moans, as if someone had a hand over their mouth. Michael's whole body tensed—he didn't know what to do, what to make of it. His friends might be in trouble, but it seemed odd that neither one had called for help.

More sounds of struggle: a flurry of footsteps, a crash like bodies hitting the fridge. The thunderous boom of gunshots. Someone shouted something he couldn't make out, then ran, footsteps fading in the hallway. A man, close by, groaned in agony.

Finally, unable to hold himself back any longer, Michael reached out to open the door, when everything fell silent again. His hand froze in midair, uncertainty flooding him.

A few seconds later there was another grunt. Then heavy, uneven footsteps, crossing the kitchen floor, as if the person had been injured.

Thump, drag, thump, drag.

Getting louder, heading straight for the cabinet in which Michael huddled like a terrified kid hiding from a bully. He couldn't take it anymore. Wishing desperately that he had a weapon, he pushed open the door and crawled out—he'd hoped to leap to his feet, ready for a fight, but instead he tumbled and tripped over the lip of the cabinet's bottom.

Sprawled across the kitchen floor, he looked up to see the

figure of a man looming over him, eyes hidden in shadow. The man clutched at his chest with both hands. Michael started to scramble, trying to get his arms and legs under him, a bolt of fear like lightning in his chest. The man groaned, then fell, crumpling in a heap on Michael before he could back away. Then a last gargled breath escaped the stranger's lungs and he went totally still.

Michael froze, trying to digest what had happened.

The red emergency lights from the hallway didn't do a thing to cut the darkness in the kitchen. He crawled partway out from under the intruder and squeezed his EarCuff. His NetScreen came to life, casting its glow on the man who'd collapsed into his lap. A cop. He had blood on his face, on his uniform, smeared on the shiny badge pinned to his shirt, his hands, everywhere. And his eyes stared at the ceiling without a spark of life shining within. The man was dead.

Michael looked up and realized that both of the cabinet doors of his friends were open, and Bryson and Sarah were still inside, staring out at him. Bryson looked as stunned as Michael felt, but Sarah had an odd expression on her face. Relief more than horror.

"It worked," she whispered.

CHAPTER 13

HAPPY DANCE

1

It finally hit Michael that he had a dead, bloody guy sitting in his lap, and with a shudder he pushed the man off and scrambled away until his back slammed into the far wall of the kitchen. The NetScreen bobbed up and down as he moved, throwing spooky shadows across the room. His breaths came in ragged bursts, and he looked at Sarah, not even knowing how to respond to what she'd said.

She and Bryson were crawling out of their hiding spots and getting to their feet at the same time. Sarah was already working at her NetScreen before she was standing. Michael took in the rest of the kitchen and saw a dead woman perched up against the fridge with a bullet hole in her forehead. The woman was a cop, too. What *had* Sarah done?

When he looked back at her, she returned his gaze as if she'd read his mind. She stopped typing and swiping, and her shoulders sank as her expression melted into sadness.

"What happened?" Michael asked quietly.

Sarah's eyes fell to the man on the floor and she recoiled as if she'd just realized what had happened. Then she looked to the right and saw the dead woman. Squeezing her eyes closed, Sarah crumpled to the floor and buried her face in her arms.

Michael and Bryson exchanged a quick look of alarm and then they were both beside her, helpless but there. Michael rubbed her arm, feeling like a fool. He didn't want to push things, but he knew more cops could be on them at any second. Especially after . . . whatever she'd done. Two people dead. Two *police*. It didn't get much worse than that.

Bryson did the asking. "Sarah, what in the world happened? We need to get out of here."

"I know, I know," she said, lifting her head. Michael had expected tears but there were none. Just a look of perfect heartbreak. "Don't worry, I've got it all figured out." She stood up and composed herself, brushing off her pants. "Just follow me and we'll be out of here in five minutes."

"But . . ." Michael couldn't find the words.

Sarah walked toward the hallway. "I'll explain along the way."

2

A half hour later, the three of them were walking through a subway tunnel, on a raised platform above the tracks, heading for an exit that was far from the scene of action. And Michael's heart ached for Sarah.

He remembered the thousands of times he'd thought

about why he loved the *Lifeblood* game so much: nothing was more exciting, more brutal, more like real life. What an idiot he'd been. The only reason it had been so fun was because it *wasn't* real life. Not even close. Nothing like this.

"Maybe we should take a break," Bryson said. "Sit our butts down."

They reached a station full of people heading to or coming from their trains, eyes glued to NetScreens, avoiding each other in a fashion that had always seemed like magic to Michael. But then, walking and Netting at the same time had become as much a part of life as walking and breathing.

They found a bench and took a seat, Sarah in the middle. No one said a word. Michael leaned back against the cold brick of the subway wall and closed his eyes. He needed to somehow come up with the right words to make Sarah feel better. It wasn't her fault. It wasn't her fault at all.

She'd done what she had to. Hacked her way into the communications system, sending out a top-level alert to every officer in the building. It said that the "perps" had stolen uniforms and were in the kitchen of the fifty-fourth floor, planting a bomb.

All she'd hoped for was some confusion and a sense of panic—she'd figured someone might call all the police back long enough for the three of them to escape via a hidden route she'd already mapped out from the building schematics. A route that led to a private maintenance entrance to the tunnels of the subway system.

Not the greatest plan ever, but they'd been desperate. There had been police a few feet away, and it had only been a matter of moments before they'd checked those cabinets. The fact that someone came in, guns blazing, not even taking the time to make sure they were firing at the right people . . . how could you expect that?

Because of Sarah, they had escaped. Stairwells, service elevators, back rooms, heating ducts, fire escapes—Sarah had figured out the best and most secret way to get down to the subway. And they'd been able to do it. But Michael didn't feel safe at all. It felt like every person in the world was on the lookout for the three fugitives.

The Trifecta to Dissect-ya, he thought. It should've made him smile, but instead he felt even sadder.

"We can't sit here like this," he said. "We need to get away. Hide. Not be seen." The sense of urgency almost overwhelmed him, made it hard to breathe.

"Relax," Sarah replied. He'd never heard her voice sound so hollow. "They think we're still in the building. I took care of it."

Bryson stood up. "We can never relax again. Michael's right. Come on. Let's get on a train and take it as far as it goes."

They boarded the very next one that pulled into the station.

3

They huddled in a corner, leaning close together in their seats to work out what came next. So far no one seemed to recognize their faces, despite their being plastered over the NewsBops.

"What're we going to do?" Sarah whispered, so softly that Michael wondered if she might be talking to herself. "How can we possibly find my parents, much less save them?"

He shrugged. His mind kept wandering to Gabriela, wondering if somehow she could help them. She'd said she'd be with her dad in Atlanta.

As if Bryson had been reading his mind, he said, "There has to be someone out there who can help us."

Sarah breathed out a heavy sigh. "Maybe we should've just turned ourselves in."

"Don't even go there," Michael warned, still not ready to tell them about Gabriela. "Seriously. This isn't just about some lazy detective looking to blame you for your parents' kidnapping. People are out to get us. Kaine is out to get us. And who knows how many Tangents he's downloaded by now. Or why in the world he's doing it. We turn ourselves in, we'll be dead come morning."

Sarah slowly turned to face him, as if it took all her energy to move that much. "A bit dramatic, don't you think?"

"You really need to ask that? After what we've been through? I can't look at anyone anymore without wondering if they're a Tangent, dying to test out their new human hands and squeeze my throat closed."

Sarah sighed again. "*If* that's what's happening," she murmured.

Michael knew where they had to go. And he knew that his friends wouldn't like it. "We need to try the VNS again."

Sarah shook her head. "After that sweet, warm reception we got at the junk-hole with Cigar Man? I don't think so."

"Yeah, it didn't go so well," Bryson added.

"I'm telling you," Michael insisted, "we have to try."

Neither of his friends looked convinced.

"I'm serious!" Michael half shouted.

"You just said we shouldn't turn ourselves in!"

"To the *cops*." Michael breathed in, then tried to exhale his frustration. "Look, I know. This is different. I'm not going to waltz into some random VNS branch again. We need to go to Atlanta and find Agent Weber. Break in if we have to. In fact, I think we *should* break in, because I don't want to risk getting caught by guards or cops. She's the only one we can risk talking to." And if that didn't work, he'd have to contact Gabriela.

Bryson wore an expression of genuine disbelief. "We already did that, Michael. You were there, remember? She blew us off."

"I know. But there was something weird about it. Maybe our mission on the Path was top-secret, or maybe what happened to *me* is top-secret. I'm sure of it, actually. I bet only she and a few others know about the Mortality Doctrine, especially that it worked. She came to me, guys. She came to my—to *Jackson's* apartment and said that she'd be in touch with me. For all we know, *she* was threatened by Kaine and now she's backing off. There's a ton of possibilities. But she's the only person on this planet I can imagine giving us a chance. They need us because we're so close to the situation, and we need them. Someone has to stop what Kaine's started."

Sarah took on a contemplative look. "Maybe she can also help find my parents."

"Exactly." Michael had her. He tried not to show too much relief. She'd come to his side far more quickly than he'd expected. Now they just had to convince Bryson.

"What do you think?" he asked him. "She's in Atlanta."

Bryson nodded slowly, reluctantly coming on board. "I guess we find a sneaky way to buy bus tickets, then. We can sleep on the road."

4

It was a long, long bus ride ahead of them, and Michael couldn't get comfortable in his seat. A plane, train, or car—anything would have been a better option, but they couldn't risk it. A bus seemed the most anonymous mode of transportation. No one seemed to care too much about three shabbily dressed teenagers riding the lonely road to visit some faraway grandma.

His friends had dozed off quickly, Bryson's head hilariously bobbing all over the place, and Michael seized the opportunity to contact Gabriela. He wanted to see if she had any value to them before he bothered telling his friends about her. Had to.

Michael couldn't risk staying connected to the Net for a long time, but if he could quickly convince her to meet him when they got to Atlanta, they could talk in person. After igniting his NetScreen, it didn't take long to find her information and send a message, using a brand-new fake ID. She responded almost immediately.

MichaelPeterson240: Gabby, it's Jax. We need to talk.

GabbyWonderWoman: Hi.

MichaelPeterson240: Oh. Hi. That was fast.

GabbyWonderWoman: I noticed all your accounts vanished.

MichaelPeterson240: My Jackson accounts?

GabbyWonderWoman: Yeah.

MichaelPeterson240: Yeah. Look, I needed WAY more time to explain everything.

GabbyWonderWoman: No. No one could possibly be that stupid.

MichaelPeterson240: Exactly.

GabbyWonderWoman: Consider me the most confused girl in history. Since the Big Bang.

MichaelPeterson240: I know. I'm just as confused about most of it.

GabbyWonderWoman: Are you really trying to tell me you're not Jax?

MichaelPeterson240: Give me a chance to explain in person.

GabbyWonderWoman: Okay. I need to see you, too. I'm going crazy.

MichaelPeterson240: Okay. I'm sorry. About all this. Bye.

GabbyWonderWoman: I love you.

Michael saw that last line and let out a breath. Not knowing what else to do, he quickly exited the conversation and turned off his EarCuff. He stared at the now-dark spot where the NetScreen had been hovering, his heart hammering, his thoughts flying. The bus hummed and bounced along the night-black road.

Gabriela's dad worked for the VNS. VNS security, which was redundant, like she said. Things made a little more sense now. Kaine wanted that inside track for some reason, which was why he'd sent Michael into Jackson's body through the Mortality Doctrine. And now, no matter how guilty it made him feel, Michael was going to take advantage of the connection himself, if for nothing else, to find out more about the VNS. And at best, to find a way inside their headquarters for a meeting with Agent Weber. In person.

Michael settled himself and closed his eyes, leaning against the cool glass of the window. The vibration of the bus, the thrum of the tires on the road, the inviting darkness— it all started to lull him to sleep. On some level, he knew the real reason he wanted to see Gabriela again. Gabby. She was real, a tether linking his new life to its origins. And . . . she loved him. It was all messed up.

Feeling ridiculous, he let dreams take him away.

5

They had to change vehicles in a town right outside the Kentucky border and found themselves with a couple of hours to kill. Hungry and tired, their options limited, they headed for a dump of a café. A full day had passed, and darkness had settled on the small dusty town. Maybe it was the humidity, but Michael felt damp and itchy and dirty.

And now he had to tell his friends about Gabby.

They were in a booth, Bryson across from Michael and Sarah. Michael had just taken a bite of a turkey club sandwich, washing it down with warm water—the bored waitress had graced him with all of one ice cube—when he got up his nerve.

"So," he began, swallowing, wiping his mouth with a napkin. "Turns out Jackson Porter had a girlfriend. I actually ran into her a couple of times before I found you guys." He waited, acting casual but feeling like he'd just revealed his dirtiest, darkest secret.

Bryson and Sarah just looked at him. But they'd stopped chewing.

"I think she might be what Kaine was talking about," he continued, "when he said he chose Jackson for a reason. Her dad works for the VNS. Does security for them. In Atlanta, actually. Maybe we can use the connection ourselves, to our advantage." He took another big bite of his sandwich, glad he'd finally gotten that off his chest.

Bryson had an astonished look on his face. "What are you talking about? You're just bringing this up now?"

Sarah stayed silent, the fuming kind of silent.

"Uh, yeah," Michael replied. "I didn't think it was a big deal until Kaine hinted at it. So I, uh, told her to meet us in Atlanta. I think we should talk to her. See if she can help us.

Or if she knows anything. And she's not being hunted by the media and cops, either. I don't know." Now that it was all out, it suddenly seemed like the worst idea ever.

Sarah dropped her fork. "Michael. How can you possibly risk bringing someone else in on this?" She leaned back in her seat and folded her arms.

Bryson was shaking his head. He looked confused.

Michael tried to smooth it over. "Guys, don't worry. I was careful. And I feel like I owe it to her to try to explain what happened. I really feel like we need to talk to her. Together."

"You should've asked us first," Sarah said sharply.

Michael looked at Bryson, and he nodded, once, in agreement.

"I'm sorry," Michael said. "You're right. I should've. It just didn't seem like a big deal, and I . . . wanted to make things right with her. Make her feel better. And I just had a feeling that she can help us somehow. I don't know. I'm sorry."

They lapsed into silence, picking at their food. Michael felt like an idiot.

He took another sip of his drink, almost choking when he noticed a young couple a few tables away staring straight at him. The man had dark hair, swept back in a gel-hardened style that looked either cutting-edge or fifty years out of date; Michael couldn't tell. The man was thin, his cheeks packed with acne scars. His companion, a woman with short red hair and eyes the color of dying grass, had leaned her head against the man's shoulder. No food—not even a drink—sat on the table in front of them. And they were both staring at Michael.

"Check that out," he said to Sarah, voice low. He gave a slight nod in the direction of the couple. A chill worked its way up his spine.

Sarah stiffened. "We better get out of here."

Bryson had his back to the man and woman. He noticed his friends' attention, though, and turned to take a look. He swung back, face a little pale.

"Okay, that's just not right," he said. "Let's skedaddle."

Michael grabbed his sandwich and a handful of fries as Sarah paid the waitress, and continued eating as he walked toward the exit, the strangers' stares like lasers between his shoulders. He fought the urge to look back at them.

Although his friends hadn't said it, Michael knew what they were thinking. That it couldn't be a coincidence, this odd pair staring at them right after Michael had contacted someone using the Net.

He hoped he hadn't made a terrible mistake.

6

Michael finished his food just as he found a seat on the new bus. He brushed the crumbs off his lap and wiped the grease on his jeans like a five-year-old, then leaned his head against the window, keeping his eyes on the café down the street. Somehow, deep down, he knew what was going to happen. It wasn't a minute later when the couple came out the door, their hands clasped, arms swinging in a sweet romantic gesture. They turned and walked toward the bus station.

"Crap," he said.

"They're following us?" Sarah asked.

Bryson was across the aisle, and he got up and leaned over them to look out the window. "If they get on this bus, I'm getting off."

"That makes three of us," Michael agreed, thankful no one was mentioning his girlfriend. *Jackson's* girlfriend.

He watched as the man and woman got closer.

Bryson went back to his seat and plopped down with a sigh. "You know, all those years we talked about getting together in the Wake . . . this wasn't exactly what I had in mind. Being chased across the country. On a bus."

Michael only half listened to Bryson complain, concentrating on the mysterious couple. They kept meandering about, oddly crisscrossing the street a couple of times, but they still headed for the bus. The driver had boarded by then, and was cranking up the engine. Most of the other passengers were in their seats as well, and Michael wished they could just get on with it. He wanted to be as far away from the spooky man and woman as possible, as *soon* as possible.

But they kept coming. Soon they abandoned any pretense of exploring the town and started walking briskly toward the bus. Toward Michael. They even seemed to be cutting a direct line to his very window.

"Who *are* these people?" he said under his breath, goose bumps standing up on his arms.

"You think they're Tangents?" Sarah asked.

Michael shrugged. He willed the bus to start moving, but nothing was happening. Step by deliberate step, the couple approached.

"Come *on,*" Michael said tightly, glancing up at the driver. The man shifted about in his seat, checking instruments and moving things around, adjusting himself. Everything *but* driving.

A look back at the man and woman showed them only a few feet away. Michael almost gasped—it was like they'd sped up time, leaping ahead in a quantum burst. And then they were right below his window, craning their necks to see him, though he didn't know how well they could in the darkness. But their eyes found his and they grew still.

Michael's nerves were officially on fire. "What should we do? Get off?"

Sarah squeezed his shoulder as she leaned in to get a better view of their visitors. "I don't know. Maybe?"

He looked once again at the driver, who had finally settled down. It seemed that he was finally about to pull out. The man reached for a lever.

Michael returned his attention to the couple outside his window. The woman slowly raised a hand, fingers slightly crooked but outstretched, palm outward, until her arm was fully above her head, the index finger pointing at Michael. Both the man and the woman had dazed expressions on their faces. They stared at Michael as if in wonder. His throat clenched.

Before anything else could happen, the bus lurched into motion with a grumpy roar, jolting everyone on board, and pulled away. The couple stood in the street, holding hands, watching longingly as the bus left them behind.

They rode through the night, making it to Atlanta in the early morning without further incident. Michael, exhausted, slept well despite the creepy chills from the strange encounter at the diner. He and his friends got off the bus, ate a quick breakfast, then made their way through the city, doing their best to keep to themselves. Their destination was close; they could see it in brief glimpses between buildings as they walked.

The parking lot of the Falcons' stadium.

Where everything had started.

Michael had only one thing to go on when it came to finding Agent Weber and forcing her to meet with him, and he was banking on the fact that *Lifeblood Deep* had been created to replicate the real world as much as humanly possible.

It was weird to remember that day when he'd been taken to the stadium parking lot, where a secret entrance opened up to reveal a massive VNS headquarters down below. It was weird because he'd been in the Sleep, and none of it was real. When Agent Weber came to see him after he'd been inserted into a human body, she'd pretty much told him that everything they'd discussed had been real, that his mission was real. Just not the world in which it had taken place.

He needed to talk to her. Desperately. Right before getting off the bus, he'd messaged Gabby, telling her to message him the second she could meet. Meanwhile, Michael and his friends meandered through the city.

They were just passing the windows of a small coffee shop when someone banged on the glass from inside, startling Michael so much that he jumped away from it, stumbling. He caught himself before he fell to the cement. Looking back, he saw a teenage girl gazing through the window, her eyes glued to Michael.

Spotted, he thought miserably. Someone was bound to recognize them from the NewsBops. Or was she like the couple at the diner? There was something about her eyes. . . .

"You friends with that chick?" Bryson asked.

Michael shook his head, panic rising in his chest. "Let's keep moving."

But even as he said it the girl had swept away from the window and come charging out the door of the coffee shop. Michael braced himself, knowing he should run but wanting the truth. Were there others out there like him?

"Whoa, hold tight," Bryson said to the girl as she walked right up to Michael. Bryson stood in front of her with hands held out, like a cop ordering someone to step away from the scene of a crime. "Back off."

Sarah had come to Michael's side, her hand gripping his arm. She leaned closer to whisper to him. "Come on, let's get out of here. Don't even talk to her."

But he was mesmerized. The girl was odd-looking, with long blond hair framing a strange, elven face with dark eyes. She looked . . . distant, like the couple in the diner. She was peeking over Bryson's shoulder, smiling at Michael, and he found himself unable to move.

"But I just . . . I wanted to say hi," she said, her gaze never leaving Michael. "My name is Carol. I just want to say hi to the First."

Bryson turned around, an expression of total confusion transforming his face. "Dude, do you know this girl or not?"

Michael shook his head slightly, still tingling with fear but feeling like he had an opportunity to learn something. There had to be a connection between this Carol person and the man and woman who'd stared at him before. He had to know what it was. It could be as simple as their recognizing his face from the NewsBops, but he meant to find out.

"Let her talk," he said quietly. "Maybe she can tell us something."

Bryson gave him a questioning look and shook his head. Sarah squeezed his arm even tighter, until it hurt. But Michael ignored them, addressing the stranger.

"Who are you?" he asked her. "How do you know who I am?"

She smiled again—had never really stopped. "I . . . He showed you to us. He . . ." She paused, flicking her eyes toward Bryson and Sarah as if she wanted to say something they shouldn't hear. "I saw you walk by and I knew. The First. That's what he calls you."

Michael swallowed a lump in his throat. He knew who she was talking about, but needed to hear her say it. "Who?"

"Kaine, of course! Isn't it all so . . . exciting?"

She giggled—a little-girl, straight-from-the-playground giggle. But her happiness made Michael's stomach turn. Sarah had let go of his arm; she was swaying as if she might faint.

"Remember my name," the girl said. "It's Carol. I'm sure we'll meet again soon. The world's changing, you know. Thanks to Kaine. Thanks to *you*." She gave a little squeal of delight, then turned and ran off down the street, dodging people as she disappeared.

Michael stared after her, speechless. The sun had finally come up, but the world felt darker.

CHAPTER 14

THE HORIZONTAL DOOR

1

Michael turned to Sarah, placed his hands on her shoulders.

"Look at me," he said. "Is it really that obvious? That I'm a Tangent?"

Sarah's face fell with pity, as if she were visiting an old relative at a nursing home, watching someone she loved sink into dementia.

"No," she answered. "You heard what she said. Kaine showed you to them."

Michael shook her, more fiercely than he meant to. "What's wrong with me? Why did he choose me?"

A tear welled up in her eye. "You're hurting me, Michael. Just stop and breathe. We'll figure this out."

"Yeah," Bryson added. "Chill, man. Let her go."

Michael did, his hands dropping to his sides. Bryson's words made him angry—mostly because he knew his friend was right. And a dreadful, weighing sorrow made him want to sit down and cry. So many emotions at once. His mind didn't know how to handle this. He was a freak. Nothing more than an experiment. A computer program shoved into a human body. A murderer. And then this creepy girl had to come by and make him some kind of hero for the other Tangents. *The First.* He wanted to puke.

"Michael," Sarah said softly.

He had closed his eyes without realizing it. He was leaning against a building, though he didn't remember moving. He rubbed his face, then looked around, expecting to find Carol or someone else staring at him, but there was only Bryson and Sarah, both of them clearly upset.

"Let's just go," Bryson said. "Let's break into the VNS and strap Weber to a chair if we have to. Make her listen. Make all of them listen. We can figure this out, dude."

Sarah nodded but didn't say anything. That tear from earlier had spilled down her cheek, leaving a trail.

"I just feel . . ." Michael tried to find the right words. "I feel all this pressure inside, and I think it's going to explode. It's hard to breathe." He pulled in long breaths, one after another, filling his lungs, then exhaling. He was as panicked as he'd ever been, just because some flighty girl had giggled.

Sarah hugged him and spoke into his ear. "It doesn't matter what you are or where you came from. You understand me? And none of this is your fault. The three of us are going to save my parents and stop Kaine once and for all. Got it? Don't worry about anything else, no matter how many people stare at you. No matter what anyone says."

Michael's breathing and the ruthless beating of his heart started to even out. He felt like a moron now.

"Sorry," he muttered. "Kinda lost it there for a second."

"Kinda?" Bryson repeated, smiling halfheartedly.

"Okay. Now, which way is the stadium?" Sarah asked.

Michael knew very well that she didn't need to ask—she had everything mapped out to the inch. But he appreciated the gesture and the show of confidence.

"That way," he said, pointing behind her. A few minutes later, his EarCuff blinked on, revealing the alert he'd set up. Gabby was in the city, ready to meet.

"She's here," he told his friends. "Gabby."

Neither Bryson nor Sarah looked very happy. Michael knew they were still worried that meeting up with her was a huge risk.

"Don't say anything about the stadium yet," Bryson said. "Have her come to that coffee shop over there." He pointed across the street.

Michael sent the message.

2

They waited nearby, hiding behind a crowd of people until Gabby showed up. They wanted to make sure she came alone, though Michael didn't doubt she would. He'd seen the look in her eyes when she'd first found him in Jackson's body. She was an innocent victim in all of this, just like him.

Once she was inside the coffee shop, Michael, Bryson, and Sarah crossed the street and followed her in. The place was only half full, and Gabby had already found a booth, where she sat looking around anxiously. When she spotted Michael, such a look of relief spread over her face that he felt terrible for dragging her into all this.

"Hi," she said when they walked up, eyeing Sarah and Bryson.

"Hey, Gabby," Michael replied, hating the awkwardness. The restaurant was warm and smelled of burned coffee. "This is Bryson. And Sarah. Guys, this is Gabby." Her nickname already came naturally.

They all said hello somewhat guardedly as they sat down. Sarah studied Gabby from across the table, and Michael couldn't tell if it was out of jealousy or mistrust. Or both.

"Well?" Sarah finally pressed. Everyone focused on Michael.

He swallowed, wishing they'd had a chance to order drinks. "Okay, listen. Gabby . . . I'm sorry about all this weirdness, but everything I've said is true."

Her eyes moistened a bit.

Bryson nodded, murmuring, "Crazy stuff. Crazy, crazy stuff."

Michael glared at him, trying to convey that he wasn't helping.

Then, surprising Michael, Sarah took charge. She reached across the table and grabbed Gabby's hand. "Do you want us to call you Gabriela or Gabby?"

"Gabby." The girl pulled her hand out of Sarah's grasp, clearly uncomfortable.

"Okay," Sarah said. "Gabby, then. Look, the three of us have been friends inside the Sleep for a long time. But then we found out that Michael was a part of the *Lifeblood Deep* program. You've heard how realistic that place is, right?"

Gabby nodded but wouldn't make eye contact with her.

Sarah continued. "These Tangents . . . some of them are completely lifelike. And now they're beginning to become sentient. Michael had no idea any of this was happening." She looked at him apologetically, but he was deeply relieved that she was doing the talking. "He was a Tangent. But there's another Tangent—Kaine—he's figured out this process that downloads the intelligence of a Tangent into a human brain. Essentially the human brain's just a biological computer. People have been saying this is possible for decades. Am I making any sense?"

Sarah spoke so calmly, and so matter-of-factly, that Michael looked on in awe. He actually thought she had a chance of convincing Gabby. Which was a good sign. They might even have a chance with the VNS.

Gabby leaned on the table. "So all three of you, right here, right now, are telling me that a Tangent named Michael was . . . downloaded into my boyfriend's brain?" She turned and faced Michael. "That this . . . person . . . is no longer Jax? That Jax was just drained, like a flushed toilet? That's what you're telling me?"

Michael felt sick having to explain again. "We don't know how it works exactly. I'm actually hoping that somehow he's, I don't know, *stored* somewhere. I mean, if it can happen in one direction, why not the other? Maybe he's still . . . maybe he still exists. Who knows, maybe we can save him."

Gabby laughed, but there was no trace of humor in it.

"Honestly?" She shook her head and folded her arms, leaning back with a heavy sigh. "I just don't know how I can possibly believe all this."

"Just think about Jackson," Michael said. "Jax. If you really knew him that well . . . I mean, do I seem like him to you? At all?"

She shook her head. "Nope. You most certainly do not." She paused, considering. "So keep talking."

They talked for another hour. Bryson got coffee and pound cake for everyone, and they swapped stories, showed her things on Bryson's old NetPad—even pulled out the ancient NetTab for a while to share some of the odd stories they'd researched about possible Tangent sightings around the world. Michael told Gabby about his old life, about his family, about Helga, about everything. Sarah brought her up to speed on Kaine and what he'd done to them. Bryson told her how they needed to get into the VNS and confront Agent Weber.

They talked and talked and talked, and Gabby listened.

Finally, as if they'd exhausted the English language, silence fell upon the table. Michael waited anxiously to see if they'd been able to convince Gabby.

She sighed and put her hands on the table, picking absently at a fingernail. "I know this sounds corny, but I don't care. I love"—she faltered, flickered a glance at Michael—"*loved* Jax. I did. I do. It's so confusing! You guys have seriously screwed up my head forever."

Michael didn't say anything, and wisely, his friends didn't, either.

"Listen, I don't know what I believe," Gabby continued. "But I know Jax, and this guy isn't Jax." She jabbed a thumb at Michael. "No offense. It's just that . . . I can tell he's *missing*. Ya know? And all those stories you showed me . . . If nothing else, you've got me freaked out."

Suddenly a composure came over her that was transforming. She sat up straighter; her eyes brightened; her skin seemed to glow. Michael could tell she was on the cusp of making a major decision, and he waited breathlessly to hear it.

"I can't be spotted anywhere near VNS headquarters," she said. "Too many people there know me because of my dad. But I can help you get in."

They leaned closer as she kept talking.

3

The Falcons' stadium was a massive thing, all glass and shiny metal. It looked like some mother spaceship from a sci-fi movie, ready to blast off for the stars. Since it was the off-season, the parking lot was an empty sea of asphalt, surrounded by multilevel structures erected to hold even more cars. It seemed that they had available parking for every person on the planet to come to a Falcons game.

He and his friends ran across the wide lot, the surface under their feet beginning to heat up from the morning sun. "In *Lifeblood Deep,* there was a space toward the front— a private parking spot that opened up like a trapdoor. That must be what Gabby was talking about." He hoped they could find the right one.

Sarah already had her NetScreen lit up. It was hard to see in the sunlight, but visible enough. Gabby had said that once they got within the range of the thousands of signals that floated around the stadium, they'd be able to find the crack they needed to dive into. They'd gone over everything in the coffee shop as best they could.

"Man," Sarah said. "This place is swarming. It makes our home signals look like cheap old radio stations. There's more information flying around here than I've ever seen before. Even deep in the Sleep itself."

Bryson clicked his tongue. "Well, there you go. We must be in the right place. Let me get linked up with you."

The two of them worked at their screens, making Michael feel a little left out. He knew what they were doing. He'd noticed it on several occasions. They were worried about him, thought he was fragile. On edge, especially after the strange encounters during the last day or so. He couldn't blame them for treading lightly with him. It was almost as if he were a newborn.

They stopped at the last—or first—row of parking spaces, closest to the hulking stadium itself. Michael looked around, took it all in. The structure loomed above them like a mountain of metal.

"This is where she said it'd be," he said. "Northeast corner."

Sarah sat on the curb, her eyes never leaving the faint glow of her NetScreen, and Bryson sat right next to her. Gabby had given them a few leads based on things she'd learned on her frequent visits to see her dad. As his friends worked those leads, Michael stood in front of them, feeling dumber by the minute.

"Anything I can do?" he asked. "Last I remember, I was pretty smart when it came to things like this."

Neither Bryson nor Sarah acted like they'd heard a word he said. He forced a laugh, but that didn't work, either. Giving up, he clicked on his own NetScreen and started dinking around to see if he could find something they might have missed.

They'd all been working for about five minutes or so when Michael heard the strangest sound. A slow but constant . . . *clopping*. He looked up just in time to see a horse come around the curve of the stadium a few hundred feet away, a police officer perched on the animal's saddle. The horse's shoes smacked against the sidewalk, an eerie, echoing noise that felt out of time and place with the hustle and bustle of the city.

Michael felt a little sting of alarm, even though the cop showed no interest in them. Yet. It was so strange. Human civilization had gotten so advanced that virtual reality was hardly distinguishable from real life and machines could hover in the air like alien spaceships. Yet some police evidently still walked around on horses, as if they were sheriffs looking for outlaws. He remembered the hovercop's story about his great-great-something-or-other-grandpa.

"Guys," Michael whispered. "We might want to pick up the pace. There's a cop over there. On a horse."

Bryson snickered at that but didn't look up. Neither did

Sarah. They were working feverishly, which Michael hoped was a good sign.

"Just saying," he murmured. He returned his attention to his own NetScreen, but he felt like anything he did would be a waste—his friends were already way ahead of him.

Two things happened, so close together that Michael couldn't tell which was first. A loud clank sounded just as the parking lot trembled close to where they sat. Then a rectangular section nearby separated from the surface around it and started lowering into the ground, groaning sounds of machinery coming from below.

Thank you, Gabby, Michael thought, hoping desperately he'd see her again to thank her in person.

The cop yelled something in the distance, and just as Michael looked over at him, the man started charging in on his horse. The sound of the horse's metal shoes striking the asphalt reminded Michael of gunfire.

4

"Quick!" Sarah yelled, on her feet. "Now's our chance!"

Michael was already on the move, getting there before either of his friends. He jumped down onto the descending section of asphalt and turned around, watching as the cop approached. Bryson and Sarah joined him; then they dropped down to their hands and knees and crawled toward the edge of the platform. They peeked down, trying to get a glimpse of where they were going. It was dark below—pitch-black—

but unless the VNS had tricked him with their re-creation in *Lifeblood Deep,* there was a second parking garage down there.

Michael got on his stomach and swung his legs over the side; then he held his breath and pushed off, landing just a few feet below on smooth concrete. He heard Sarah land nearby, and then Bryson landed on top of him. They scuffled until everyone got back to their feet. The light from above illuminated the garage well enough now to see that there was no sign of people.

The secret entrance halted with an echoing screech of metal that rang though the air, then immediately started moving up again. It had only come halfway down.

"Did you do that?" Michael asked Sarah.

Before she could answer, a man's voice boomed at them from above. Michael turned to see the cop leering down.

"What the hell are you kids doing? Get back up here!" He pulled out a gun, but the horse shied away at the sound of groaning machinery. The cop worked at the reins to steady the animal. In a few seconds they'd be safe, cut off by the rising section of parking lot.

"Stop this thing!" the cop yelled. This time he *did* point the gun as best he could. "What's going on? Are you . . ." His words faded and a look of recognition came over his face. He knew. He knew who they were.

The secret door slammed shut, plunging them into darkness.

Thank you, Gabby, Michael thought one more time.

5

Sarah's NetScreen flashed to life, casting its green glow over the dank garage in which they stood. Michael didn't know what to say. Everything was a jumbled mess in his mind. But at least the place looked familiar.

"Why did the platform stop halfway down? Did you program that or something? You'd turned your screen off."

He knew the answer before Sarah replied. "No. I couldn't even tell if Gabby's stuff was what made it open in the first place. I was working on it, but it might've just opened on its own."

"Maybe someone *let* us in," Bryson said. "And now we're trapped."

"Isn't this what we wanted?" Sarah countered. "We're in, aren't we?"

Michael sighed. "Yeah, but I bet some beefy security guards are on the way. They could lock us up before we get within a hundred feet of Agent Weber."

"Not to mention the dude on the horse," Bryson added. "He's probably calling every cop in the city. Do we have the worst luck on the planet or what? Just one lucky break. That's all I ask." He blew out a frustrated breath. "A cop on a freaking horse. You've gotta be kidding me. Seriously."

Michael almost laughed, the final proof he needed that he was losing it. He had no idea what to say.

"Well," Sarah said, "it's not going to help if we sit here and wait. Come on. Let's at least try to get inside—we can hide or something."

"Ladies first," Bryson offered, sweeping out an arm and bowing.

"Not the best time to test out being a gentleman. I'm happy to let *you* go first."

Michael rolled his eyes and headed for the exit, a set of doors he remembered from his virtual visit to the place. Bryson and Sarah fell in line behind him.

Not so shockingly, the doors weren't locked. Someone *had* let them in.

Bryson made an exaggerated exclamation of joy. "Hey, that lucky break I asked for!"

Sarah huffed. "I hope we get something a lot better than this."

Michael swung open the door and stepped into a hallway dimly lit with distantly spaced emergency lights glowing along the ceiling. It was just like the *Lifeblood* version of itself.

"Do you remember the way to her office?" Sarah asked.

Michael shook his head. "No," he said absently. He was thinking. In the middle of a workday, why wasn't the place abuzz with life? The VNS should have been busier than ever now, what with everything Kaine was up to.

"Do we really want to keep going?" Bryson said. "This is obviously some kind of trap. And even if it isn't, no one else is here, so why would that Weber lady be here? Maybe it's company picnic day."

"We're not turning back now," Michael said. "I don't care if it's a trap. I need to talk to her, and this is the only way it's going to happen."

Sarah shushed him, raising her hand as her brow creased in concentration. She was straining to hear something.

"What?" Bryson whispered.

Michael heard it. A faint, distant clicking sound. Growing louder, getting closer. More of a tapping. He suddenly knew exactly what it was.

"Footsteps," he said. "Someone's coming. And I've heard those shoes before."

"What do we do?" Bryson asked. "Should we hide?" He tried a couple of nearby doors, but they were locked.

Michael crossed his arms and waited. "There's no reason to hide."

The footsteps grew to a crescendo just as a figure appeared around the corner up ahead: a tall, stylish woman in a skirt. Long hair flowing over her shoulders. It was too dark to see her face very well, but Michael had no doubt.

Agent Weber clickety-clacked her way down the hall until she stood right in front of Michael. He could see her eyes now, dark, unfriendly. She had them trained on him so fiercely it seemed as if she saw only him.

"Michael," she said in a commanding voice. "Not exactly how I thought we'd meet up again, but I guess it will do."

"I . . . We have to talk to you." Michael's words tumbled out. "About a lot of things. But why did you act like you didn't know me before?"

She smiled, then turned and started walking away. She spoke to him over her shoulder.

"Come. I'll explain everything, but we need to hurry."

CHAPTER 15

EVERY SPECK

1

Michael and his friends followed Agent Weber down hallway after hallway. Finally, they took an elevator down several floors, then climbed a staircase. Weber remained silent the entire journey. The VNS seemed shut down, its rooms dark and deserted. It was unsettling, especially as they descended deeper underground. Michael highly doubted that every employee had decided to take the same day off.

The reason for the empty facility ended up being the first question Weber answered, one of the few.

"All my agents and analysts are inside the VirtNet for a three-day job," she said. "They Lifted from their homes—we only have a skeleton crew here to run things." They entered a small, simple office furnished with nothing but a round table and four chairs. There was another door at the back of the room, made of metal with a heavy locking mechanism, which piqued Michael's curiosity. "I don't need to tell any of you that the stakes have been raised in the Kaine affair. We're sweeping the virtual world—every speck of it—until we find him."

Michael expected Weber to offer them seats around the table, but instead, she walked to the heavy door and turned to face them. "I know you have questions, but the answers are . . . difficult. I had no choice but to pretend I didn't know you back when we last spoke. There are . . . factions within my agency that disagree with my course of action. I don't trust them, and they don't trust me. Yes, you contacted me over a secure communications line, but it was only secure from the outside world. Many within the VNS might have seen our conversation, and I couldn't let that happen. You have no idea just how secret your mission was."

Michael thought he understood perfectly. "In other words, you guys screwed up big-time and you're trying to cover it up. Make us go away."

Agent Weber was a beautiful woman, no doubt. But something washed over her face when he said that, that made her terrifyingly ugly. It was gone in a flash, and she was answering Michael.

"Like I said, we don't have time to talk. There are many, many levels to this, Michael. The politics are only a small part of it. Ultimately, what matters is the security of the Virt-Net and the safety of the people who frequent it. That's my mandate, and I'll do anything—*anything*—to fulfill my obligations. Do you understand?"

Michael flinched and took a half step backward, then tried to recover and make it look like he'd just repositioned himself to get more comfortable. This lady was scary, and he found it hard to trust her. But he didn't know where else to turn.

Bryson chimed in. "You keep calling him Michael. Why? His name is Jackson Porter, right? You know everything, don't you?"

That flash of anger showed on her face again as she directed her look at Bryson. "Listen to me. We don't have time for this. Yes, Kaine duped us. In a monumental way. In ways you don't even understand. Yes, I know Michael was a Tangent and was inserted into the body of Jackson Porter. I know it's happening all over the world. I know we need to stop it. Now, are you here to help me or waste my time?"

"How can we trust you?" Sarah asked. "After you led us to the Path, led us right into the trap Kaine set for us?"

Weber showed no anger this time, just a look of genuine frustration. As if she had a thousand things she wanted to say and no time. "If the three of you would just take a moment to reflect on the sequence of events, I think you'd see that we were fooled just as you were. We tried to find Kaine, and we used you. And it worked. Not in the way we hoped, but it *did* work. We got our answers—we know more than we ever could have otherwise. Now our problem is to figure out how to stop him before things get out of control. His influence is spreading even though we don't know his ultimate goal yet. And I'm not just talking about the Tangents he's humanizing."

"What else?" Michael asked. He reminded himself not to trust her too quickly, but she seemed sincere. He could see the stress in her every movement. She was scared, and that was a good thing in Michael's book. "What could be worse than that?"

Agent Weber shook her head. "I didn't say anything was worse. But the problems inside the VirtNet are just as bad as the problems in the Wake. Kaine is taking over, in ways you'll realize soon enough."

"We will?" Sarah asked.

"Yes," Weber replied. "Look, I went well out of my way to visit you, Michael, after we realized what had happened. We're all on the same side. I had to tread carefully for reasons we don't have time to discuss right now. I knew you would come to find me after our admittedly odd conversation over the communications uplink. The timing is good, and I need you—all three of you—more than ever."

Michael started to say something, but she held up a hand to cut him off.

"No, please," she said. Any sign of wanting to intimidate them had washed away completely. She was almost trembling. "We don't have time, I'm telling you, we don't have time! I need to get you three inside the VirtNet, and I need you to use those skills of yours. You'll be protected like never before, I promise."

"Wait," Bryson said. "What do you mean? You want us to go inside . . . here?"

Weber seemed relieved. "Yes." She turned and motioned toward the heavy metal door at her back. "Everything you need is waiting in there. It's all set up."

2

The place looked like a morgue. Two rows of at least twenty NerveBoxes were lined up against both walls, looking just like the coffins from which they'd gotten their nickname. The low hum of machinery filled the dimly lit room, giving the place an otherworldly feel. It was almost like they were already in the Sleep.

"I've prepped three Coffins for you," Agent Weber said, marching toward the back of the facility. Michael and the others followed. "I'm afraid I don't have much information to give—Kaine has eluded my best people from the start, and the deeper we dig, the more elusive he becomes. I wish I could've brought you in immediately, but it was just too risky. There are people who'd be very . . . upset if they knew I was bringing you in at all."

Michael didn't let on how much doubt he felt. A huge part of him thought it would be the most absurd thing ever to trust this woman and get in a Coffin that was under her control. But this was the VNS. If he couldn't trust them, whom *could* he trust? And if he left now, he was sure he'd spend the rest of his life in jail. At least this way he had a fighting chance.

"You haven't even told us what you want us to do," Bryson said. "And don't tell me that our only instructions are to jump into the Sleep and stop Kaine."

Agent Weber frowned at Michael's friend. Somehow it was the sincerest expression she'd borne yet, half pity and half remorse. She appeared to feel genuinely guilty that she had to ask them to risk everything once again.

"No, I don't expect you to stop Kaine," she said. "In fact, quite the opposite. If you do find him, it'd be way too dangerous for you to try anything by yourselves. I can't afford to tag you like we did when you went on the Path."

"Because of your enemies inside the VNS," Sarah offered.

Weber nodded but then seemed to regret it, catching herself. "They're not enemies. They just feel—they very strongly feel—that using a Tangent is out of the question. No offense, Michael, but you're a creation of Kaine now. You can understand why some people would find it hard to trust you."

Michael shrugged. What she was saying made more sense than he cared to admit.

"I'm just hoping you can find out where he is," Weber continued, "without actually *going* there. If we can discover the location of his central coding—if there even is such a place—then I have a plan for how to destroy him. *Literally* destroy him. We have a program that could set off a chain reaction in his programming and erase him from existence. But it won't work unless we find his central port."

She stopped then, seemingly done. Michael almost laughed. And he thought she'd given him hardly any instruction the *last* time. Mission Number Two looked to be a complete wild-goose chase. But he had his own reasons to pursue it, to find out more about Kaine: Sarah's parents; *his* parents; discovering what, if anything, had happened to Jackson Porter's essence. He could do that for Gabby, if nothing else.

"That's it?" Sarah asked. "You don't have leads or anything?"

Weber gave an apologetic smile. "Leads are exactly what we're looking for."

Michael looked at Sarah, then Bryson. It was hard to read their faces, but he could imagine what they were thinking—the same things he was. A little fear, a lot of doubt. And, of course, he knew they, too, had that old feeling that swelled up inside: The urge to game. To jump in feetfirst and conquer the Sleep from top to bottom.

But he didn't say anything. He couldn't be the one to decide this time; he'd already dragged Bryson and Sarah into too much. The decision had to come from them.

"We have a big problem, though," Sarah said. The tone of her voice told Michael what Weber might not have sensed yet: they were in, one hundred percent.

"Just one?" Weber replied. "We should be so lucky."

Sarah ignored the comment. "Every time we've gone into the Sleep, Kaine has been able to track us down. No matter how many layers of protection we've coded around ourselves. He wants us for something. He wants Michael, anyway. We've been trying to avoid Sinking back in."

"Trust me, I understand," Weber said. "All too well. Kaine is more powerful than we ever would've thought. But I think you'll feel better once you're in. Since we figured out that Kaine is a Tangent, I've spent hours building a new Hider program. It's several layers deep—virtually invisible. No one will be able to tell you're in there, I promise. Especially combined with the fake identifications I'm sure you guys have built yourselves."

Instead of responding, Sarah turned her attention to Michael. "What do you think?"

"Consider me curious," he said. Which was completely true.

"The only drawback," Weber added, "is that you won't be able to see code like you normally would once you're inside. That's the only way it can work. To hide you from the code, the code ends up being hidden from you."

"Drawback?" Bryson repeated. "You saved that little nugget until the end? That's more like a deal breaker! What good are we if we can't manipulate the code?"

Michael's hopes had crashed as well.

The agent's face didn't reveal a thing—she was solemn, her expression focused, her demeanor calm. "Don't be a child. All I meant is that you won't be able to access the code in the way you're used to. You can still use your NetScreens—old-fashioned, I know. But three people as skilled as you are—I think you can handle it."

"Unless we get into a pinch," Michael countered. "Whatever we can do on a NetScreen will be slow—probably too slow."

Agent Weber gave the slightest of nods, conceding the point. "It's that or risk Kaine being able to find you. The choice is yours. Both have their pros and cons, I'll admit."

Bryson said exactly what Michael was thinking. "I'll take the pro of keeping Kaine off our butts, I guess."

"Then it's settled," Agent Weber said, even though Michael wasn't sure they'd quite reached that point. But no one argued. "I'll pull you out in twenty-four hours, see if you've learned anything. Now let's get you in those Coffins."

Michael was a gamer at heart. True-blue, dyed-in-the-wool. He'd heard his dad say that once about how much he loved the Falcons, and he'd had no idea what it meant. But it seemed to apply to how he felt about Sinking. Before his life had been ripped to shreds by the VNS and Kaine, Michael had eaten, slept, and breathed gaming. It was the blood that pumped through his veins, program or not. It was a part of who he was, human body or none.

Gaming had been everything to him, and his love for it took over as he lay down in the VNS Coffin. It was ridiculous, considering all the danger and trouble, but he felt an overwhelming, familiar rush as the device did its magic—NerveWires and LiquiGels activating, AirPuffs extending, bubbling, and injecting. His *life* had become a game, the stakes ever higher, and he was ready to enjoy the thrill of it in the Sleep.

Agent Weber Sunk them to a Portal at an intersection of two streets lined with shops and businesses that he didn't recognize. When he opened his eyes, the first thought he had was that it was good to be back. Weber had said that they wouldn't be able to access the code like they normally could—and a quick check proved her right—but the world around them still had that overall feel of the code: the blurry edge of a building here and there, the static-like quality of some of the clouds in the sky, small sections of the road where you could see pixels if you looked hard enough. Not even the greatest programmer caught everything, and often they left glitches on purpose. Make it too realistic and people could really get screwed up in the head.

Except for *Lifeblood Deep,* of course. All the rules changed when it came to *Lifeblood Deep.*

"Where do you guys think we are?" Sarah asked, slowly turning in a circle to take everything in. Her Aura—and Bryson's—had been disguised, leaving just enough of their old selves to make them recognizable to each other.

Michael, who assumed he was an altered version of Jackson Porter, studied the street a little more closely. A few people moved about here and there, but it appeared to be a quiet town, the buildings small, the businesses typical and unexciting. A barbershop, a café, a social club, a coding school. There was even a furniture store, which meant someone really wanted the place to feel like a real town.

"I've never been here before," Bryson said.

"Me neither," Michael said.

Sarah pointed randomly down one of the streets, mostly empty. "There are hardly any people around. And it's the middle of the day." Just to punctuate the point, a slight breeze picked up and scattered a few pieces of trash, which skittered across the road almost loudly enough to echo. It made the place feel utterly vacant.

"This place is like a ghost town," said Michael.

"Spooky," Sarah agreed. "What should we do first?"

"It's driving me nuts not being able to see the code." Bryson kept opening and closing his eyes, blinking as if to dislodge an eyelash or a particle of dust. "We're going to look like idiots if we open up our NetScreens in the Sleep. Doesn't

Weber realize how important it is for us to look cool?" He shook his head.

Sarah patted him on the back. "Your ego will survive. Come on, let's start exploring."

4

They headed toward the more built-up part of town, where several tall buildings loomed in the distance. Oddly, though, the farther they went, the fewer people Michael saw. And even stranger, the few they *did* come across didn't react to them at all, almost as if they didn't see them. One woman walked by with a blank look on her face, and if Bryson hadn't jumped out of the way, she would've run right into him.

"Wait a second," Michael said. "Are we literally hidden from everyone? Can they not see us?"

"That's about as illegal as it gets," Bryson replied.

Sarah was gazing after the woman as she walked away. "I guess the VNS can do whatever they want. Check that out." She pointed at the lady.

Michael watched as the woman stopped, then turned in a circle as if she were lost and trying to find her bearings. Her feet scuffed the ground as she turned around like a zombie several times, then started walking across the street, not bothering to check for cars first.

Cars, Michael thought. Those were just as common in the Sleep as in the Wake—you especially saw a lot of them in a place like this, which was trying to replicate a real town as closely as possible. But he'd yet to see even one drive by.

"What is *wrong* with that lady?" Bryson asked.

"What's wrong with this whole *place*?" Sarah added.

Michael turned his back to the wandering woman. "Let's keep moving. She gives me the creeps."

Things got weirder the closer they got to the downtown area. People all but vanished. Cracks appeared in the buildings and sidewalks, then disappeared. One second they were there; then they were gone; then there again. Michael looked at a wide window of an unmarked business as he passed by and saw no reflection. Of anything, not just himself. He felt off-kilter looking at it—the surface was like glass in every way, tinted, shiny, almost opaque because of the light outside. But no reflection. He hurried past.

More glitches showed up. A light post shimmered in waves, as if it were made of water. A manhole floated up from the street like a flying saucer, then burst into a million pixels, digital butterflies that fluttered away, disappearing around a corner. The pavement buckled in places before going flat again. More and more splotches scarred the faces of the buildings, as if the code itself was starting to decay. Or someone was changing it, weakening it.

"What do you guys think is going on?" Bryson asked very calmly.

Michael wasn't surprised at his friend's calmness. Even though everything was a little weird, it didn't feel scary. At least, not yet. They'd been through plenty of stranger stuff. "It might just be a part of this place," he offered. "Weber could've put us in an actual game instead of a gathering spot. Maybe it *is* a ghost town."

Sarah stopped. "Do I dare bring up my NetScreen?" She

shot Bryson an annoyed look. "And not because I give a crap if people think I'm cool or not. Do you think Kaine will be able to track us if we start connecting to the code?"

"I'm sure Weber thought of that when she said we could do it the old-fashioned way," Michael replied. "If our Auras are as protected as she promised, our NetScreens are safe. Don't you think?"

In answer she squeezed her EarCuff, bringing her NetScreen to life. After a few seconds of poking around, she said, "Man, it's hard to see much. Everything keeps flickering and bouncing. I'm not used to coding with the NetScreen in the Sleep, but something seems wrong."

Michael clicked his own EarCuff to take a look, and it was just as she described. He'd rarely seen the code of the Sleep from this vantage point—from the dinky square of a NetScreen—but it did seem off. The code randomly jumbled up in some places and bounced across the screen in others, mixing itself even more.

"Weird" was the best he could offer. He tried entering a line of code here or there, but nothing seemed to work. The letters and numbers just got swept up into the chaos of the screen, to no effect that he could see. "Very weird."

"Do I even need to open mine up?" Bryson asked. "You two seem to be getting nowhere fast."

Sarah started to answer him but barely got out a word before she was interrupted by a drawn-out scream coming from around the corner of the closest building. Michael looked up, an icy shiver running down his spine, just in time to see a woman run out from behind the building, clutching at her throat as if someone were trying to strangle her. She lurched forward a few steps at a time, struggling against some unseen force. She staggered into the middle of the street, then collapsed.

The fall revealed her back, and Michael sucked in a quick breath. Little rectangles of sparkling blue light covered the area between her shoulder blades, leading all the way up to her neck and the back of her head, swarming her hair as they fluttered. He remembered all too well where he had seen such a thing before: the Black and Blue Club. KillSims. They'd eaten Ronika's digital soul, not only devouring her code, but also permanently damaging her brain in the Wake. The same thing appeared to be happening to the lady on the street. Like burning embers, the bright blue rectangles spread over the woman's body.

"They're eating her," Bryson whispered, and Michael realized it was the creepiest thing he'd ever said.

5

Sarah moved forward as if to help, but Michael snagged her by the arm, pulling her back. She slammed into him and they both stumbled.

"What're you doing?" she asked, working to break free of his grip. "We have to . . ." But then she stopped in defeat, slowly turning to watch as the woman was consumed by the attack on her code. She shone from within, brilliant blue lights pulsing like a heartbeat.

"There's nothing we can do," Michael said. "Who knows—it might spread to us if we touch her. And if there are KillSims around, then we need to get out of here, fast." Like he even needed to say it.

The ground beneath his feet bounced, throwing all three of them a full foot into the air. Michael caught his balance, holding on to Sarah, but Bryson fell to his knees.

"What wa—" he started to say, but then the street jumped beneath them again. This time, Michael and Sarah fell, too.

The ground trembled, small vibrations at first but then stronger, until Michael felt like he was on a boat being tossed about on an angry sea. The buildings around them shook, then swayed back and forth in a way that made no physical sense. They seemed almost rubbery, bending and warping, yet cracking in places. Streams of broken rock shot out from the stress. Noises filled the air, great booms and groans of metal. It reminded Michael of the visions he'd had during the Decay process of his Tangent programming, but it was obvious that his friends were being affected as well.

He placed his hands on the rocking surface of the street and steadied himself, then slowly rose to his feet, balancing as if he stood on an AirSurfer. He reached for Sarah and helped her up, too—it almost felt like they were dancing.

"I'm not in the mood for this!" she yelled sarcastically over the thunderous noise. But her face had paled with fear. Michael wondered if she'd momentarily forgotten that they were in the Sleep.

"Guys, look!" Bryson shouted, pointing down the street in the direction they'd been heading.

Michael had to take a step to his right to see around Bryson, and the movement almost made him fall down again. But he caught his balance and surveyed the scene, not sure what his friend had meant to point out. There was a lot to see.

The woman who'd been digitally attacked was now nothing more than a roughly human-sized form of flashing blue planes of light, and some of them had started to drift away, caught in a wind that Michael didn't feel. He had no clue what had happened to her—there was still no sign of KillSims.

Beyond the woman, farther down the street, weird streaks of odd colors were falling from the sky like lightning. It looked as if the skyline were made of paper and claws were tearing it apart. Green and blue and yellow light flashed so brightly that spots danced in Michael's eyes even when he turned his head. He timidly glanced back and saw that the tears in the skyline were growing, lengthening to touch the ground, spreading toward where he stood.

He understood what was going on. At least on some level. Someone, somewhere, was literally erasing the place from existence, and Michael wasn't so sure what would happen to them if they waited around to witness its destruction.

"Get back to the Portal!" he yelled. "Now!" Visions of the three of them back in the VNS Coffins, brain-dead, haunted his mind. "Go!"

He didn't need to tell them. They were already running, stumbling back down the street in the direction they'd come. A distinct sound filled the air, overtaking everything else—

a high-pitched, grating squeal. Michael looked over his shoulder and saw a huge gap in the road arrowing toward them, the pavement faded into a jagged line of fuzzy digital static. The world itself was coming apart, and his ears felt like they might start bleeding from the horrible noise of it all.

The land jostled beneath their feet, gashes in the programming fell like lightning all around them, and the noise got impossibly louder. Michael saw the silver column of the Portal up ahead, and even it seemed less substantial than normal.

Something warm and wet landed on his arm. He looked down to see one of those blue fragments of light fluttering across his skin. He swatted it away, watched it tumble to the ground and disappear into an abyss of crumbling code.

"Faster!" he yelled, barely hearing himself over the din of wrenching squeals.

Sarah was right next to him, sprinting hard, fists clenched and arms pumping. Bryson ran a few steps ahead, pounding the loose pavement. The expanding chaos was about to overtake them.

Michael focused on the Portal. Only forty or fifty feet away. It was fading, a ghostly pillar from a dream. And then a chasm opened under it, a massive hole in the ground that faded into a crumble of pixels and a swirl of gibberish code. He watched in shock as the Portal fell into the abyss. Just like that. Gone.

Michael stopped. He sucked in huge, gulping breaths as he turned in a circle, watched the world disintegrate around him. Sarah was there, and he pulled her into his arms. Bryson joined them, and they clasped each other in a group hug. Noise and destruction everywhere.

Sarah had leaned close to Michael's ear, and he was sure she said something, though he didn't hear it. Just as he felt her warm breath against his skin, the ground below them collapsed and they fell into the chasm of infected code.

Light.

Sound.

Wind.

Falling.

Michael lost hold of his friends and was swept away.

CHAPTER 16

THE INFINITE LADDER

Michael didn't know how or when it ended.

There was no crash landing. His Aura didn't find itself broken from falling onto some hard-packed land miles below the old dusty town. The noise was gone. There was no sound at all. Only a numb silence. A silence so complete it hurt his ears. Yet he lay on his back in a dark, still space.

He gently rolled over onto his side, then sat up and assessed how he felt. He expected pain, or at least a few aches, but he was fine, if a little dizzy. The darkness around him was so heavy it almost felt like it was pressing down on him. Reaching his arms out, he got to his feet and shuffled around, hoping to find a wall, a chair, something. But there was nothing except the solid ground under his feet and that blaring silence.

"Sarah?" he called. His voice sounded strange to his own ears, as if he had a cold and his head was stuffed up. "Bryson? You guys out there?"

"Mi-chael."

He jumped back a few steps, swung around in a circle, desperate to see. That voice. It was unsettling . . . mechanical and haunting, like something you'd imagine hearing from another dimension.

"Mi-chael."

He sucked in a quick breath, turned in a circle again. "Sarah? Bryson?" he whispered. Then he yelled. "Guys! Is that you?"

"Mi-chael." The voice was so odd and otherworldly he couldn't tell if it was male or female.

"Sarah!" he shouted. *"Bryson!"*

No response.

He remembered his NetScreen, hurriedly clicked his Ear-Cuff to flash it up. The green glow almost blinded him but revealed nothing in the darkness. He shut it off, realized it would be better for his eyes to be sharp and adjusted—the screen would only blunt his night vision.

Shuffling forward, arms before him, he headed toward where he thought the voice had come from. Only there was nothing. He walked and walked, sure he was going to smack into a wall at any second, but still nothing.

"Mi-chael."

He stopped. This time the voice sounded like it had come from above him. Michael froze, calmed his breathing, and waited, head tilted back to look up, searching the darkness. Finally, after a few seconds, he thought he saw a faint light hovering a hundred feet or so above him in the black, starless sky.

He cupped his hands around his mouth and yelled as loudly as he could. *"Sarah! Bryson!"*

Nothing.

But that light was still there. It was faint, but it was there.

He sat down on the ground and lowered his head. He had to think. Being cut off from the code was driving him nuts. Never in his life had he been forced to use a NetScreen to program within the Sleep, and he didn't know if he'd be good at it. The code in the VirtNet was so different from back in the Wake. It was more visual and intuitive. But he had to try. He had to get up to that light. Somehow.

He brought his screen blazing to life and got to work.

2

It took an hour. Possibly the longest, most excruciating hour of his life. Sweating, concentrating, digging through endless lines of code, surrounded by that awful darkness and pressing silence. And what did he get for all that effort?

A ladder.

He ended up stealing it from a game he'd played long, long ago called *Donkeys on Platforms*. One of those games that was so outrageously silly that everyone fell in love with it. The player had to navigate an intricate maze of bridges and ramps and arches and landings, all of it complex and jumbled, barely rational, avoiding an endless array of traps and freaky creatures. All to find lost donkeys and bring them back home to a guy named Scooter.

Eventually Michael had gotten bored and programmed gigantic, gravity-defying ladders to beat the system. Now, as Jackson Porter, it wasn't that hard to duplicate it.

One of those ladders now loomed above him, stretching into the darkness toward the light far above.

He started climbing.

3

The light in the distance got brighter as he ascended, its boundaries more defined. It was a cold light, almost blue, and it shone through an opening that appeared to be a perfect circle. He had to stop several times to adjust the programming of his ladder, make sure it led him in the right direction. Far below, it scraped along the floor as it moved at his will. *The wonders of the Sleep,* he marveled.

Up, up, up Michael went, always toward the light. He was sure someone wiser could come up with a really good philosophical parallel, but all he could think about was how sweaty his hands were and how much he missed his friends.

After a good thirty minutes of climbing the impossible ladder, he reached the edge of the light source. He stopped a few feet below and looked up to the fake sky—gray clouds cutting across the blue. He paused, took a final deep breath, and went the rest of the way, like a worker climbing from the sewers through an open manhole to a busy city street, hoping that nothing came by to swipe off his head.

Two rungs below the light, he stopped, so shocked by sound that at first he didn't know what was happening. He'd become used to the silence, even in such a short time. What he heard now was distinct and familiar: the majestic, rolling swells of the ocean.

The ocean?

Intrigued, he bolted up the last few feet and carefully peered out the circular hole. His eyes had slowly adjusted to the glow of the light coming from above, but he still wasn't prepared when he fully emerged. Blinded by the brilliance and deafened by the sound, he needed a few seconds to get his bearings. And when he did, his jaw dropped.

He emerged at the top of an angular sheath of black rock, jutting out of the churning waters of a massive purple ocean. Waves crashed into the stone to create great crystalline plumes that looked like sparkling wine. The noise of it was a rushing boom, filling the air. A spray of the plum-colored water washed across his face. It was so cold he gasped. He wiped it out of his eyes, felt the slight sting of salt. It was exhilarating and made him feel more awake than he had in a long time.

Squinting, he studied the endless sea stretching in every direction, its choppy surface full of whitecaps, like frosting on a purple cake. There was no ship, no birds or sea life or land to speak of. Two other rocky spits were the only things that broke the monotony. They stood equidistant a few hundred feet away, forming a triangle with his own perch. He didn't catch it at first, but as he gazed out at the other rocks, he realized that a person sat on each one. And he was pretty sure who those people were.

Bryson and Sarah.

Michael climbed out and kneeled down at the edge of the hole. He waved his arms, shouting his friends' names as loud as he could, but the roar of the wind and the ocean swept his voice away. Eventually both of his friends noticed him waving and motioned back to him. Michael couldn't imagine where they'd been sent—or why—but he didn't really care at that moment. He was just relieved to be reunited with Bryson and Sarah.

He looked back down at the hole he'd climbed out of and watched as it disappeared, only to be replaced by rock congruous with the rest of the little island. The area looked as if nothing had ever been there.

What is *this place?* Michael wondered.

He scanned the choppy waters below, wishing he had the courage to swim across, and realized there was something strange about the ocean, besides the fact that it was purple. There was a static look about it, sparkles and flashes and fuzzy lines, all moving in the water like sea creatures. And when he really thought about the color itself, it reminded him of times he'd been immersed in areas of naked programming material within the VirtNet—undeveloped places waiting to be molded by code.

Swimming seemed like a bad idea. He was thinking about the possibility of coding a bridge when Sarah beat him to it: a green beam of light suddenly stretched from her rocky perch into the air. It was simple, a flat plane about three feet wide, and it was crossing the distance between them as if someone were drawing it with a giant marker. Michael smiled, still feeling the rush of the cold water that had splashed over his body. He knew exactly where she'd gotten the code for this beauty. It was from a game called, simply, *Bridges*. It was about as exciting as it sounded, and they'd only played it a couple of times before moving on to bigger and better things.

Even before it reached Michael, another bridge started connecting Sara's rock to Bryson's, where he sat like a sun-bather, leaning back with his face open to the gray sky even though clouds hid the sun. It made Michael think Bryson spent way too much time inside.

Michael stood up, bracing himself against the wind, just as another wave crashed into his island and sprayed him good. Laughing, he wiped his face again. For a moment he forgot about everything that had happened and just smiled, feeling like the king of the world.

As soon as Sarah's bridge of light reached Michael, he jumped onto it and sprinted toward her. The surface was rubbery, just like he remembered from the game. Goose bumps covered his skin as the wind ripped at his wet clothes, and the feeling gave him even more energy. He picked up his pace.

He was about twenty feet away—almost there—when the bridge vanished, leaving nothing below him but air. He yelped as his heart leaped into his throat and he plummeted into the angry purple water.

4

The ice-cold water swallowed him, igniting his nerves and making his heart pound from the shock of it. He kicked and pulled himself upward, breaking the surface in a sparkle of purple light. Treading water, he looked up at Sarah's rock, only a few feet away now, to see his friend staring down at him, Bryson standing beside her.

"Sorry!" she yelled. "I forgot those things had unpredictable timers on them in the game!" She laughed, tried to cover it up, then laughed again. Bryson didn't even bother trying to hide his glee. Michael would have laughed, too, if he didn't feel like his nether regions were about to freeze solid.

"I didn't know you were *that* slow!" Bryson shouted down to him.

Michael wiped his face and spit out some of the strange purple water, then swam toward his friends. Suddenly he saw something out of the corner of his eye. Something slithering—and there were more than one. In a flit of panic, he burst forward, swimming frantically until he reached a slab of low black stone angling into the ocean and climbed onto it. He scrambled away from the edge of the water until he backed into a wall of jagged rock.

He ducked as a huge wave slammed him against the stone. When it receded, he quickly climbed even higher, finding plenty of places in the rocks for hand- and footholds. About halfway up, he found a flat outcropping and stopped. He got onto his stomach so he could lean out and look down at the water, madly curious about what lurked in this bizarre ocean.

Another cold wave crashed below, its crest splashing over him as he ducked his head. When it receded, he wiped his face and spit, slicked his hair back. And then he stared.

It wasn't eels or fish slithering around in the water. They

were spliced lines of code—actual, literal lines of numbers and letters—squirming and bouncing around like electrocuted worms.

He called out to his friends, the words ripping through his throat. "Get down here!"

5

By the time Bryson and Sarah clambered down to him, Michael had gotten to his feet. He crouched over, hands on knees, studying the water below. There was just enough room for the other two to squeeze in beside him, both of them taking a seat on the ground, legs dangling over the edge of the rock. A wave crashed, spraying them all. Sarah shrieked and then laughed.

"Whoa!" Bryson shouted, pointing at several different spots. "What was that? What are those . . ." Michael knew Bryson had seen the same thing he had. And Sarah, too, because her face had grown as immobile as the wet stone on which they sat.

"It's code," Michael said, even though he knew they'd figured it out. There was no denying what they saw. It was just too familiar, far too familiar—something they'd seen thousands of times, those combinations of letters and numbers. This purple ocean was full of swimming, wiggling, slithering lines of code. And they behaved as though they were all desperate to create a program. "Infected or destroyed somehow, which is probably why we can see it. But it's code."

"Okay," Sarah said, holding her hands out as if steadying

herself. "Let's put our heads together. What exactly are we looking at here?"

"And how did we get here?" Bryson added. "What happened to that town we were in? Where are we? And while we're at it, where can I get a burger?"

Michael felt like he was in a trance—he barely heard his friends. He stared at the frothy purple water below them, waves crashing into each other, spray filling the air. Everywhere he looked, those lines of code bounced off each other. There were so many of them, he thought the water itself might be made out of the things.

Bryson gently shoved him with an elbow. "Hey, wake up, maestro."

Michael shook his head a bit—he had to recalibrate his vision after concentrating to focus on such small things for so long. "Sorry. It's just so weird."

"Yeah" was all Bryson said. But then a few seconds later he added, "Guess I'm not getting that burger any time soon."

"Guess not."

"The water's just an illusion," Sarah said, seemingly out of nowhere. Michael knew she'd been thinking fiercely since they'd arrived in the strange world, and she had a theory already. He wanted to hug her, wet clothes and all, because his mind was worthless mush at the moment.

"Care to expound on that?" Bryson asked.

Sarah looked over at them just as another wave crashed below, buckets of purple water splashing over them. Michael quickly wiped it out of his eyes, eager to hear what she had to say.

She rubbed her face with both hands, then squeezed as

much wetness as she could from her hair. "Well," she said, "I think Kaine is destroying parts of the Sleep. I think he's marching in and just wiping out the code, ripping it to shreds. And I think it's all draining into this place." She waved her arms at the vast ocean around them. "All of this . . . it's literally a dumping ground of code and that purple building-block stuff that holds it all together. If we hadn't been protected by Agent Weber's programs, I think we could've been in serious trouble."

"Wait, what do you mean?" Bryson asked. "You think we would've been pulled apart and dumped in here as nothing but a bunch of code splices?"

Sarah nodded. "Something like that. I don't know if Kaine . . . what's the word . . . *manifested* this ocean like this on purpose, or if it's just some kind of natural result of what he's doing. But because of the way we were protected, I think we somehow formed—without meaning to—these islands of rock. Otherwise we might be swimming with the fishes, too. And brain-dead, for all we know, back in our Coffins. Or something else just as bad."

"That lady we saw," Michael said. "Back in the town. Dissolving into those blue spark thingies, just like what happened to Ronika. Maybe that would've been us, too." He shivered at the thought.

"How in the name of Gunner Skale did you come up with all this?" Bryson asked Sarah. He seemed genuine, like he believed her. It made Michael realize that he did, too. And he wondered if on some subconscious level he'd created this escape—it made him think back to how he'd instinctively manipulated the code right before Kaine triggered the Mortality Doctrine and sent him into the mind of Jackson Porter.

Sarah saw him thinking and just shrugged, smiling sheepishly. "Sometimes I amaze even myself."

The three of them didn't speak for a minute or two, soaking it all in. Michael knew how Sarah had come to the conclusion—when you'd spent countless hours digging through the raw materials of the Sleep, you came to understand its workings on an instinctual level. It made sense. And so did what came next.

"I know what we have to do," he said.

And then he told them.

CHAPTER 17

CORKSCREW

1

The icy chill when they dove back into the churning waters of the purple ocean took Michael's breath away. He gasped for air as he fought the whitecaps. Bryson and Sarah were right next to him, struggling to stay afloat.

"This better work!" Bryson yelled at him over the roar of the sea.

"You know it will!" Michael shouted back.

Sarah's lips quivered in the cold. They were almost the same color as the water sloshing about her. "Just remember that we're not really breathing the air here anyway. It's all an illusion. Once we've . . . gotten past the hard part we'll probably feel more at home than we have since we Sank after seeing Weber."

"The hard part?" Bryson repeated. "Try horrific. I think that's a better word. It'll be the worst few seconds of our entire lives."

Michael smiled, which creased his frozen face in a way that hurt, made him feel like he was about to crumble into shards. But he totally agreed with his friend. What they were about to do went against every human instinct.

Hopefully it wouldn't kill them.

"Let's do it," he said to his friends. "I'm pretty sure it'll work." He flashed another grin at that last part.

"Pretty sure, huh?" Bryson asked, not amused.

"Ninety-nine percent." That was the honest truth. He just hoped that one percent wouldn't mean the end.

Sarah found his hand underwater and squeezed.

"Okay," she said. "I was the one giving the pep talk, but I'm actually scared. I don't know if I can do this."

"You can," Michael insisted. "No more talking about it."

He sucked in a huge breath, then submerged himself, pulling her down with him. Opening his eyes, he felt the sting of salt, but he forced his lids to stay up, telling himself that he was only imagining the substance around him as ocean water. Abruptly the sting disappeared and his vision cleared.

Sarah and Bryson floated before him, eyes closed, cheeks puffed out, hair floating in halos around their heads. Sunlight slanted in shafts through the purple water, illuminating millions upon millions of strings of code—numbers and letters and symbols sewn together. They were everywhere. Like minnows, they darted back and forth and swirled around each other.

Michael and his friends continued to sink, slowly but steadily, the physics of the situation seeming to have vanished now that they'd decided what to do. Down, down they went, arms waving, legs kicking.

Michael reached out, tapped them both. As he did, they each opened their eyes. And then they were all staring at one another. Michael knew that the fear on his face and in his eyes matched what he saw in his friends'. Terror. They were about to do the one thing every human feared, no matter how brave.

Drown.

Michael pointed at his mouth, trying to show them they had to do this. It was now or never. His lungs burned, begging him to take a breath. If they didn't psych out their bodies soon, they might very well die of asphyxiation.

Sarah nodded, and so did Bryson.

It had been Michael's idea, so he felt like he had to do it first. Every molecule of his body screamed at him to shoot back to the surface, breathe in that rich air that filled the world above the ocean. But he fought back. With one last, desperate look at his friends, he opened his mouth and let the water rush in, then sucked it down his throat and into his lungs.

There were a few seconds of sheer panic, his chest filled with agony and a wrenching need for air. Spasms riddled his body, and his heart suddenly felt empty and lifeless, slowing down, forgetting how to beat. He twisted left, then right, instinctively sucking again and again at the sea around him, as though if he tried hard enough he could pull in the oxygen from the water like a fish. He saw his friends beginning the process, bubbles of air streaming from their mouths, their eyes wide with fear. Just when Michael thought he might choke, he felt a sudden and sweeping rush of calmness spread through his muscles as his lungs filled with air. His heart was whole again, thumping and thumping, if a little fast.

The transition was instant, nothing like that of a newly surfaced man who'd been close to drowning, and he knew what had happened: his body and mind—safe and sound back in the VNS Coffin—had switched from the state of illusion within the Sleep to normal function. From edge-of-death fantasy to all-systems-okay. As a result, he was no longer submerged in anything like water. The cold, the wet, the ocean pressing down on him, the muted sounds—all gone, replaced by open air. Michael still felt buoyant, as if he were floating, and was still surrounded by lines of code, but he could breathe. And each lungful of air felt like heaven.

Sarah was just a few feet away, and he could see by her ease that she'd completed the transition herself. Bryson came along a few seconds after her, though he was farther away. Together they floated in a surreal world of purple lights and code, in desperate need of someone to splice it all back together.

"That *was* the worst few seconds of my entire life," Sarah said. Her voice was a little . . . *off.* Almost robotic, like it had been charged with static. "Remind me to never go swimming again."

Bryson flapped his arms, looking like a deranged oversized

bird, but somehow it worked to move him closer to the other two. "I'm gonna have to say that was about a nine on the old sucky scale. I'd rather get eaten by the *Lizards of Laos* than go through that again."

"But it worked, right?" Michael asked. He didn't mean it in an I-told-you-so way. He was just filled with a ridiculous amount of relief that they hadn't drowned. Of the countless times he'd been virtually killed throughout the years, for some reason this one had felt most real.

"Uh, I guess," Bryson murmured, gesturing with his hands at the bizarre world around them. "If you call this working. I was kinda hoping for a library or something. At least a chair."

Sarah spoke in that manner that showed she was doing some seriously deep thinking. "It's weird, you know? Because of all the programs Weber drenched us in to make sure Kaine couldn't find us, it was like we were cut off. At least from what we were used to. But then here we are. Code all over the place. It's almost like normal, when we close our eyes in the Sleep and access whatever program we're in."

"*Almost* being the key word," Michael replied. "I hope we can do something with all this. Otherwise Weber will bring us back and all we'll have to say for ourselves is that we got to go swimming and feel what it's like to drown. We've got nothing on Kaine."

"How much time has passed, anyway?" Bryson asked.

Sarah pulled up her NetScreen, its glow odd-looking in the world of flying code. She scanned through a few things, then shut it back down.

"We have tons of time before she pulls us back out," she said. "Like thirteen hours. So what do you guys want to do?"

Michael had no doubts. "There's only one choice. We need to put some of this code together. If it's all stuff that was destroyed by Kaine, like that town we were in, then it'll have traces of him. Or whoever works for him. Or whoever did it for him. Anyway, I think we can work backwards. Maybe even find out where he's hiding, if we're lucky."

Bryson snorted. "You make it sound like we're going to make sandwiches or something. This is going to be harder than *Devils of Destruction,* my friend."

"Yep," Michael replied. It would be.

"It won't be that bad," Sarah said. "We only need our brains for this, guys. Time to put on your big-boy pants and get to work."

Bryson looked at Michael. "Are we sure *she* wasn't the Tangent? One of those pain-in-the-butt sidekick programs in the *Ancient Digs of Runeville* game? I'm pretty sure she was one of those."

Michael responded by waving his arms enough to turn himself around, putting his back to his friends. Purple lights shone in front of him, and mysterious figures lurked in the distance, obscured and fuzzy. Lines of code buzzed about him like a million marching caterpillars, ready for him to dissect and put back together. It was programming in a way he'd never done it before, and he was more than a little excited.

Squinting with concentration, he reached forward and literally dug in.

3

It took a while to get used to this new method of manipulating code. It brought Michael back to his childhood days—his fake, fabricated, programmed childhood days—when, while living his life within the virtual world of *Lifeblood Deep,* he'd played with toys. Actual, tangible toys. SealBlocks and ViviCars and SimLasers and the countless figurines of those games the "big kids" played in the Sleep. Kids weren't allowed to immerse themselves in the VirtNet until they were eight years old. Everyone was worried about proper brain development and acquiring social skills, so they'd made a law, though the age changed every few years.

Back then he'd played with his hands, developing the imagination that would end up taking him so many places virtually.

It was like that now. Playing. Physically playing. Touching the building blocks of programming, feeling them, squeezing them, trying to reach into their essence and read their origins, understand the bigger picture of what they used to be a part of.

He'd been a part of *Lifeblood Deep.* Literally. No one was more qualified to do this than Michael.

Piece by piece, he examined. He deduced. He built. He manipulated.

He played.

4

Time sped by, Michael oblivious to it. He was lost in the fun of the programming. He might've worked forever, his body back in the Coffin weakening until even that device couldn't keep him going.

A tap on the shoulder snapped him out of it.

"Got anything?" Sarah asked.

He waved himself around to face his friend. She seemed weary but satisfied. Bryson had drifted off in the distance, his enthusiasm for manipulating the code making him completely unaware of his surroundings. An indecipherable shadow loomed behind the purple lights beyond his body, as if a giant whale were making its way in their direction.

"I got a lot," Michael answered, returning his attention to Sarah.

"Me too. I think it's time we linked up." She paused and looked around. "Well, guess we can't do that here. Put our heads together, then."

"Sounds good."

They flapped their way toward Bryson, the insane-bird dance bringing smiles to their faces.

5

By the time they were finished, Michael's entire body ached and his stomach was growling. It had taken both mental *and* physical effort to piece all their programming together, and he was starving. Such was the nature of the Sleep. Yes, the Coffin would feed him the nutrients he needed, keep him alive and fairly healthy. But that didn't mean his mentally infused virtual body didn't get to the point where he'd kill a roomful of people for a hot dog.

An entire world of logical code extended farther than Michael could see. It was a beautiful, beautiful thing, and the three of them had worked furiously in the last hour or so, copying the details of what they'd learned onto their own NetScreens so they wouldn't forget. And so they could share it all with the VNS once they returned to the Wake.

Michael clicked off his NetScreen. As fun as the process had been, he was done. Officially done. There wasn't a molecule in his body that didn't ache for food, only before settling down for a long nap.

"I can't believe this guy," he said, almost used to the tinny echo of his own voice. "I guess I can understand why Kaine wants to be human. But wanting to wipe out half of the VirtNet doesn't make a whole lot of sense to me."

"You know what I still don't get?" Sarah asked. "Why he *wants* to be human. I mean, even if he downloads into someone our age, he's gonna be dead in a hundred years. In the Sleep, he's immortal, right? He could live forever."

"Well," Bryson said, "there's the Decay that'll hit him."

Sarah shrugged. "If he can download a Tangent's brain into a human, I bet he can figure out how to avoid that."

Bryson laughed. "That'll be hilarious if he does all this, wakes up in some dude's body, then gets hit by a bus the next day. I'd even go to his funeral."

Michael shook his head slowly—something Bryson said had struck him. "No way," he murmured as his thoughts started coming together. "No way it's that easy—that Kaine just wants to try out a human body. Something else is going on. Something a lot bigger. Remember what he said about the Mortality Doctrine being a plan for *im*mortality? I mean, he could be planning to switch his intelligence to a new, younger human every twenty years and keep a backup on the VirtNet in case he *does* get hit by a bus."

"Well, at least we've got a line on him," Sarah said. "We know where he's been, what he's done, and where he's hiding when he . . . does whatever he does after a hard day's work."

"Do you think that guy even sleeps?" Bryson asked. "You did, Michael, but your programmers wanted you to think you were human."

Michael shrugged, looking absently into the distance, where all those odd shadows grew and shrank and coalesced behind the spray of purple lights. Despite his fatigue, he was excited at the wealth of information they'd gathered from the broken code. *The VNS should bow down and worship the Trifecta to Dissect-ya,* he thought.

"How much time do we have left?" Bryson asked.

Sarah looked at her NetScreen, which was still illuminated. "About forty-five minutes. Let's just hope we're still connected to her. I don't see a whole lot of Portals around these parts."

"We're connected," Michael said, so confidently that they didn't even respond. Sometimes he just knew.

Sarah started to say something, but her mouth snapped shut when the lights around them dimmed. It didn't take long for Michael to understand, and an uneasy feeling crept into his belly.

The lights that kept the strange world of code illuminated were flaring, then winking out of existence. One by one they were popping like burst lightbulbs. The darkness deepened, or maybe those weird shadows were getting bigger. Either way, it didn't matter. Something was wrong.

"I don't think we can wait for Weber," Michael said. "We need to get into another program." He already knew exactly what Sarah's response would be, and that she'd be right.

She didn't disappoint. "There's no way. There's no link from here—this place is nothing but a dumping ground. It'd take us just as long to figure out an escape as it did for us to work backwards to find Kaine."

"Even if we could get into another program," Bryson added, "where would we go? Chances are we'd still be about to get chomped on by Kaine's kill programs, and end up washed right back down in this cesspool. And maybe we wouldn't quite live through it a second time."

Michael grumbled. "You guys are downright pleasant to be around."

Lights flashed all around them, increasing in rapidity, as if struck by a virus that multiplied exponentially. And the shadows grew. The darkness rolled in like a fog, blacking out the world, which had once been full of purple light.

"How much time?" Michael asked anxiously.

"When did I become our official stopwatch?" Sarah responded, but even so, she checked her NetScreen. "She should be pulling us out in twenty minutes. Keep your diapers dry."

Michael held back a smile that would have given her too much satisfaction. When had she become so uppity?

"That's going to be twenty long minutes," Bryson muttered under his breath.

As if some cosmic holder of the code heard his remark, a wind picked up. The purple fragments began to swirl into wispy clouds of a darkening blue. The gusts, stronger and stronger, tugged at Michael's clothes, his hair. The lights continued their dance, flaring, then dying. More than two-thirds of them were gone now, the darkness almost complete.

And then, in a thunderclap of an instant, everything picked up.

The wind blew with the force of a hurricane, ripping at Michael and his friends. Clouds and streaks of black mist swirled around them, and a discordant symphony of sound filled the air, threatening to deafen Michael once and for all.

And then, out of the corner of his eye, he saw it. He jerked his head around to get a better look. A hole of darkness, deep and pure, the blackest thing he'd ever seen, yawning wider and wider until it was dozens of feet in diameter.

And somewhere within it, Michael thought he saw yellow eyes.

A boom sounded behind him, a concussion of noise that shook the substance he floated in, pushed him several feet forward in the purple code. He turned around to see *another* hole opening, maybe a hundred feet away, but this one wasn't black. This one glowed with an ethereal orange light that cut through the darkness. Figures appeared within it—silhouettes of people of all shapes and sizes. They were moving, heading straight for Michael and his friends.

He spun again to see the black hole—the eyes. Shadow upon shadow. There were figures there, too; he could sense them more than see them. Coming. Coming fast. Dark shapes suddenly leaped out of the gaping hole.

Stunned, Michael didn't have time to feel fear. He reached out and grabbed his friends, pulled them closer.

"What in the world!" he shouted.

"What do we do?" Sarah shouted. "We still have ten minutes before Weber Lifts us out!"

Bryson wrenched free of Michael's grip and held up his fists. "We have to fight. That's not long to hold them off!"

Michael didn't know what to do but get in a defensive position himself. He held his arms up, feeling totally useless. Figures emerged from both sides: people from the orange light, creatures of darkness from the black hole. What would happen, he wondered, if they did get killed? This place seemed like a wild card. And what if Kaine was behind it all? What if the life could be sucked out of them?

He wanted to run, but there was nowhere to go. The wind roared, noise filled the air, and from two opposing directions, enemies charged in.

His life was ridiculous.

There was but an instant of time to decipher those who charged at Michael and his friends. From the blackness came dark-skinned creatures, loping and slithering and pouncing, all shapes and sizes, no beast the same as another, and none Michael had seen before. They looked like KillSims morphed into twisted, unnatural shapes with yellow eyes.

From the blinding orange light came more recognizable—if strange—characters. All of them appeared to be from famous VirtNet games: warriors with axes; fully suited astronauts with laser guns; giants with wooden clubs; a woman on a deathcat, brandishing a staff lit with fire; a mechaknight on his robotic horse; a sunpyre and his brood of white lions; the fighting priest of Grendelin; and countless others. They charged in formation, rallying behind someone who was obviously their leader.

It was a woman. Tall and powerful, decked out in all kinds of futuristic, gleaming armor, she had four arms, and four weapons. In one hand, she gripped a thick cylinder with spinning blades on the end. In another, a shaft of pure blue light, pulsing as if ready to fire. In yet another, a menacing black box with a gaping hole at one end. And the fourth arm cradled a long barrel that looked exactly like a cannon from ancient wars.

As she ran, bricks appeared beneath her, one after the other, forming a path under her feet. The rest of her army charged atop their own surfaces—flat beams of light and rocky gravel and patches of stone or grass. Their battle cries filled the air and their eyes shone with anger.

Michael took it all in, in what could only have been a few moments. Time seemed to slow to reveal one of the strangest sights he'd ever seen. He thought that it really *did* slow, as if the programming itself, this cesspool of countless destroyed virtual lands, wanted to witness the spectacle. Michael's friends were still beside him, seeing what he saw, their movements sluggish, as if they were flies trapped in molasses.

And then, with a burst of wind and a screeching noise, everything ripped back to full speed.

The warriors rushed in. From one side: yellow eyes like raging fires, set in snarling and snapping, slithering and pouncing, blacker-than-black forms. From the other: heroes from decades of gaming, charging along on their magic paths. The fierce woman leading them was only a few dozen feet away from Michael and his friends, and she yelled at the top of her lungs, a sound like crushing rocks and booming thunder.

"Out of the way, pips! It's not your day to die!"

Who were these people? Where had they *come* from?

Instinct took over Michael before his mind could catch up. He grabbed both of his friends, pulled them close. And then he reached out and scrambled the code, manipulating it with his mind, understanding on some deep level what he'd once done in the Hallowed Ravine. Everything around him was a fabrication, a visual manifestation of sequenced letters and numbers and symbols, including Bryson, Sarah, and himself. He attacked it all with nothing but thought.

He and his friends suddenly catapulted to the sky, three

human missiles rocketing upward, just as the armies of light and darkness crashed into each other below like two out-of-control freight trains.

8

Michael stopped their flight several hundred feet above the clashing battle, suspended in the ethereal world of goop. His mind was a cyclone, spinning with a million thoughts, backed by a fierce rush of adrenaline through his body.

Sarah looked at him almost as if she were afraid. Of *him*.

"I just did what she told me to," he said.

"Look!" Bryson shouted, pointing downward.

A couple of stragglers had separated from the battle—one a long streak of blackness with yellow eyes, the other a bulky mass with at least a dozen arms and legs. Both were coming at Michael and his friends, flying fast.

"Take us away, Superman," Bryson said.

"Weber should be Lifting us out any second," Sarah added.

Michael's mind felt as if it was shutting down, as if the quick explosion of effort to code them away from the armies had sapped him of all mental strength. He halfheartedly tried to repeat what he'd done, but he knew it was hopeless as soon as he began.

"Sorry," he muttered. "That was a one-act play, folks."

"What in God's name happened down there?" Sarah asked in a rush, as if they didn't have two hideous dark beasts coming right at them, rising like heat. "Who are those people who came to help? And how did Kaine find us?"

"Maybe we can talk about it later?" Bryson yelled. "Looks like we're going to fight after all." He balled his fists—as if they'd do any good.

And then the creatures were on them.

The long, snakelike form went at Michael, its battering ram of a head slamming into his chest. He barely had time to see the flash of yellow eyes before he was hurtled head over feet through the darkening purple goop. Swinging his arms wildly, he righted himself just in time to see those eyes again, directly in front of him. A gaping mouth opened, black teeth glistening, and it snapped at him.

Michael jerked away, throwing his hands out to grab the horror by the neck. He squeezed its smooth, muscular skin, holding the thing back as it opened and shut its jaws, snapping again and again in its attempt to bite Michael's head off. He dodged left, then right, wrenching the neck of the beast back and forth to keep it away.

The thing wrapped itself around the length of Michael's torso, then his legs. Soon he was wrapped head to toe, sheathed in blackness, and the creature tightened its grip, squeezing the breath out of him. Michael gasped for air, searching for a way to get some help, but there was nothing. With every bit of strength he had left, he fought, trying to rip the foul thing's head right off.

The flurry of movement sent the pair spinning like a corkscrew. Dizziness overwhelmed Michael and he lost his grip, the creature's neck slipping from his grasp. In an instant, the creature opened its jaws and struck, lightning fast. It clamped down, and suddenly the world was black. Michael's entire head was inside the beast's mouth. Its jaws tightened and its teeth pierced Michael's skin. He couldn't even hear his own screams—it was all a muffled fog of terror and pain.

He flailed, half inside the mouth of the creature, as their death spin continued. Michael fought the overwhelming dizziness and struggled to grab hold of the enormous fangs puncturing his neck. His muscles tensed and his stomach quivered with nausea. The creature's long, muscular body continued to squeeze the life out of him, tighter and tighter, making it impossible to breathe. The dizziness turned into light-headedness; stars and flashes swam in his vision. His pulse pounded in his head, and he remembered the KillSims. How they suck the digital life out of their prey.

How they'd killed Ronika and almost killed him.

This stupid thing wrapped around his body was some sort of cousin to the KillSims; Michael knew it. He wasn't just dizzy from the spinning and the pain. It was an all-out attack on the essence of his life.

He tried harder, screaming with the effort as he pulled on the mouth of the giant snakelike beast. Its teeth started to move, to slowly slip out of his skin; blood oozed from the wounds on Michael's neck. He pulled harder. Farther and farther apart creaked the jaws, the gap widening, the pressure on his head weakening, the dizziness and lights subsiding, feeling returning to his body, surging through him as though a dam had been breached—pain and adrenaline and elation and fire. Michael screamed again, and this time he heard it, a raw, piercing, strangled sound. And still farther he opened the creature's mouth, the world of purple returning to view around him.

With every inch the monster's jaw opened, Michael's confidence grew. He could hear the cracking of bone, the ripping of tendons, the cry of the creature as it lost the struggle. The pressure of its body on his weakened, then fell away altogether. Michael braced himself for one final burst of effort, readied to tear the monster's head apart.

But there was a popping sound. A sweeping rush of noise and a blur of streaming colors. The world tilted, bent, spun. Darkness swept it all away. And then Michael was blinking, gasping for air, staring up at the lid of Agent Weber's Coffin.

She'd Lifted them out of the Sleep. Across his body the NerveWires prickled as they receded from his skin, slithering into their hidey-holes.

He was back.

CHAPTER 18

THE LANCE CODE

1

Michael was soaking wet—partly from the LiquiGels, but also from sweat slicking his every inch of skin. His chest heaved as he gasped for air, feeling like he could never get enough to satisfy his lungs. Somehow he composed himself enough to find the release, and he sprang it, then waited, impatiently, the hundred years it took for the lid to swing open on its hinges. Warm light spilled in from the room, and he saw Agent Weber herself standing there, looking down at him, her face blurry. His vision hadn't quite adjusted yet.

On the edges of his consciousness, he had the thought that he was glad he'd worn shorts for the trip, at least. Usually he went stark naked to experience the full effects of the sensory elements within the Coffin. But lying down in his birthday suit had seemed a bad idea this go-round. He'd been right.

"Are you okay?" Agent Weber asked.

Michael blinked a few times and she came into focus. The look of concern on her face seemed genuine enough. And she'd fulfilled her promise to bring them back.

He sat up, ignoring how wildly his head spun from the movement.

"Sarah!" he shouted. "Bryson!"

"They're fine," Weber said, kneeling down next to the Coffin. "I was able to get them out a little early—I'm not sure why it was so hard to Lift you. There was . . . something interfering, as if the system couldn't quite lock on to your signal. I'm sorry. I really am. Things must've gotten bad in there."

Michael waved his hand, as if swatting away her concern. He knew very well what had happened, and why it had been such a struggle to Lift him. That creature—that twisted version of the KillSim—had been sucking away his digital essence. He felt such a rush realizing how close he'd come to permanent brain damage that he found it hard to breathe. Fumbling and slipping, he scrambled out of the Coffin, stood up, swayed, sat down, breathed in deep pulls of air. What if he hadn't yanked the thing's jaws apart, gotten it off his head? How close had he come to dying?

Agent Weber was at his side, touching his shoulder.

"That bad?" she whispered.

He nodded. He tried not to think of Ronika and what had happened to her. "I'm fine. It was just . . . I was attacked by one of those . . . one of Kaine's creatures. How did he find us? I thought your hider codes were supposed to be super complex."

Weber stood up, maneuvering deftly in her heels, then helped Michael get to his feet.

"It wasn't you specifically that he found," she said. "I've talked to Bryson and Sarah about it. Kaine noticed the massive amount of programming you three were doing and he sent in his cavalry. But Sarah said she was able to wipe away the code structure before he could see that you'd been backtracking to find his information. Still. I didn't expect things to go so wrong in just twenty-four hours. Again, I'm sorry."

"It's fine," he said. He could hardly blame Weber. They'd been reckless once again. And most importantly, she *had* brought them back to safety.

Weber motioned to the door. "Well, you're all back, and you're all okay. And from what Sarah said, it sounds like you found some pretty incredible information. Am I right?"

Michael felt a surge of pride and hoped Weber didn't see it on his face. "Yeah. We did. And we need to work fast. Before he catches on and moves his home base."

Weber walked toward the door, her heels clicking. "I'm already gathering the few people I trust. I've called them to the War Room. In the meantime, you need to shower and eat. And this is going to take everything we've got—so get some sleep."

To Michael, that sounded good. Really good.

2

It felt like he'd only shut his eyes for a moment when someone gently nudged him awake. He jerked up to a sitting position, looking right and left. It was as if his body had been waiting for the moment Kaine's monster would return.

"Whoa, there, cowboy!"

It was Bryson, Sarah standing beside him. It was odd to see their real selves again. "No need to get feisty."

Michael closed his eyes and, relieved, slumped back onto the bed. It was actually more of a cot, stowed away in a dark, cool room alongside several others. His friends had already been sound asleep and snoring by the time he'd showered and eaten, and he hadn't had the heart to wake them up. He'd wanted to, wanted to wake them and hug them—well, Sarah, anyway—but instead he'd collapsed and fallen asleep almost instantly.

Sarah was standing, arms folded, at the foot of his cot, looking down at him with a smile he could tell she was trying to hide. She was happy to see him—it showed in her eyes.

"How're you feeling?" she asked.

Michael groaned and sat up again, swinging his legs to the floor, rubbing his eyes. And then told the truth. "Like crap. Groggy. Achy. My muscles feel like a granny's." But at least he felt no pain in his head, other than a foggy, dull throbbing from where the Coffin had simulated the struggle with the KillSim. If it had even *been* a KillSim.

"How do you know?" Bryson asked.

"Huh?"

"How do you know what a granny's muscles feel like?"

"I used to play *Grannies at Teatime,* and don't say you didn't."

He and Bryson started snickering like middle schoolers in the back of class.

Sarah threw her hands up. "Are you guys finished? I know more about that game than you think. Now come on, we need to talk about slightly more important things."

"Yes, we do," Bryson said, suddenly serious.

Sarah sat on the cot next to Michael, leaned in, and kissed him on the cheek. "That's something Bryson will never get," she whispered, obviously not caring that their friend had heard.

"Who said I'd want it?" he countered, though his cheeks turned red.

Sarah just smiled, not taking her eyes off Michael's, and he suddenly felt much, much better.

"All right," he said. "What's the plan? Where's Weber?"

"She woke us up and said she'd be back for us in a minute," Sarah answered. "Apparently she has a team of people waiting to meet with us. We're going to a place she called the War Room to tell them what we know."

Michael nodded. "Yeah, she mentioned that to me, too."

"What're we going to say?" Bryson asked. "I barely got through my presentation on amphibians last fall without squeaking."

"Squeaking?" Sarah repeated. She gave him a little pat, then turned to Michael. "How about you do all the talking?"

"Me?" Michael's voice rose an octave. "Why me? Last fall when Bryson was . . . squeaking through his amphibians report, I wasn't even human. I might not know how to use my vocal cords properly."

Bryson snorted.

"Fine, I'll do it," Sarah said.

Michael and Bryson exchanged a look: it was clear she'd known all along that she'd be the one. Before Michael could thank her, there was a knock on the door and it swung open. Agent Weber walked in, confident as always.

"It's time," she announced. All that humble sorry-you-were-almost-killed sentiment had vanished. She was back to being all business.

"We're not ready," Bryson said. "We need to plan what we're going to say."

But Sarah was already off the cot and walking toward the door. She stopped when she reached Agent Weber and turned to face her friends.

"Come on," she said. "We'll wing it."

3

The War Room.

Michael found himself not breathing for a few seconds after Agent Weber ushered them inside. He stopped for a moment to take it all in. On one side of the giant room, there were several tiers of seats—almost like a theater or a stadium—the rows roughly half filled with men and women of every race. In front of each glowed a NetScreen, at which most of the people were busily working, oblivious to the newcomers. Michael wondered why the room was only half full.

On the other side of the room, one of the largest three-dimensional displays Michael had ever seen hovered in mid-air. Displays like that were usually reserved for games and movies, but this one was enormous, at least a hundred feet wide and nearly as tall. It was impossible to tell how deep it went; it looked like it continued on forever. There were maps and diagrams and live feeds of places both real and programmed. A massive, detailed globe of the world hung right in the middle, slowly turning, symbols and dots scattered across its glowing surface.

Michael felt like a high-level spy, ready to take on the world. And then he realized that Agent Weber and his friends were all looking at him.

"Sorry," he muttered. "Just thinking."

Weber motioned to a podium that sat directly below the flying globe of the Earth, with several chairs lined up right next to it. "Please," she said. "My people are dealing with a lot of situations that need attention. I don't want to take any more of their time than necessary."

Michael stared at her in disbelief. For her to say such a thing made him wonder if she could possibly understand what was at stake. He was about to say something when Bryson went ahead and did it for him.

"A lot of situations?" he asked. "Are you kidding me? Do you—"

Sarah interrupted him. "Let's just get started. Please?" Michael was surprised that she looked nervous.

He looked back at their audience and realized that most of the VNS agents had stopped what they were doing and turned their attention to the new arrivals. He waved feebly, feeling like the stupidest person who'd ever lived. No one waved back.

"By all means," Agent Weber said, once again motioning

to the podium. "The floor is yours. I'll be at the controls—just link with my system if you want anything displayed on the War Board."

"War this and War that," Bryson murmured under his breath to Michael. "Seems kinda weird for people who're just supposed to be monitoring the VirtNet. This place gives me the willies."

"The willies?" Michael repeated.

"The willies."

Sarah had already made her way to the center of the vast room. Agent Weber matched her stride for stride. Michael grabbed Bryson by the shirt and hurried after them. The whole situation seemed a little off, but what could they expect? The entire world was a little off when a computer program tried to take over the human race.

Weber stepped up to the podium and pulled the microphone closer to her mouth, just as Michael and the other two settled in right behind her. Before she said a word, the room quieted, the murmurs of conversation cutting off instantly.

"Good afternoon," Weber began, her voice echoing. "Thank you for gathering today, especially on such short notice. Some of you are here virtually, but I'm glad that as many of you as possible are actually present. I've only invited those with whom I've built a solid relationship of trust over many years."

Curious, Michael scanned the room, and sure enough, he could see what he hadn't before: about three in ten agents were holographic projections in their seats. It was hardly noticeable except for an odd glow to their faces or an occasional glitch here and there interrupting the feed.

"As we are all well aware," Weber continued, "the VirtNet is faced with perhaps its most dangerous situation since our agency was formed nearly fifty years ago. To share a very old quote, 'We have before us an ordeal of the most grievous kind.' And I wanted all of you here today so that . . ."

Michael tuned out, looking around the room as she droned on. Something had been bothering him, and his unease was growing. As he studied the faces of all these agents—men and women, dressed in a cornucopia of cultural attire—it suddenly hit him. Hit him hard. Something wasn't right, and he knew why.

"Sarah," he whispered, leaning closer to her.

She shushed him with an angry look.

Michael shook his head. He thought back to Agent Weber's performance on the uplink they'd used in that dingy office they'd found. How she'd denied everything and then explained later, when they broke into the VNS headquarters and confronted her, that she'd had no choice, that she was worried about people within her agency who might have shady intentions.

So why, then, were they standing here, in front of everyone, being presented like winners at an awards ceremony? And what about all the warrants for their arrest? And the search for the missing Jackson Porter?

Michael had the sudden urge to grab his friends by the hands and drag them out of the room. To run while they still could. But so many people had seen them. They didn't have a chance. Not here.

Sarah was stepping to the podium by the time he returned his attention to her. She cleared her throat and opened her

NetScreen, pulling up her notes. Weber came over to stand beside Michael and, as if she'd hacked into his mind, leaned in to whisper to him.

"I've only brought in the ones I can completely, utterly trust. But even they don't know everything. You're going to have to trust me."

She paused, scanning the room with a thoughtful expression, as if considering everything one last time. Then she spoke in a low voice, "I have a plan."

"Well," Michael said, "don't you think you should've let Sarah in on it before you threw her to the wolves like this?"

Weber shook her head ever so slightly. "These people will think their way around an ice cream cone before ever giving it a lick. Once they get far enough with whatever Sarah tells them to actually accomplish anything, the matter will probably be settled anyway. They're essentially my backup plan."

"What do you mean?"

"You'll see soon enough."

4

Michael looked at her, not knowing what else to say. He had no idea if he could trust her yet, but all he could do was nod. Weber seemed satisfied, and she walked toward the back of the room, where a large systems console waited. Michael turned his attention to Sarah, who finally began speaking.

"I'm glad we—" She stopped when the microphone squawked, pushed it away a bit, then tried again. "I'm glad we have the opportunity to speak about what we've seen. Because my friends and I"—she turned and gestured toward Michael and Bryson—"have seen a lot. A lot of things we should all be worried about. What we're about to tell you should be the top priority of this agency, and we need to act quickly."

Michael almost groaned. He loved Sarah, he really did, but the faster she got to the facts, the better.

"I think all of you are far too familiar with the Tangent known as Kaine by now," Sarah continued. "My friends and I have seen firsthand that he is self-sentient and not exactly out for the good of humankind. The complicated part of this is that unlike traditional Tangents, he seems to be everywhere at once, not just part of one specific program.

"I'm not sure how much you've been briefed on the Mortality Doctrine, but I assume you know what's happening. Something you may not know, however, is that Michael, here"—she gestured again—"was the first example of the Doctrine's being successfully implemented. He was once a Tangent, but his consciousness, his intelligence, his memories—everything that makes him who he is—were transferred to a human body. My colleagues and I are ready to share vital information on how we can stop Kaine."

This time Michael did groan a little. My *colleagues*? Bryson just stared out at the audience, his thoughts well hidden.

Sarah pressed on, picking up steam as she went. "We visited a town within the Slee—within the VirtNet that was almost completely empty of players. And the ones we saw seemed troubled or emotionless. We witnessed a lady who'd been attacked by something we've seen before—a program designed to digitally rip her apart. The next thing we knew . . ."

Sarah went on and on, her confidence growing as she spoke, as if she'd done this a thousand times. Michael thought that maybe she'd end up being the boss at VNS someday. He had no doubts that she could do it. Piece by piece, she told the agents—most of whom seemed rapt with attention—all the details of what she, Michael, and Bryson had seen, what they'd been through. From the destruction of the town to the purple sea to the massive pool of code they'd swum through to build a picture of Kaine and what he'd been doing. Michael listened intently but found his thoughts wandering from time to time. He couldn't stop thinking about Agent Weber. The woman was an enigma.

". . . were able to trace the code back to see just how many places Kaine had destroyed. Why he's doing it, we don't know. Another thing he's doing is taking over commerce sites, stealing personal ID codes, manipulating financial markets. Why he'd be doing that is obvious: the Tangent is accumulating a good chunk of wealth."

Accumulating, Michael thought. She really did sound like a professional. Someone tried to interrupt Sarah to ask a question and she told him—didn't ask, *told* him—to wait until she'd finished talking.

She continued, saving the best for last. "After all the coding we assembled—which I recorded, and I've sent a copy to Agent Weber—we know where Kaine is. And I don't mean where he's walking around, or where he's eating his virtual food, or where he's sitting, scheming what to do next. We found something much more important." She paused, making sure everyone was listening. "We know where Kaine's central programming is located."

This set off quite the buzz among the agents, and Michael couldn't help but feel that surge of pride once again. How educated were these people? How experienced? How many hours and days had they spent searching for Kaine, ever since back when they still thought he was an actual gamer, a human, not a Tangent? And yet it ended up being three punk teenagers who'd found him. Michael, Sarah, and Bryson, the Burn-and-Pillage-y Trilogy. He had to fight hard to keep a smile off his face.

"We know where it is," Sarah continued. "We found his source code, his intelligence. One would think it'd be part of—or near to, at least—the massive array of code that makes up the VirtNet's structure itself, so that he could easily be wherever he needed, whenever he wanted, but that's not the case."

Another pause, and Michael wondered if she was hamming it up just a bit too much. And then she finally said the one sentence that probably would've sufficed from the very beginning.

"Kaine the Tangent is inside a game. He's inside *Lifeblood Deep.*"

5

Another flurry of questions and conversation erupted around the chamber. Michael heard a *tap-tap-tap* behind him and he turned to see Agent Weber walking toward the podium, holding a small remote device. She pushed a button just as she reached Sarah's side and suddenly the rotating globe above them vanished, replaced by an aerial, three-dimensional view of a city, zooming in toward one section. Standing beneath it, and so close, sent Michael's stomach pitching. He quickly looked away since he already knew what it was.

Downtown Atlanta. Zeroing in on a small building no one would ever think twice about as they passed it. Kaine had hidden his virtual home right under the virtual equivalent of VirtNet Security's noses. He'd probably done it just to make a point, to display his power.

A small, stupid thing, but it made Michael hate him just a little bit more. The Tangent seemed to learn all his moves from old films.

"Kaine's presence is felt all over the Sleep," Sarah said, not bothering to correct herself with the more proper term this time. She was too much in the zone. "But he's just like any other Tangent, no matter how powerful he has become. He's still a program, and he's still made up of code, no matter how complicated, and that programming is centrally located somewhere, just like any other. He's hidden it well. But my friends and I have become very familiar with him. And by comparing the sea of code we just escaped from and cross-analyzing it with all our other experiences, we were able to construct a back door to his home base. It wasn't easy, but we did it."

"Who programmed him in the first place?" someone yelled from the audience.

Sarah looked over at Michael. He shrugged, because it was a guess at best.

"We don't really know," she said. "But it seems his origins go all the way back to the beginning of the Internet age. Programmed to learn and to grow, he's been working toward sentience ever since, from what we can tell." She cleared her throat and hesitated, obviously worried that they'd gotten off track. "Now back to his code's location . . ."

The giant image hanging above them zoomed in on the building in question—a small, three-story structure wedged between two skyscrapers. Being *Lifeblood Deep,* Atlanta was an exact replica of the real deal, and Kaine's home had been classified as a historical building. That was the only reason it hadn't been demolished a long time ago. The perfect hiding place for a rogue Tangent.

"Because he's spotted in the Sleep all the time," Sarah continued, "I don't think there's any way Kaine has used the Mortality Doctrine on himself. It's way too early. He'll want a lot more testing done before he dares do it. So we're pretty sure he's here."

Agent Weber stepped up to the microphone, and Sarah moved aside as naturally as if they'd practiced. It bugged Michael. He was sure the agent wanted to take all the glory now that it was time for the meat of the presentation.

"Thank you, Sarah," the woman said, giving Sarah one of

those professional smiles that said her mind had already moved on to the next thought. She turned to the audience. "I don't think I need to tell you how much we owe Sarah and her friends. They're under an incredible amount of stress. Suffice it to say that they've undertaken incredibly dangerous assignments for us on more than one occasion, and our debt to them is significant."

She paused, and the other agents took the cue, finally erupting into applause. Michael swore he even heard a couple of hoots out there.

When it quieted down, Weber continued. "The information that our young friends have gathered is astounding. I think we can all be impressed—*should* be impressed. In twenty-four hours they've done something that none of us has been able to accomplish: they have isolated the central code of Kaine's Tangent programming. I'll be sending it to all of you so that we can begin the full analysis and develop a plan of attack. Our goal, and I don't say this lightly . . ." She let that last word hang out there for a few seconds. "Our goal is to make a move within seven days' time."

This elicited a wave of fierce whispering, as if the idea was preposterous. Michael frowned. Was that too much time or not enough? In his mind, they should be acting yesterday. Kaine could move his base at any time. But they'd need to be prepared.

Weber held up her hands to quiet them down. "Time is of the essence. I'll go through the final details and then let you get straight to work. As you can see from the map of Atlanta . . ."

Bryson leaned in to Michael. "These people are gonna screw everything up. Gah-ron-teed," he whispered. He stepped back, not waiting for a response.

Michael hated how thoroughly he agreed.

6

An hour later, Michael was sitting in a small room, at a table, eating hot dogs. Not the most glorious thing to be doing after attending a meeting in the War Room of the VNS.

Bryson was next to him, picking through a salad, of all things. Sarah sat across the table, eating hot dogs slathered in chili and cheese. Weber had told them she needed to take care of a few details before they decided on a plan of action—after all, the three of them were fugitives from the law, even if they'd apparently convinced the VNS they were innocent of cyber-terrorism and kidnapping.

When Weber dropped them off in the break room, she'd introduced them to a man from the cafeteria, then instructed him to get the three whatever they wanted. And so it was that they ended up eating hot dogs and salad.

"I gotta admit," Bryson said, talking through a bite of lettuce. "I tuned out big-time once that lady got going. Stuff we already knew anyway."

Michael plopped a half-eaten dog back onto his plate. He'd had enough, though he figured that out a few bites after his stomach did. He leaned back in his seat and groaned. "Ugh. Ate too much."

"Oh, really?" Bryson said snarkily. "I would've never guessed." He gave Michael's plate a disapproving look.

"Next time we'll order one of your dainty salads," Sarah responded. "And then a half hour later when we're starving we'll get some more hot dogs."

Bryson responded by taking a huge bite of his rabbit food; he chomped on it and moaned with pleasure.

"You were good up there," Michael said to Sarah. "Seriously. Official prediction: you're the head of the VNS by the time you turn thirty. Then president of the country by forty. You heard it here first."

Bryson made a *pssshaw* sound. "If we're all still alive."

It came off way more somberly than he'd probably intended, and the room plunged into silence. For just a few seconds, Michael had forgotten about all their woes.

"Thanks for reminding me," he grumbled.

"Huh?" Bryson asked.

"Nothing." As if in an act of defiance, he took another bite of his now-cold hot dog. If his stomach could talk, he would've gotten an earful of complaints.

The room went silent again as they all allowed themselves to be lost in their thoughts. Michael jumped when someone rapped loudly on the door. It swung open immediately—of course—and Agent Weber walked into the room.

"Are we finished?" she asked a little too cheerfully to sound genuine.

Michael exaggerated a groan while he doubled over, holding his stomach. He was getting too comfortable around this woman. Sarah snickered.

"I'll take that as a yes," Weber pronounced. She moved closer to the table, looming over Bryson's shoulder. He didn't look up, though he obviously wanted to.

"I'm glad you've had a chance to eat and rest," their host continued. "Because we need to get going."

That perked Michael up. "What? Go where?"

"I need to get the three of you back into the NerveBoxes."

Michael didn't know if he'd heard that right. He exchanged confused looks with his friends. Sarah finally voiced what they were all thinking.

"What do you mean? I thought you and the agents were going to run through the data before doing anything."

"Why do you want *us* in the Coffins, anyway?" Bryson added. "I thought our job was done. Isn't that why we just spilled everything to your agents?"

Michael stared at Agent Weber, waiting for answers. Once again they were on the edge of a huge cliff, about to be tossed over.

"There are plenty of things my agents will be doing," Weber said. "Trailing you, supporting you, providing backup the second you need help. Most importantly, trying to locate Sarah's parents. I'll stay here and work with them—for one thing, we need to hunt down any person who's been transformed by this Mortality Doctrine. Start figuring things out. In the meantime, I'm sending *you three* back into the VirtNet to get the job done. You've proven yourselves over and over—I wouldn't dare trust the lead on this to anyone else. You know Kaine like no others, and it needs to be a quiet operation."

Michael looked at his friends, who appeared as stunned as he was.

"And I'll take *that* as a yes on the mission, then," Weber said, folding her hands together in victory. "Now come. I have something to show you."

7

The thing she wanted to show them didn't even exist.

Not in the real world, anyway.

They were in Weber's office, huddled around a large projection. It was a collection of images and words that were slowly swirling in a circle. Michael saw a picture of a dog—a golden retriever—with a little boy kneeling next to it, the biggest smile you ever saw splitting his face. So many thoughts went through Michael's head seeing that picture, but mostly it made him feel like Agent Weber was a real person after all.

Without any kind of introduction, she tapped and swiped at the projected sphere and moved things around until it all suddenly flew away and was replaced by one lone image: a long, rectangular metallic box, wires and anodes lining its surface. As Michael and the others stared, it revolved in place.

"What's that?" Bryson asked.

Weber reached forward into the projection, and it looked as if her fingers touched the two ends of the box. She grabbed them and stretched the whole thing out so that it was much bigger. Michael had no idea how large or small the device would be if it weren't just an image.

"This is what you're going to use to bring Kaine down," Weber said, her voice filled with satisfaction. A little too much, Michael thought, even though it didn't bother him. She obviously disliked the Tangent as much as he did. "This is a project I've been working on for a long time. A very long time. And it's a grand achievement, if I do say so myself."

The woman stared at the box, pride on her face. Then she blinked hard and cleared her throat, as if she'd just realized there were other people in the room.

"Sorry," she said. "It's just that . . . I've put a lot of blood, sweat, and tears into developing this. You'll have to forgive me if I'm a little excited that it'll finally be put to use."

Sarah asked the obvious question this time. "What *is* it?"

The agent sat back in her chair, leaving the image to continue rotating. "I call it the Lance. It seems to fit."

Bryson and Sarah didn't say anything, just stared. Michael knew it was his turn to ask, but it seemed stupid. So he stubbornly waited for the agent to tell them what the thing did. She took a few moments to admire her creation before speaking again.

"It's a program, of course, the most complex collection of code I've ever been able to put together. I gave it this visual manifestation to make it as easy as possible to place and trigger."

Michael broke his silence, so intrigued now it was like an itch. "Place and trigger?" he repeated.

She nodded slowly. "Yes. I'm going to meet you inside the

VirtNet, where I'll literally hand you this program, in the form of this device. It won't be as easy as I've laid out, but all you'll need to do is get to the location of Kaine's programming, insert the Lance, activate it with an eight-digit password to initiate the countdown, then get out of there. When it detonates, the Lance will annihilate the Tangent. Not only his central code, but it'll set off a chain reaction that will wipe him out wherever his Aura may be."

She paused, letting the information sink in. There was an awful lot to sink in, Michael thought. Then she continued. "I've spent years programming this. I knew we'd need it someday. It will kill him. I know that's a bold claim, but I stand by it. All we have to do is get you inside *Lifeblood Deep*, into its version of Atlanta, and into this building. The Lance will do the rest."

Michael was waiting for the inevitable catch. "And how do you expect us to get inside the Deep, much less the building, without being seen? The Hider programs make us blind to the code, for the most part. . . . If we do what we did in that purple sea, it'll be like hanging up a big sign that says 'Hey, Kaine! Come and get us!'" He didn't like the hesitant look that was coming over her face as he spoke. "I'm guessing you have a plan?"

Her expression matched exactly what she said next. "Yes. And you're not going to like this part."

Michael waited for the bomb to drop.

Agent Weber let out a huge sigh; her excitement about the Lance had disappeared. "There's no easy way to get you inside. There's a reason it's called the Deep, and the *Lifeblood* section is the toughest by far. Its whole purpose is to keep you out unless you have proper access, and all three of you know how hard that is to get—even you, Michael. You're not who you used to be. Alarms would spring up all over the place if we put you three in without taking . . . extreme measures."

Bryson and Sarah shifted in their seats, but Michael stayed stock-still. He was ready to hear just how bad things were going to get.

"We have to Squeeze you in," Weber finally said.

Michael looked at Bryson, then at Sarah. They looked at each other, then back at him.

Squeeze.

Michael had only heard the term *Squeezing* a few times in his life, mostly in off-the-cuff remarks from little kids, talking about things they knew nothing about. People didn't speak about Squeezing because it was illegal. It was nearly as bad as messing with someone's—or even your own—Core programming. No one Michael had ever met had Squeezed or been Squeezed. He almost asked Weber to repeat the word, just to make sure he'd heard her right.

But he knew very well that he had.

Agent Weber was going to *Squeeze* them into *Lifeblood Deep.*

God help us, he thought.

CHAPTER 19

SQUEEZED

1

Michael sat on the toilet lid, fully clothed. He didn't need to use the bathroom, but he desperately needed to be alone, even if for just a few minutes. Agent Weber had been serious about wanting them to Sink back into the Sleep immediately, and his friends were pretty much ready to go. But not him. He wanted a little time to himself—time to gather his thoughts.

Weber had dropped so much news on them, so many plans at once, that he could feel every single tick of his pulse, throbbing in his head, his neck, even down to the veins in his ankles. They'd done plenty of dangerous stuff, and going back out into the world and risking arrest just wasn't an option. But he didn't know if he felt ready for *this*.

The Lance—that ordinary-looking rectangular metal box that was supposed to solve all of their problems. Going back to the Sleep right away, when they'd just risked their lives for what they thought was the last time. The job of finding that building in *Lifeblood Deep,* getting past its security firewalls, planting the device, triggering it, and getting away. It was so much to accomplish. Not to mention the Squeezing it would take to get them inside the *Deep* in the first place.

Squeezing.

It seemed like such a simple word for something that was supposed to be utterly terrifying, painful, horrific. Michael had never been through it, of course, but the stories out there were awful, and even if only half of them were true—and those exaggerated—Squeezing was not a pleasant experience.

The process itself was just like it sounded. Your Aura, wrapped tightly in Hider codes, would be jammed through a space the width of one line of programming. Even knowing all he did, he didn't quite understand how the process worked, but in many ways it was a literal thing. To avoid the massively complex firewalls protecting *Lifeblood Deep* from outsiders, and to avoid detection, you had to squeeze yourself through a virtual crack in the wall. Most people described it as trying to walk through a wall by stretching yourself out so much that you fit between the atoms. It sounded impossible, but in the world of code, you could do just about anything.

As long as you were willing to suffer the consequences.

And evidently, Agent Weber had decided that Michael and his friends were willing.

The bathroom door creaked open, then thumped shut.

"Michael?"

It was Bryson.

"Yeah?" Michael mumbled. Did they really have to go? Now? Couldn't they get one more night's sleep? He laid his head in his hands.

"We need to get some more fiber in that diet of yours," Bryson said, standing right outside Michael's stall door. "You've been in there for twenty minutes, dude. Sometimes it just doesn't flow, my friend."

Michael snickered, bursting into a laugh before he knew it.

"At least you're still alive!" Bryson responded.

Michael stood up, sighed, then walked out of the stall.

"Uh, sir?" Bryson asked. "Aren't you going to flush?"

"No need. I was just sitting there, planning how to add more fiber to my diet."

Bryson gave him a good, hard look. "Hey, man, you okay? If it helps, I'm more scared than either of you two. I just hide it well by being obnoxious."

Michael took a deep breath and exhaled. "Yeah, I'm fine. Just seems crazy that they're asking us to do this. With all those fancy agents at their disposal. Sarah's mom and dad— their lives are on the line, here."

"But we've proven ourselves," Bryson said with a shrug. "Honestly, would you really trust someone else to do this? It's us, man. The Burn-and-Pillage-y Trilogy. If anyone can pull this off, it's me, you, and Sarah. Slip in, do our business, save the world from a psycho, slip out. Weber's agents find Sarah's parents. Boom. We can retire."

Michael had the sudden, embarrassing urge to hug his

friend. He'd needed a pep talk, and he'd gotten it. Bryson punched him in the arm, and Michael guessed that would have to do.

They walked out of the bathroom together, ready to destroy Kaine.

2

No one spoke much as they prepared for the Coffins. A few bites of protein-rich granola bars, a full-sized bottle of nutrient-saturated liquids, stripping down to their underwear. Handshakes and hugs—Michael hated that part. Without meaning to, they were acting as if this would be the last time they ever saw each other.

If anyone was bothered by Agent Weber's being in the room while they stood there almost naked, no one showed it.

"I'll be in my own private NerveBox," Weber said, "just upstairs in my office. I'll meet you at the rendezvous spot in fifteen minutes. I'll give you the Lance device, and you can be on your way."

That was it. No more explanations, no more time for questions.

Weber left. Michael stepped into his Coffin, closed the lid.

The NerveWires snaked their way across his already moist skin and he closed his eyes.

3

When he opened them, he stood in a large white marble room. The veins in the stone pulsed, as if some kind of toxic liquid were pumping through them. Sarah was there; Bryson, too. And Agent Weber—all three of them dressed just like they'd been in the Wake before stripping down.

"So we meet again," Weber said with a stiff nod. She turned away from them and walked to one of the bright walls, where she reached out and tapped a pattern on its surface. After a moment something hissed and snapped; then a drawer slid open.

"Here we are," she said as she pulled out a black bag with a strap, handling it carefully. Inside was something boxy, making it obvious what the bag contained.

The Lance.

Weber turned to face them, taking a long look at Michael and his friends, as if assessing whom she trusted most to carry the precious device. The device she'd spent years programming.

"Take this, Michael," she said finally, handing him the bag.

He accepted it after the slightest hesitation, wondering why she chose him, then slipped the strap over his shoulder. With the bag resting against his hip, he unzipped it and peeked inside, to see exactly what he'd expected: gleaming metal and colorful wires. Weber leaned over, her hair brushing his face. She reached in and pointed to a small keypad on the side of the device, then flipped up its protective case.

"You see that?" she said. "Once you have this open, it's

eight numbers. I trust you have the password memorized by now."

"That's it?" Michael asked, feeling stupid. "Activate this and all our problems are solved?"

Weber stepped back and nodded. "Just like I told you— find the building, break in, find whatever it is that represents his central programming. Insert the Lance device, enter the code. The results will be messy. Get out fast and either find a Portal or I'll Lift you myself once I know you're clear. I just wish it were less dangerous."

"Why do I get the feeling things probably won't go so smoothly?" Sarah asked, her arms folded as she stared at the bag on Michael's hip.

"That's why I'm sending you three," Weber replied. "I trust you. I've seen what you can accomplish. Things are . . . very complicated among my agents. This needs to be a quiet, small operation."

"And the Hider codes?" Bryson asked. "Those are still all in place?"

Weber nodded curtly. "Of course. Kaine should have no idea you're coming. The same applies as before—you won't be able to see the code like you're used to, and *Lifeblood Deep* is realistic on a level you absolutely won't believe until you see it for yourself. Use your NetScreens if you have to."

She directed a sheepish look Michael's way. He'd lived most of his life thinking the Deep was the real world. It was a painful reminder of everything he'd lost.

"Now, any questions before I send you off?" Weber looked eager for them to get to work.

Michael and his friends traded looks. And shrugged. Agent Weber appeared satisfied, almost smiling.

"Good," she said. "Time to Squeeze you into the *Deep*."

Michael's back was pressed against the marble wall between Sarah and Bryson. Weber had told them to hold hands, to not let go no matter how bad things got. Bryson's hand felt meaty and sweaty, Sarah's dainty and soft. Michael liked hers a lot better.

Weber faced them, standing a few feet away, a grave look on her face. "I'll be doing most of the work," she said. "All you have to do is close your eyes and endure the . . . intense sensations you're about to experience."

"You mean the unbearable pain," Bryson muttered. "Pain that's going to make me cry."

Michael smiled a little, but his heart thumped like the foot of a nervous cartoon rabbit he'd seen on the Vids years and years ago. He wanted to get this part over with.

"Pain, yes," Weber replied. "But there are also things worse than pain. Just keep hold of each other, try not to panic, and . . . endure. It won't last as long as you might think. Once you're in, get the job done as quickly as possible." She looked at the bag on Michael's shoulder—he'd slung it across his chest to make sure it didn't fall off. "You know what to do, right?"

He nodded stiffly, impatient to get going.

The agent gave them a warm smile, her face creased in what Michael could swear looked like sympathy. It helped, a little, and if Michael had been alone he just might've hugged her and said goodbye.

"Okay," Weber said. "Close your eyes."

5

A good minute or two passed before the process began. Michael counted the seconds down for a bit, then abandoned the idea when his anxiety spiked even more. The first thing he noticed was the dimming of the lights. Darkness swept over them, and he had the urge to open his eyes. He didn't really know if Weber had meant they *needed* to keep them closed, or if that would only help. *Crap,* he thought. He should've asked her.

"Do you think—" he started to say, but a loud humming cut him off.

It felt as if the air suddenly had weight, as if it was pressing in on his eardrums with a heavy buzz. His skin tingled, and he shifted on his feet, feeling more and more uncomfortable. All he could do was hold on tightly to Sarah's and Bryson's hands and not let go. No matter what. He needed them—he was far more scared than felt natural. Maybe it was the uncertainty that made it so bad.

The world pressed in, the sound getting louder. Michael imagined the LiquiGels back in the Coffin, pressing in on his skin as if he'd lain down in water that was freezing solid.

He tried shifting again, but it did no good. The strain made him feel every pulse of his heart beating, feel the pumping of the blood in his temples, his neck, the crooks of his elbows, everywhere.

Thump.

Thump.

Thump.

Something pulled him away from Bryson and Sarah, but he held on to his friends. He curled his fingers tightly around theirs, refusing to let them slip away. His eyes popped open on instinct and darkness filled his vision, so he closed them again. That tugging sensation continued, but instead of trying to yank his friends out of his grip, it worked on his body, every part of it, as if some force was trying to pull his muscles and bones and skin and sinew—everything—apart. *Stretching* him, impossibly. It hurt, an achy strain turning worse by the second. Then came the pain—little jolts that made him gasp. Parts of him were *snapping*.

It's the Sleep, he told himself in a rush of panic. *It's not real, not happening. Endure. Don't let go.* He thought he might've heard Bryson trying to say something, but it was lost in the humming buzz that pulsed in rhythm with his heart, felt in every vein he had.

Thump.

Thump.

Thump.

The pulsing of his heart. The pulsing of the noise, pressing into his ears, his face, his skin.

Thump.

Thump.

Thump.

The force continued to work on him, stretching him forward and backward into a long trail, making him shudder when he thought of what his body must look like, how thin and grotesque. The pain intensified, lancing through his nerves, becoming unbearable. A constant rush of brutal agony, as if something wanted to rip apart every molecule in his body. He screamed, but he let out nothing but a dull memory of sound swallowed by the buzz. The force pulled him, thinned him, stretched him to infinite lengths, making the pulse of his blood stronger and louder.

Thump.

Thump.

Thump.

On some distant edge of his mind, he knew that his fingers were still clasped around Sarah's and Bryson's, but everything was like a string, a thin cord of tissue, full of pain.

Thump.

Thump.

Thump.

Thinner.

Harder.

Pain.

A storm of humming, buzzing, thumping.

Screams.

Holding on to something that made no sense, lines of code, barely there.

The world, collapsing.

Pain. Oh, the pain.

Spinning.

Crushed.

His mind, finally unable to handle any more, gave up and shut down.

All was nothing.

Not even a thump.

CHAPTER 20

PLANT AND TRIGGER

1

He floated in emptiness, completely unaware of time passing, barely aware of anything at all. But the pain faded, and the darkness held him, and he slept.

He sensed a brightness, a glowing red that woke him up. He blinked several times, then squinted to keep his eyes open. He lay on his back. The sky hovered far above him, several buildings converging to a point up in the blue, as if they were fingers reaching for something he couldn't quite see.

His head swam with grogginess, and when he rolled over onto his side, that didn't help. Woozy, he paused and saw Sarah and Bryson close by, still asleep. They were at the end of a long alley, no one in sight, and not much of anything else except cement and dust and trash. The wet warmth of the air made him feel sticky, greasy.

The crisp realness of his surroundings made him realize that Agent Weber had done it. She'd really done it.

Michael and his friends were inside *Lifeblood Deep*. She'd Squeezed them through the intense complexity of its code. He was home—back where he'd always lived. He didn't know how to feel or what to think. Maybe, just maybe, his parents and Helga were somewhere in the Deep. Trapped, imprisoned, or something. Had they really just vanished, their code wiped away? He swore to look for them, to search every last digit of code if he had to. As soon as they dealt with Kaine.

Which reminded him of everything in a flare of panic.

"Bryson!" he yelled, quickly checking his side to make sure Weber's bag was still there, the strap across his chest. He felt the bulk of the Lance, the sharp, hard edges giving him a small dose of relief. "Sarah! Wake up!"

Michael's friends groaned, rubbed their eyes. Blinked and squinted as much as he had. But soon they were all on their feet, the ordeal of the Squeeze in the past, become a mere memory more quickly than Michael would've guessed.

"This place is fantastic," Sarah said, turning in a circle as if she'd landed on another planet. "It's so . . . *real*." She reached out and touched the rough cement of the closest building, which towered dozens of stories above them. "You can barely tell we're in the Sleep."

"Tell me about it," Michael muttered absently. Images of his family filled his head, but they needed to get moving, no time to waste. No matter what Agent Weber had said about their Hider codes, he'd never again make the mistake of thinking Kaine couldn't find them. "Let's get this over with."

Bryson had his eyes closed but opened them when Michael stopped talking. "Just like the last time she sent us in. No code. Her programs are stronger than ever."

"I've got all the info loaded," Sarah replied. "Just a sec." A quick squeeze of her EarCuff and the green NetScreen projected in front of her. She made a few swipes and taps. "Wow. Weber's good. Squeezed us in really close. It's less than half a mile from here."

Michael looked down at the bag again. He wanted to get rid of the Lance as soon as possible. "Let's go, then." It seemed like he should've said something a little more pep-talky, but that was all he had.

Bryson cupped his hands around his mouth and yelled, "Kaine! We're coming to get you!"

Sarah slapped him on the shoulder. "What're you doing?"

"Yeah," Michael added. "That might be the stupidest thing you've ever done."

Bryson shrugged. "I hate that piece of rat-trash." And it was hard to blame him.

The three of them ran down the alley toward Kaine.

2

Plenty of pedestrians walked the sidewalks in front of the building they wanted. It looked just like it had on the huge map Agent Weber had pulled up back in the VNS War Room. Wedged between two tall buildings, three stories, a few small windows, made of an ugly mixture of steel and cement—the thing was an eyesore, and Michael couldn't guess what possible historical significance it had. Maybe as one of the most hideous, nondescript, useless buildings ever constructed?

"Huh," Bryson said. "I would've thought he'd live in a palace or a castle." The three friends studied Kaine's home from a block or so away.

"Too obvious," Sarah replied.

Bryson spit on the sidewalk. "I can't wait for this to be over."

"I get to do it," Michael said, anger rising in him like a red sun.

"What?" Bryson and Sarah said at the same time.

Michael broke his gaze from the building. "I get to place the Lance. And trigger it." He paused, trying to find the best way to say it. "I'm glad I get to kill him."

His friends didn't say anything. Bryson nodded; Sarah looked down at the ground, as if she was worried about him. Or thinking about her own mom and dad. But Michael had to do this. Kaine had taken away his family, his life, Helga. It didn't matter that Michael was a fake, that he was nothing but a program. He'd loved his parents; he'd loved Helga. He'd been happy. Getting a bag of real flesh and bones to wrap around his intelligence would never make up for that.

He was going to kill Kaine, even if the Lance's effects were as messy as Weber predicted. Even if every last KillSim in the Sleep came at him, he'd set the thing off before going down.

"We ready for this?" Bryson asked. "Time's a-wastin.'"

"I'm ready," Michael said.

Sarah looked firm again. "Me too. I just wish we had a

better plan. It's going to be so hard doing this without swimming in the code." She flicked a hand up by her EarCuff, as if disgusted by it. "I guess this stupid old thing will have to do."

"Yep," Michael said. "It will." He had no doubt they could get inside that building and get the job done. The part that worried him was getting back *out*—Kaine would have his creatures swarming the building as soon as he realized there were intruders. "The skyscraper next to it has a sunken alcove in front of the doors. We can hide there while we work on Kaine's security system."

"Sounds like a plan," Bryson said. "Try to look like goofy *Deep* tourists while we walk up to it. And don't stare at the building we wanna get into."

"And don't walk fast," Sarah added. "Or slow."

"And—" Bryson started to say, but Michael had already started walking.

"Just come on," he said, unable to wait a second longer.

3

They made it to the alcove of the neighboring building without incident, and no one seemed to give them more than a passing glance. Teenagers, one with a bag strapped across his chest, Sarah with her NetScreen already blazing—they looked like students, and sitting down to work only added to the appearance. Michael wondered about all the people around him—weirdly envious that they'd all worked their way inside *Lifeblood Deep* somehow. Of course, a lot of them were Tangents, programmed to make the world seem as real as possible.

They'd divvied up the jobs, and Michael's was to shut down any alarm systems—both the audible kind, which might bring guards and curious people running, and the communications kind, which would bring Kaine's army of who-knew-what this time around. Sarah worked away at the firewalls, trying to find ways to slip past them. Bryson went at the cameras and locking systems.

As he worked, Michael kept thinking back to when they'd tried to break into Ronika's Black and Blue Club. It seemed like a million years ago. He longed for the day when they were able to break by doing something as simple as tricking a couple of idiot bouncers.

"This is . . . weird," Sarah said after they'd all been working for a while.

Michael knew what she meant. The systems were unlike anything he'd ever come across—very basic, and despite being multilayered and heavily fortified, there was hardly any of the usual sophistication.

"I know why," Bryson replied, looking intently at his screen. "My dad's taught me a thing or two about the old days of programming. This is patterned after a *super*-old system. Like, from decades ago. Why would Kaine do that?"

"To avoid suspicion," Michael said. He glanced at his friends, but they were too busy to look up. "If he had something really advanced and heavy, that'd just make people *really* want to know what's inside. And considering he's in the place that has the best-of-the-best gamers and hackers in the Sleep, that's not a good thing. It's like the old hiding-in-plain-sight thing."

Sarah appeared doubtful. "Seems too easy. Another thirty minutes and we'll be ready. I expected to work at this for eight or nine hours, and then be lucky if we got in after all that."

"Yeah, no doubt," Bryson said. "You'd think he'd choose buff security over trying to trick people into just walking on by."

Michael shrugged. "I don't know. Maybe. I think what I said makes sense, though. Let's just get in there and blow his mind to bits."

Kaine was inside that stupid building—he'd helped trace the Tangent there himself—and he wanted to get this over with. Kaine might move his central programming if they wasted any more time. Michael kept working, excitement building to match his rage.

4

True to her word, thirty minutes later, Sarah turned off her NetScreen. With a click of her EarCuff she let out a huge sigh. "Okay. I'm ready."

Bryson had shut down a few minutes earlier. "Me too. Cameras are all showing old loops from an hour ago. There's a back door we can get to through a tiny alley next to the building. It's unlocked and ready to welcome three crazy people eager to blow the place up. And there aren't any guards on-site, as far as I can tell."

Michael finished up just as his friend said those words. "All the alarms are shut down." He clicked off his screen in triumph. "And you're right, that was way too easy. Once we're inside, we better be ready for whatever little booby traps he has for someone who *does* come snooping."

"I actually think you're right," Sarah said. "I can't see Kaine trusting anyone—gamer or Tangent—to work as a guard here. I bet there are plenty of traps. Who knows what'll spring up once we're in. KillSims for sure."

"Are we still a go?" Bryson asked.

Michael spoke quickly. "Absolutely."

Sarah paused before giving her answer. "One hundred percent."

"Then let's get on it," Bryson said with a tight smile.

5

Bryson hadn't been kidding when he said the alley leading to the back of the building in question was tiny. Michael had to turn sideways, his chest and back brushing against the brick walls as he shuffled along. He led the way, Sarah and Bryson right behind him, nothing but a canyon of concrete in front and decades' worth of trash at their feet, making each step an adventure. The sun barely penetrated the high cliffs squeezing them in, and the entire walk had a spooky, twilight feel.

When they were about halfway to their goal, Michael

paused and looked back. "So far, so good. Nothing's jumped down and ripped our throats out."

"I keep thinking," Sarah replied, "about *Lifeblood Deep*. When they say they want to replicate the real world, they sure mean it, don't they? Can you imagine? Michael, you didn't even know it was fake! I just can't believe how amazingly lifelike the programming here is. It's like you have to follow the same rules as life in the Wake."

Bryson made a scoffing sound. "Don't jinx us. If anyone's going to break those rules, it'll be Kaine. I bet he's just waiting for us to step through that back door, and then he's going to throw everything that's ever caused pain in the Sleep at us."

"Always looking on the bright side," Michael replied. He turned away and continued down the alley, stepping over a dead rat, hoping Sarah didn't see it. It ended up being Bryson who squealed before he could stop himself.

They finally reached the end of the narrow passage. Michael was surprised by how far back the building went—it looked so small from the front. But it was the Sleep, and there were two giant skyscrapers throwing off their perception.

He steeled his breath, then leaned out from between the walls to take a look. Another alley, this one much wider, crossed the back of the building and the others beside it. Michael heard cars and people in the distance, but this area was deserted, dark, and silent. A sudden rush of wind sent the cover of a Dumpster swinging, and the noise made Michael jump. The hinges creaked until it slowed to a stop again. All was clear.

"Come on," he whispered to his friends, stepping out into the wider alley. Bryson took over from there, leading them to the back door of Kaine's building, the one he said he'd been able to unlock. It was a simple metal door with a silver latch for a handle. Three cement steps, cracked and worn, led to the entrance. Bryson pressed his back against the outer wall right next to the stairs, and Michael and Sarah lined up beside him. Michael fingered the hard edges of the Lance in his shoulder bag, eager to use the thing.

"Should we try to code in weapons?" Sarah asked. "Who knows what's waiting in there?"

"It won't work," Michael said, and he knew that despite the suggestion, Sarah already knew they couldn't. They'd had a hard enough time Squeezing themselves into the Deep; there was no way they could risk trying to bring something else in. "Use your fists and elbows, and if they shoot bullets, lasers, or bombs, duck."

"Thanks," Sarah responded. "Helpful."

"Nothin' to do but go in," Bryson said, his chest puffing up with deep breaths that he blew out far too noisily. He gave a stiff nod to Michael and Sarah then pushed himself away from the wall and quickly moved toward the steps, ran up them. Sarah was next, then Michael, waiting right at the bottom. He watched as Bryson lifted the latch, hesitating just a second before doing so. It clicked and the door popped open.

All three of them froze, expecting some monstrous beast to emerge, roaring, ready to suck the lives out of them. But nothing happened. Michael leaned over to see a line of darkness where the door stood ajar. With a pang in his heart, he remembered a joke Helga had once told him, when he was a little boy.

When's a door not a door? she'd said in her thick accent.

When? he'd asked

When it's ajar.

He'd loved her, just as much as he loved his parents. And Kaine had taken that away from him.

"Let's go!" he whispered fiercely. "Now!"

Bryson tore the door open and the three of them slipped inside.

6

They entered a room that looked like nothing more than a storage area—big and dusty and full of boxes, mostly on warped shelves that sagged in the middle. A lot of the stuff looked mechanical—wires and pieces of metal and exposed circuit boards. For the few seconds it took to cross the room, Michael admired the almost perfect programming of the Deep once again. Crisp and real, even in its deteriorated parts.

But they didn't stop and stare. Sarah had her NetScreen on, a map and schematics of the building glowing brightly before her.

"No sign of people," she said, right before stepping into a long, dark hallway. "Anywhere. At least according to the heat sigs."

"Are we sure this isn't too easy?" Bryson responded. "I'm getting nervous."

"Getting?" was all Michael would say to that. "Come on,

Sarah, lead us to the mainframe. Or whatever his programming looks like here." His finger itched on the surface of the bag, as if there were a trigger there that he could pull at any second.

"It's on the top floor," Sarah said. "In a column at the center of the building—looks like it goes down the entire length of the building, even into the basement, but the easiest way to access it is from above. Like a silo. I can't really tell what it looks like."

It sounded strange to Michael—but it didn't matter. They'd come this far, and all they could do was move forward.

"The stairs," Sarah said, suddenly bolting forward, down the hallway.

Michael was at her heels, Bryson right next to him. They turned a corner and ran into another dimly lit hall. Sarah stopped at the first door and opened it, went through. A stairwell. They started up, running, skipping every other step when they could. So far, no one had made an appearance. All Michael could hear was their own footsteps. If there'd been guards, they would've been on top of them by now— there was no doubt in Michael's mind.

So, no guards.

Which meant there was probably something worse once they got to where they were going. He remembered the Kill-Sim's mouth, its jaws, its breath, its terrifying digital growl. He put it out of his mind and climbed.

Second floor, third floor. Another set of steps led to a roof, but instead of climbing, Sarah opened the door to the top floor and they stepped into a hallway. She had her NetScreen on, brightness up all the way, map shining. Down one hall into the next. Turn, then turn again. Still no sign of people. Still no sounds but their own. Michael studied the ceilings, the walls, the corners, searching for anything suspicious, but there was nothing. The building was like any other he'd set foot in.

Sarah stopped at a big metal door that appeared to be slightly newer than anything else. She yanked on the lever and the heavy thing swung open—Bryson had done his job well. A bluish light spilled into the hallway, pulsing like a heartbeat, and for the first time, they heard noise. A deep, mechanical growl that throbbed along with the light, keeping the same rhythm.

"It's in there," she said.

Michael didn't hesitate. He stepped past Sarah and Bryson, directly onto a catwalk that circled the room. Below his feet he could see that he'd entered what Sarah had said looked like a silo on the map—a round room that seemed to descend for miles. The drop took his breath away for a moment, and the space itself was jarring. The pulsing light, the smell of ozone and metal. There was machinery everywhere: walls lined with circuits and buttons and switches and wires and pipes, all covered in blinking lights.

And that pulsating hum that sounded more like a heart now that he was inside and near the source.

Vwoomp.

Vwoomp.

Vwoomp.

Vwoomp.

Vwoomp.

Michael noticed Bryson and Sarah at his back and he jumped. It was as if he'd been temporarily hypnotized by the surroundings, but they hardly registered him, staring down into the humming throng of sights themselves.

"Okay," Michael whispered, mostly to himself, as he got down to his knees and pulled the bag off his shoulder. He placed it carefully on the metal grid of the catwalk and unzipped it, opening its top wide. Then he reached in and pulled the Lance from its resting place, handling it as if one wrong move might set it off and kill them all.

It's not real, he told himself. *None of this is real.* How strange was that? After all the years, after all the gaming, after everything—for the first time it hit him just how odd life in the Sleep could be. How much their world had changed, a world that wasn't even really his.

He placed the Lance on the catwalk just as Sarah said, "Uh-oh."

He looked up at her. "What?"

"I think our luck finally ran out," she said, staring at her NetScreen. A bead of sweat trickled down her cheek. "I've got heat sigs all along the outside of the building. At least a dozen, maybe more."

Bryson clenched his jaw and shook his head. Michael felt a roll of panic in his chest.

"Whoever it is, they're coming inside," Sarah said.

Michael's mind switched off. There was no time for thought, only instinct. No chance of turning back. Only forward now.

Place and trigger the Lance.

Kill Kaine.

Whatever happened after that didn't matter.

Settling his mind to the task, he picked up the device carefully and examined it. He found the keypad, flipped up the cover, typed in the code. His friends stood patiently beside him, knowing better than to urge him to hurry.

A glance showed him that there was a ladder on the other side of the room. It led from the catwalk into the depths of the machinery. He headed that way.

"Our visitors are spread out across the bottom floor of the building," Sarah said, amazingly calm. Michael knew she was doing it for his benefit. She had to keep him informed, but she'd try her best to make it sound like she was giving him directions to bake cookies. "They are clearly in search mode, scattered in some kind of military formation."

Okay, Michael thought, *not so much like baking cookies.* He made it to the ladder, leaned over the railing to search the maze of machines and wires and tubes. Those pulsing, blinking lights that seemed to be trying to lull him to sleep. Kaine's central programming appeared to descend to the very depths of the Earth, a tunnel straight to hell. An apt description. And Michael was ready to blow it up.

Sarah continued her play-by-play. "They've started up both flights of stairs—the ones we used and a set on the other side of the building. A few are also coming up the elevator. They appear to have divided into groups of three. They're human, though, by the looks of it—not KillSims."

They were coming. They were coming fast.

"Do they have weapons?" Bryson asked.

"Um, I think so," Sarah responded, her voice hard to read.

Michael had turned around, his back to his friends, and lowered his foot until he felt the first rung of the ladder. He cradled the Lance in his right arm as he gripped the railing tightly with his left hand.

Vwoomp.

Vwoomp.

Vwoomp.

The pulsating sound filled his entire body.

Vwoomp.

Vwoomp.

Vwoomp.

He climbed down another rung, and then another. He kept going, being careful to hold on tightly to the Lance. His back scraped an outcropping of circuitry behind him—the whole place was a jumble of metal and wire. He took another rung down, his palms beginning to sweat.

Sarah and Bryson had walked around the catwalk at some point and were standing directly above him.

"They're almost to the third floor—on the stairs," Sarah called down. "The ones on the elevator—they're here. The doors are opening now."

Michael had gone down a few more rungs while she

spoke; he paused and looked up. Sarah was calm, Bryson a nervous wreck, shifting his weight from foot to foot.

Vwoomp.

Vwoomp.

Vwoomp.

Michael kept going. He somehow knew he was almost there. Weber had said the location didn't matter so much, just to plant the Lance somewhere in the heart of it all. That he'd know when he'd arrived. So down he went, his neck and shoulders strained, his arms aching.

And then he saw it.

He'd descended at least twenty feet. Twisting carefully around, hugging the closest rung with his left arm, the Lance still cradled in his right, he stared at a cluster of burning blue lights that slowly flashed along with the throbbing hum of noise—*vwoomp, vwoomp, vwoomp*—that filled the world around him. Everything was brighter, hotter, shinier in the cluster, packed in and thrumming. The air vibrated; he could feel it buzz on his skin, and goose bumps broke out across his neck and back.

If this place had a heart, this was it.

"Running down the hallway!" Sarah shouted down; he couldn't even see her anymore. "You've only got a few seconds!"

Bryson finally lost his cool. "Hurry, man! What's taking so freaking long?"

Michael ignored him, steadied himself on the ladder. He slipped the Lance down his arm a little, then carefully slid his hand to the corner of the device until he could get a good grip on it. His fingers slipped from the sweat and the Lance almost fell from his grasp; he jerked forward and caught it against his ribs.

"They're at the door!" Sarah yelled.

"Almost done!" Michael shouted up.

Time seemed to stretch out, measured between those pulses of sound.

Vwoomp.

He strengthened his grip on the Lance, then held it away from his body, stretching his arm out, leaning forward into the cluster of lights and wires.

Vwoomp.

Muffled shouts filtered down from above. A door slamming open.

Vwoomp.

Michael found a little nest of wires among the throbbing lights and gently pushed the Lance into them, wiggling the device until it lodged firmly. Slowly, he let go, making sure it wouldn't slip before he pulled his hand away.

Vwoomp.

The thud of footsteps rattled the catwalk and a man yelled, a woman shouted.

"Do it, Michael!" Sarah yelled. "Weber will Lift us out!"

Vwoomp.

His hand slipped on the ladder behind him and he lurched forward, face-planting into the hot cluster of Kaine's mind. He was tangled in a sea of wires, metal burning his skin. The Lance was right in front of him, the keypad at his fingertips.

Vwoomp.

Sarah screamed, followed by a heavy thump that shook the catwalk above. Bryson released a strangled yell. Another thump. Rattling. Shouts. More footsteps.

Michael entered the first number of the code.

Vwoomp.

A man yelled down, a booming voice that overpowered everything else.

"Stop what you're doing! Now!"

Michael ignored him, pushed the next number. The next. The next.

Vwoomp.

He felt the rattle of someone clambering down the ladder. His fingers slipped, found the next number, pushed. The next. The next.

Vwoomp.

The man's voice again, closer, louder.

"Do not move another inch or I *will* shoot!"

Michael pressed the last number of the code and heard a click.

8

A shot rang out, the bullet pinging against something right next to Michael's ear.

"Okay, okay!" Michael shouted. He held his hands up to show he'd stopped. It didn't matter. The deed was done. *Lift us out,* he thought, almost like a prayer to Agent Weber. *Please,* now. *Lift us now.*

"Untangle yourself and slowly back away from the

device," the man said much more calmly. "Get yourself back on this ladder. Now."

"Okay," Michael said, but his eyes stayed focused on the Lance, waiting to see what it would do. As he maneuvered out of the nest of wires, he watched. Waited. Hoped. So far, nothing.

His feet finally found the ladder, and he planted them on the closest rung. He crouched on top of wires and ducts and pushed himself backward, then turned around, hugging the ladder, the man with the massive gun right above him.

"Nice and slow," the guy said. "Up we go. Don't try anything. I promise you, the next shot won't miss."

Michael nodded, then gave one last glance over his shoulder at the Lance, planning to obey the man completely. And hope that Weber would get them out of all the . . .

Suddenly his chest went cold. He'd just started to turn away from the Lance when it caught his full attention again. Riveted, he stared, not sure exactly what he was seeing. The whole thing was . . . melting. Its corners were no longer square, its edges no longer sharp. The wires drooped off the sides as the metal of the device warped and bent, turning into a goopy soup of molten silver. It started to seep through the wires it was wedged into and then transformed into droplets that fell like rain to the circuits below.

Michael stared as some of the droplets fell sideways. Some fell *up*. In a matter of seconds, the entire Lance had melted into tiny drops of silver that flew in all directions, defying physics. Michael could only think that some type of magnetism had occurred.

He looked up at the guard with the gun and realized he was staring, too. But then the man met his gaze.

"What did you do?" he asked, more nervous than angry. "What was that thing?"

"Honestly?" Michael responded. "I have no idea. Someone who gets paid a lot more than you do told me to put it there and press a few buttons. So I did."

The man had no chance to respond. A riot of sounds suddenly filled the air. Then sparks erupted from the device. The pulsing hum stopped, only to be replaced by what sounded like great sheets of metal warping.

"What's going on?" the man shouted, fear lighting up his face, which now glistened with sweat.

Michael was scared himself. All he could do was shrug.

"Get up top," the guard ordered, then started climbing the ladder.

Michael reached for the next rung above him, and as soon as he clasped it, everything began to shake. The sounds got louder.

Michael climbed as the entire building shook violently. The blue sea of lights scattered among Kaine's Core programming flared and flashed, popping and exploding, and sheets of circuits began to break off the walls and fall, rattling off other parts of the core as they plummeted. The heat rose quickly, scorching Michael as he clambered up the ladder.

He pulled himself up onto the catwalk behind the guard to see Bryson and Sarah, hands cuffed behind their backs, being herded toward the exit. The structure swayed back and forth as the world quaked and every person with a free hand held on to something for support. Flames licked up from below as the core collapsed in on itself. The noise was unbearable.

The man who'd come after Michael had his gun in Michael's face. He shouted, "We get out of this building, and then we deal with you! Now go! I'll be right behind you the whole way!"

Michael nodded. Agent Weber would Lift them out of *Lifeblood Deep*. She *would*.

And so he went. Around the catwalk, stumbling and lurching. He held on to the rail like the other guards, though hot, furious air blew up from the crumbling center of the room. Sweat soaked his whole body, and he kept moving, the guard pressing the gun into his back, pushing him.

He made it to the door. Exited into the hallway.

Something exploded behind them, a quick ripping of sound and air. The building heaved.

Michael ran down the hallway, around a corner. He tripped, caught his balance, ran to the stairwell, to his friends and the other guards.

Down they went, leaping from step to step.

Another explosion.

The building jolted.

Michael fell.

Got back up.

He was at the landing of the second floor. Down more stairs. They reached the first floor, stumbled into the hallway. Around yet another corner. They were going in a different direction this time, heading for the front door instead of the back. Several explosions tore through the air. Michael and everyone else fell down. Got back up. Dust choked them. They kept moving, made it to the exit, out into the sun and the streets.

Other men and women with weapons waited outside. Beyond them, crowds of people had gathered to watch the commotion. Fire trucks lined the streets, and cop cars, both wheeled and hovering, sat abandoned, their lights flashing.

Michael's mind spun and his muscles burned. He could barely see, sweat blurring his vision on top of the sudden brightness. Now that they were out of the building, the man who'd pushed him along grabbed him roughly and dragged him farther away, to an area where others were taking Bryson and Sarah. To a big black truck, whose doors two men had just opened.

"Weber," Michael breathed, stumbling along, barely able to keep his feet under him. "Weber." He swiveled his head, searching for a Portal, wondering if he could make a break for it. Something wasn't right. He hadn't thought this far ahead, but things were supposed to go down differently.

Plant and trigger the Lance. Get Lifted.

Suddenly, like a waking dream, *Gabby* appeared. She was in the crowd, pushing past people, running toward Michael. He stared at her. He didn't understand.

"Jax!" she screamed, her face lit with terror, sprinting straight at him. Two cops chased her. "Michael!"

"Gabby?" he whispered, barely hearing it himself. What the hell was going on?

"It's not real!" she yelled, just as one of the cops grabbed her arm. "I mean, it *is* real! They tricked you! I should never have helped—" The other cop slugged her in the head with his nightstick and she collapsed to the ground.

Unable to form words, Michael screamed, a bloodcurdling sound that pierced his own ears. It came from everywhere inside him, a banshee cry born of confusion and pain. He was pushed ahead, and he lost sight of Gabby.

They were throwing his friends into the back of the truck. Panic surged inside Michael. No, no, no. Everything was so *wrong.*

"Gabby!" he yelled.

He jerked his body, twisting away from his captor, trying to see Gabby. The man lost his grip and Michael staggered, turned, started running. Toward Gabby.

Wrong.

Everything.

Throngs of people surrounded her. If he could just get that far. Find her, help her, get lost in the crowd.

A woman stepped in front of him, dressed in all-black battle gear. She had a nightstick, too, and she swung the long, thin club directly at Michael's face. It connected with his forehead, a crushing blow that made the world erupt into bright lights and pain. He fell to the ground, crumpling in a heap, the back of his head slamming into the concrete.

The sky and the tops of buildings swirled above him. He almost lost consciousness but held on, forcing himself to stay connected. His strength was gone. Gone.

"Gabby," he whispered. "Weber. Where are you?"

And then he was being lifted into the air. Carried to the truck. Thrown inside.

They slammed the door closed, a long screech followed by a thunderous, echoing boom, leaving him and his friends in darkness.

Michael closed his eyes.

CHAPTER 21

CRIMINAL

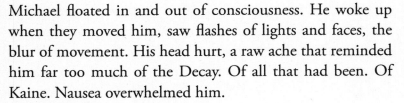

Michael floated in and out of consciousness. He woke up when they moved him, saw flashes of lights and faces, the blur of movement. His head hurt, a raw ache that reminded him far too much of the Decay. Of all that had been. Of Kaine. Nausea overwhelmed him.

He slept.

2

"Hey," someone whispered. "Michael. You okay?"

Sarah. It was Sarah. He blinked a few times, opened his eyes fully. She was staring down at him. He was on his back, lying on something very hard. His head felt better, and the wooziness had subsided. With a groan he moved to get up, and she helped him. His heart sank when he saw where they were.

He was on a bench. He was with Sarah and Bryson in a dimly lit room with iron bars all around—a prison cell. There was no one else in sight. Had they been Lifted?

"Dude," Bryson said. "That lady must've knocked half of your brains out of your ears with that blow. I saw it. You've been out for a while."

"What . . ." Michael groaned. It hurt to speak.

Sarah was next to him. Holding his hand.

"Everything was a lie," she said. "They won't tell us much. Just that we're under arrest. The cops here are terrible."

"What . . ." Michael said again. Maybe he'd suffered some serious brain damage and that was the only word he'd ever utter for the rest of his life. "Did you see Gabby?"

He turned to Bryson, who didn't seem to have heard him. His friend was fuming, rubbing his hands together as he stared at the wall of metal bars. "Weber. She set us up. Set the whole thing up, top to bottom. I just hope I get a chance someday . . . Just five minutes. That's all I need."

Michael wanted to ask what in the world he was talking about but had to focus on breathing.

"We don't know it was her," Sarah said. "In fact, it doesn't even make sense if it was her. After she Sunk us into the Sleep, someone else must've charged in and taken over operations."

Bryson just scoffed at that.

Michael was becoming more convinced by the second that he had been hit too hard to recover. "Wait . . . what's going on? What do you guys know?"

Sarah kept talking, but she didn't seem to be talking to Michael. "They must've done it right after Weber gave us the

Lance device. It was somehow linked to the Squeeze. I mean, we all passed out. Slept for who knows how long. They had plenty of time to do it."

"I'm telling you, it was Weber," Bryson said. He sat back against the cement wall behind the bench. "You can't tell me she gave us that Lance thing and Lifted out of the Sleep, and then suddenly other people took over. That's too convenient. *She* set us up."

"But *why?*" Sarah asked. "We already had tons of reasons to be arrested. Michael's supposedly a terrorist, and everyone on the planet thinks I did something to my . . . parents." She faltered but quickly recovered. "Not to mention the umpteen times we've broken laws in the Sleep. It doesn't add up. If Weber—or anyone else—wanted us in jail, all they had to do was turn us in. Call the cops."

Michael just kept looking back and forth between his friends, trying to connect the dots. Bryson was slowly nodding, considering.

"Huh," he said. And then he repeated it. "Huh."

"Guys." Michael shifted in his seat, wincing from the pain that lingered. "Call me slow. But what in the world are you talking about? What did Gabby mean back there? Have they even Lifted us out of the *Deep* yet? Where *are* we? What happened? Is this a real jail or—"

"Michael," Sarah said softly, but firm enough to cut him off. "Michael. They tricked us. Someone did."

"How?" he asked. "What did they do?"

Sarah looked terribly, terribly sad.

"We were never in *Lifeblood Deep*," she said. "They had to

have drugged us at some point—knocked us out after we got in the Coffins, I don't know—and then Lifted us and dropped us in the Wake, in the *real* Atlanta. It's the only explanation."

Michael's head started spinning again.

Sarah gave his hand a hard squeeze. "Whatever was in that building, we really did destroy it. In the *Wake,* Michael. And I don't know if it had anything to do with Kaine."

CHAPTER 22

TWO VISITORS

1

Michael lay on a tiny cot in a cramped room. The floor, ceiling, and three walls were made of stone blocks. A line of thick bars made up the fourth wall. The only light was a single lonely lightbulb, which buzzed and flared every few minutes. Michael stared at the ceiling, overwhelmed by a deep grief like he'd never known. He wished he were dead.

He didn't know exactly why he felt so despairingly sad. Things had been bad going on worse for a long time now. But being locked away—and worse, separated from his friends, which the guard had done a couple of hours earlier— gave him all the silence and time in the world to think about his problems.

And think he did.

About his Tangent parents, gone forever. About Helga, his loving Tangent nanny, gone as well. Sarah, her parents still missing, accused of being behind their disappearance. Bryson, accused of helping her. Kaine, on the loose and taking over more bodies by the second, for all Michael knew. Agent Weber, the only person he'd trusted besides Sarah and Bryson, betraying him.

He thought about Jackson Porter. The boy's life, stolen.

Michael, a murderer, whether he'd meant to be or not.

And Gabby. *He'd* dragged her into this. And all he could see was her crumpled, injured body lying on the pavement.

It was all too much.

Michael had always prided himself on not being the crying sort. That had changed recently. The lights above looked blurry, and when he reached up to scratch his cheek, his fingers came away wet.

He rolled over and faced the wall, curled up into a ball.

And then Michael cried. The kind of crying where his chest hitched and his throat closed up and his shoulders shook. The kind where snot flowed and the sound of sobs and sniffles broke the gloomy silence.

Michael *wept.*

2

At some point, he fell asleep. He only realized this when a clanging on the bars ripped him from empty dreams. Disoriented, he sat up on the cot.

A guard stood there, chewing gum lazily, his gun out— that was what he'd used to drag across the metal bars. When

Michael was awake and attentive, the man put the gun back into its holster.

"You have a visitor," the guard said, bored. "Two, actually. A man and a woman. Which one you wanna see first?"

This woke Michael completely. He stood up. "Who . . . who are they?"

"Don't know and don't care. Which will it be?"

Michael thought hard. The whole situation was odd. Who could it possibly be? Finally he just said, "The man, I guess."

The guard gave a bored nod, then walked away. Michael stayed where he was, heard a clang, a few whispers, then footsteps. Soon a different man came into view, alone, wearing jeans and a black shirt; brown hair, chin stubble, watery blue eyes.

Michael had never seen him before.

"Sure got yourself into a lot of trouble, Michael," the man said. He didn't say it kindly, but he wasn't hostile, either. Just matter-of-fact.

"Who are you?" Michael asked.

"The name's not important."

Michael expected more, but the man went silent. He stared at Michael with his icy gaze.

"So . . ." Michael searched for words. "Just how bad was it? The police won't tell us anything. We thought we were in the Sleep. Did . . . did we kill any people?" He'd been avoiding that thought, holding on to hope that everyone had gotten out okay. But they were certainly being treated like they'd at least *tried* to kill.

"People?" the man scoffed. "You did a lot worse than kill people. You killed the VNS."

"Wha . . . what're you talking about?" Michael's chest hitched and he struggled to make sense of the man's words.

The stranger gave a sad smile. "Only, *killed* is a strong word. *Crippled* is more appropriate. Severely. For a long time. Whatever that device you planted was . . . it was a beast, my young friend. It set off a chain reaction throughout all of their systems, like a physical virus, destroying everything as it traveled from station to station. Completely put them off the grid. How you knew where their mainframe was hidden, I'll never know. And honestly, I don't care. That's not why I'm here."

Michael stayed as still and silent as granite. As smart as he was, his mind couldn't compute what he was hearing.

The man stepped closer to the bars and leaned in close. "Listen to me, boy. I came to see you because the world is changing. Changing under everyone's noses. And you're a part of it, whether you want to be or not. There's no telling how long you'll be in here, but I suspect the time will come, sooner or later, when . . . circumstances may set you free. And I want you to remember my face. Remember it well."

"I . . ." Michael tried desperately to think of something logical to say or ask. "Do you work for Kaine? Agent Weber? Does this have anything to do with the Mortality Doctrine? Who *are* you?"

"Friend?" the stranger said in a contemplative tone. "Or foe? That will be determined in the weeks ahead."

Michael had no response to that.

The man continued. "I'm going to leave you now. You'll have plenty of time to think before things come to a head. I hope you've learned a valuable lesson from what happened at that building. About the nature of the VirtNet. About the nature of reality."

"What do you mean?"

"When mankind can create a world that is so like our own," the stranger said, "then how can we possibly ever know what's real and what's not real again? I could Lift you right now, pull you out of a NerveBox, and then you'd say, 'Ah! I'm back in the real world!' And then I could Lift you again, and you'd be surprised, but feel for certain that this time you're in the . . . what do you kids call it? . . . the Wake."

The man brought his hands up and gripped the bars until his knuckles turned white. "I could Lift you a hundred times. A thousand. How, Michael, could you ever know again that you are truly, truly in the real world? For that matter, who's to say there even *is* a real world?"

Michael was so bewildered that his knees went weak, almost making him crumple right onto the floor. And not because it was nonsense. But because it was the single most frightening thing he'd ever heard.

"Think on that," the man said, stepping back from the bars. "Think about whether someone is evil because they want to bring immortality to humankind. Think on all these things and more. You'll have the time." He turned to go.

"Wait!" Michael yelled. "Just . . . tell me who you are."

"I can't tell you now, Michael. It would be . . . emotionally difficult for you. But I wanted you to see my face. Someday, someday soon, it will be important. Until then." He gave a brief nod, then walked away, not looking back.

"Wait!" Michael yelled again, but the only answer was the echo of his own voice.

3

Michael sat on the cot, so dazed by the man's visit that he felt separated from his body, his consciousness floating in some ethereal world that made no sense. The air buzzed with something malicious, a feeling that he could only compare to those horrible moments when he'd Lifted out of the Sleep into another person's body.

And then he heard the *tap-tap-tap*ping of high heels.

He couldn't believe it. How did she dare show her face?

He looked up just as she walked into sight on the other side of the bars.

"Really?" he asked. "You came to *visit* me? Be thankful I'm locked in here."

Agent Weber stopped. Her face was completely unreadable.

"Michael," she said. "There are things you don't understand. Especially about me. Also about why things have come to pass the way they have."

Michael's heart beat rapidly, and his chest rose and fell with heavy breaths. He couldn't even speak.

"Everything said in here is recorded," she continued. "I have to be careful. But just know that what you think about me is not true. You and I are on the same side. I'm not . . . who I used to be, for one thing." Her eyes flared a little when she said that, as if she wanted him to get a secret message. "And the role of the VNS is much more complicated than you think."

She leaned very close and whispered so softly that he could barely hear. "The VNS *created* Kaine, Michael. But now he's gone rogue. And he deliberately led you to that building in *Lifeblood Deep* so that you'd go there in the *real* world. *I* didn't switch you. I swear it on my life. No one at VNS can be trusted anymore. And Kaine wanted all evidence of his connection to them destroyed." She took a step back, as if, with only a few sentences, she hadn't just spun the world like a top.

Michael stood still, trembling with anger. And he stared harder into her eyes. Oh man, how he missed his friends. He could do this, he could handle this moment—right there and then—if only Bryson were sitting on the cot, making jokes. If Sarah were by his side, holding his hand.

"One more thing before I go," Weber said. "And this is very important." She paused, looking left and right, then back at Michael. "You can never destroy a human intelligence. Nor a *programmed* intelligence. Do you understand me? They're stored. All of them. Both human and Tangent. The Decay may scramble them a bit, but they still *exist.* They can be put back together. This is going to . . ." She seemed to search her mind for the right way to say something. "I think it will make all the difference in the struggle ahead. If things are ever going to be made right."

That made the other stuff go away for a second. Although he couldn't imagine why she was telling him this, it made him think something that he was scared to ask. But he did anyway.

"Not that I can believe a word you've said," he said, "but are you trying to tell me that my parents—my real parents, my Tangent parents—are still alive? And that Jackson Porter is still alive? That somebody figured out how to download a human's mind?"

Weber took a step back and once again looked to the left, then the right, then back at Michael.

"Things will get worse before they get better," she said. "But I do believe that they can and *will* get better. Goodbye, Michael."

He didn't bother yelling for her to wait this time. It would do no good.

Her high heels tapped their staccato rhythm as she disappeared down the hall.

4

They'd taken away most of his access but allowed him an EarCuff, with very limited ability to use the Net. Some entertainment. Simple games. Even criminals got that in a world where reality just wasn't enough.

He lay on the cot and stared at the NetScreen absently, the glowing green plane mostly blank. His thoughts swam with all the things he'd heard from his two visitors. So much information. So much strange information. The VNS had *created* Kaine? His family and Helga might still be out there? Just as he'd dared hope.

His mind could barely handle it all. He missed the world outside his cell. Wondered what was going to happen. Worried. About everything.

But mostly, right that second, he missed his friends.

A little blip of light caught his attention on the NetScreen. He looked, but it had disappeared.

A few seconds later, it flashed again, white against green. Then gone.

He watched and waited.

Another blip—this time it lasted longer.

And then two words appeared, as crisp and bright as if they'd been there forever.

I'm here. S.

Michael's chest swelled. His mind relaxed. His heart softened.

Sarah.

Only she had the guts and compassion to do what she'd just done. Seemingly simple, but he knew how much effort it had taken, and doubted he could do it back. They were being watched like hawks. But he'd sure try.

Sarah. She was there, and for now, that would have to do.

He started working on a response. It took him an hour to break through the heavy fortifications of the prison systems without being detected. But he wouldn't let himself sleep until he'd done the deed. Finally he sent the message, then lay back to get some desperately needed sleep. What he'd sent seemed appropriate—they were, after all, gamers when it all came down to it. The message floated in his thoughts and dreams like a beacon for the rest of the night.

We will win.

EPILOGUE

Two days later, Michael received his third visitor. Except this time, no cop came to announce him. A series of buzzes and a rattling of metallic clicks echoed through the halls of the jail. Michael had been lying on his bunk, but at the strange noises he sat up and strained to listen. Heavy footsteps, getting closer. A door in the bars of the cell creaked open several inches. Then a man walked in and stood there like he owned the place.

"Come on, Michael," the newcomer said. "Your prison days are over."

It was Sarah's dad. Gerard.

Michael swallowed a lump in his throat and tried to speak, but no words came out. Surely he was dreaming.

"Or . . . you can take a nap before we go." It took a second for Michael to even get the sarcasm, confused at why he'd go back to sleep when his cell door stood wide open.

"Michael," Gerard said forcefully. "Get *up*. We're leaving."

"Okay," he managed to squeak out, standing, hurrying over to Sarah's dad. "Okay. But . . ."

"Yeah. I know. Things aren't a whole lot less confusing for me, either. Let's just go."

Michael nodded, then followed Gerard out of the cell, down the hallway, noticing that all the doors stood open. The prison was almost empty.

"Sarah," Michael said. "Bryson. Where are they?"

"Don't worry, I already got them." Michael followed Gerard through a heavily reinforced door that stood ajar. "They were in a separate wing. They're already in the car, waiting with my wife. You'll be with them in two minutes. Now pick up the pace."

Gerard broke into a jog, and Michael followed suit. Sarah's parents, alive and well. Michael and his friends, being freed. Slowly it was all starting to hit him. He felt a surge of elation that he could barely suppress.

They went through another security door and entered the lobby of the prison—the place was completely empty, not a cop or anyone else in sight.

"How?" Michael asked, running to keep up with Gerard as they headed for the sunshine that waited outside.

Gerard stopped, then turned to face Michael, his breathing heavy. "A group of people rescued me and my wife. Then arranged all this." He held his hands up, looking around. "They said something about being Tangents—that they *used* to be Tangents—which I just don't get. But you think I cared? We're safe and back with our daughter."

He started to turn away, but Michael grabbed him by the shoulder, suddenly filled with alarm. "Tangents?" he asked. "You're sure they said that?"

Gerard nodded. "Yeah, led by some woman. Said her name was Helga." He grabbed Michael and pulled him through the door, into the open air and the blazing sun. Michael followed Sarah's dad, running after him toward a car waiting on the street, its engines rumbling, a spark of hope burning in his chest.

ACKNOWLEDGMENTS

Thank you, readers. Every day it hits me a little more just how fantastic you are, all of you. Thank you, dude or lady who invented the Internet, for making that possible.

Thank you, educators, librarians, booksellers, and everyone else who pushes these books on poor, unsuspecting folks looking for a new read.

Thank you, Krista Marino, my patient, thorough, brilliant editor.

Thank you, Michael Bourret, Best Agent Ever.

Thank you, Lauren Abramo, Best International Agent Ever.

Thank you, Random House, for throwing so much incredible support my way. And for making me feel part of the family.

Thank you, Lynette, for sticking by my side. You are Everything.

Thank you, Wesley, Bryson, Kayla, and Dallin, for making Daddyhood such awesomeness.

Thank you, Mom, for raising me right and encouraging my creativity.

And this may be a strange place to do it, but . . .

Thank you, Twentieth Century Fox, Gotham Group, Wes Ball, Wyck Godfrey, T. S. Nowlin, and all the cast and crew for what you've done with the *Maze Runner* movie. Not only have you captured my vision perfectly, you've brought me many new readers, and for that I'm supremely grateful.

And again, even though twice isn't nearly enough: Thank you, readers. Thank you very much.